LIGHT

Visit us at www.boldstrokesbooks.com

LIGHT

by

'Nathan Burgoine

A Division of Bold Strokes Books

2013

LIGHT

ISBN 13: 978-1-60282-953-4

This Trade Paperback Original Is Published By
Bold Strokes Books, Inc.
P.O. Box 249
Valley Falls, NY 12185

First Edition: October 2013

Credits
Editors: Greg Herren and Stacia Seaman
Production Design:
Cover Design by Sheri (graphicartist2020@hotmail.com)

Acknowledgments

If it weren't for the effort of the editors in my life—all of whom are talented authors, to boot—I'd never have gotten this far. Every time I work with an editor, I learn something, and I've had some amazing teachers: Becky Cochrane and Timothy J. Lambert; Jerry L. Wheeler; Richard Labonté; Steve Berman; Ryan North, Matthew Bennardo, and David Malki; Amie Evans and Paul J. Willis; Kfir Luzatto and Dru Pagliassotti; R. Jackson; J.M. Redmann; Shane Alison; Tom Cardamone—and, of course, my editor for *Light*—Greg Herren. If you ever have the chance to work with talented people willing to help you with your art, take it.

I'd also never have even tried to write that first short story if it hadn't been for the Saints and Sinners crowd in New Orleans, many of whom are part of that editor list above, but also including Josh Aterovis, Rob Byrnes, Dale Chase, Marika Christian, Michael Thomas Ford, Mark G. Harris, William Holden, Jeff Mann, David Puterbaugh, Jeffrey Ricker, Rhonda Rubin, Lindsey Smolensky, Lisa Standal, and Michael Wallerstein. Beignets are on me next time.

Last—but most importantly—my husband. Dan, I love you. Yes, we can get a dog.

For Rachel. You were right: it's fun to prove them wrong.

BLACK

It didn't make sense to him that his mother looked so much better now that she was dying. Maybe the doctors were wrong.

"What are you thinking, honey?" she asked him.

The boy looked away, embarrassed. His father had told him not to upset her. "Nothing."

His mother nodded, then glanced up at the television that loomed in the corner of her hospital room like an electronic gargoyle.

"It's starting," she said.

The boy looked up and grinned. His embarrassment slipped away and he climbed onto the bed beside her, barely fitting in the bed. She moved her IV hand away from him in a move that had become an unconscious old habit. He looked at the door, wondering briefly if he should go find his dad and his brother, then snuggled down beside his mother.

"Do you think it's real?" he asked, excited.

"I hope so," she said.

He rolled his head back to look up at her, surprised.

"It's like magic," she said, and tousled his hair. "I'd like there to be magic in the world."

He pondered that, and then gave her a fierce nod.

They turned to watch together.

On the screen, a fairly plump toad of a man in his late forties stood in the middle of the room, his red receding hairline damp with perspiration. He was in an auditorium, and his name was on the bottom of the screen.

It said: "Thomas Wright—Psychokinetic."

Oh, how the boy loved that word. *Psychokinetic.* He'd looked it up, memorized the definition, devoured the syllables, and tried to find ways to use it in everyday discussions at school, much to the ongoing chagrin of his teacher. Psychokinetic. Telekinetic. Mind over matter. All of it caught his attention like nothing else. Pyschokinetic. Abracadabra. He thought the word sounded like magic. Just like his mom.

He wanted it to be real, for her, in some way that left him a bit confused.

Another man was speaking, a news reporter who had nice hair, a handsome face, and teeth that seemed to shine too brightly.

"Thomas Wright's agreement to be on live television is a landmark moment in history," the reporter was saying. "He has agreed to this evening as what will be the first public display of psychokinetic ability by any known individual, here in the his former high school gymnasium in his home city of Jackson, Mississippi."

"What about Miracle Woman?" the boy said, annoyed.

"I think they mean that they don't know who she really is," his mother explained. "She hasn't told anyone her name or where she lives."

"Oh." His mother was usually right.

On the screen, Thomas Wright was now beside a container of basketballs. The room fell quiet. Wright pointed at a basketball, and as the news reporter whispered that Thomas was pointing at a basketball—*Well duh*, the boy thought—there was a collective gasp as one of the basketballs rose about a foot into the air.

"Wow," the boy's mother said.

The boy watched, transfixed. The news people were playing

some kind of stupid music, like wind chimes, which was distracting him and making it hard to hear what the news reporter was saying.

He watched as Thomas slowly turned, still pointing his finger, and the ball rose, arced around the gymnasium as though it were attached to Wright's finger on some sort of invisible pole, and then dropped through the basketball hoop when Thomas flicked his finger. Wright didn't seem overly impressed with himself. The boy couldn't help but wonder if the toadlike man ever smiled.

The applause was loud enough to be heard even over the strange chiming.

"Why are they playing that stupid music?" the boy complained, but it stopped once the ball bounced its way back across the gymnasium floor.

"Music?" his mother asked.

"It stopped," the boy said, not noticing his mother's frown.

"Devil!" someone yelled.

Both of them looked back at the screen, shocked. The boy frowned at the television. The camera shifted around with a blurred jerk and showed a man standing and yelling angrily. His hair stuck up at odd angles, and there was a stain on the front of his shirt.

"Devil worshipper! Witch!" the man yelled.

"Honey," the boy's mother said. "Let's turn this off."

The camera panned back to Thomas Wright, who was frowning and turning red. His hands were balled at his sides, white-knuckled. The boy slipped off the bed and reached for the remote control.

The news reporter was saying something about a religious person, but the chimes were back. Louder than before. They grew in volume to the point where it started to hurt.

Hide!

"Ow," he said, and pressed his hands against his ears. He dropped the remote.

"Honey? Are you okay?" his mother asked.

The gunshot was so unexpected his mother swore—her cry would stay with the boy for the rest of his life. He looked up just in time to see the half second of red that spurted from Thomas Wright's forehead. It was surprisingly bright, and fountained once before the image on the television suddenly cut away to two people sitting at a desk, both of them white with shock and speaking in clipped and tense voices. The chiming clashed loudly, and the boy rocked to the side, tumbling against the bed, clipping his temple on the table that swung over his mother's lap at lunch and dinnertime. His world darkened as he slumped to the floor and in his head he heard a woman's voice, insistent and full of fear.

The woman's voice was an order. She said one word.

Hide.

The boy obeyed.

RED

I woke from the dream with a strangled yelp and the remembered scent of hospital antiseptic itching in my nose. I was shaking, sticky with sweat, and panting, and I hadn't even done anything fun to deserve it. I forced myself to take a deep breath and tried to calm down. It had been a long time since that dream had paid a visit. It was probably overdue.

My cat padded into my bedroom, hopped up onto the side of my bed, and stared at me with his wonderful mismatched eyes.

"Hey, Easter," I said, and shivered. It's amazing how quickly sweat cools once you're not tangled and thrashing in the sheets.

Easter lay down next to my hand and nudged his head beneath my fingers. He's very subtle, in the way of all cats. Once I started scratching, he purred for me, and I lost myself rubbing at his beautiful white fur and let the last of the dream anxiety go.

I looked around the room. My water glass was on the floor and four books were scattered over my desk. At least I hadn't broken anything this time.

Over Easter's purrs, I listened to the sounds of Ottawa coming to life. My small apartment is off the Byward Market, just far enough away to not quite hear the more raucous bars at night, but still close enough to enjoy the chimes of the Peace Tower. It wasn't bright out yet, and I could hear a few cars and the louder rush of buses. My alarm clock was on the other side of the bedroom—the only place it is worthwhile for me to place anything with a snooze button—but there hadn't been an alarm set for this morning. I had no idea what time it was. I couldn't see the numbers without my glasses.

Easter rolled over, and I rubbed his tummy. The purrs increased in volume and bass, and his paws started to curl and wiggle. I was seconds away from a pounce, I knew, where his needle-sharp teeth would give me a playful nip. It was our morning ritual, though I'm not sure who'd trained who.

My glasses were on the chest of drawers, where I put them every night. Still rubbing Easter with my right hand, I raised my left hand, palm flat.

The glasses began to glow with a faint blue light as they lifted from the chest of drawers, floated across the three feet to the bed, and landed in my palm. "Ta-da," I said.

Say what you will, telekinesis is just the thing to make an early morning bearable.

Easter pounced and nipped my thumb. I rolled him over, and his purr rumbled. He narrowed his eyes.

"What?" I said, defending my laziness with the glasses. "I'm on vacation."

Easter pounced again.

❖

Every year, I take Pride Week off from Now & Zen—the spa where I work—and glory in hitting my local coffee shop at the same time everyone else is racing off to their nine-to-fives. Seated at Bittersweets, I toast them with my tea and eat something decadent and sugary for breakfast. At the sugar-breakfast, I open my Pride Week flyer and decide which events I want to hit, and generally spend my week off feeling happy to have been born the gay child.

After showering, feeding Easter his morning kibble, and changing into my favorite shirt—a light-green short-sleeved piece of awesomeness that fits me just right—and a pair of khaki shorts, I went to my regular coffee shop where I go most mornings before work and ordered my chai tea. The barista—a cute pixie of a girl with blond hair and dimples whose name I've never managed to catch—raised an eyebrow.

"You're late today."

I shook my head and regarded all the sinful morsels in the baked goods display.

"Nope," I said. "Vacation. I'll have the lemon poppy seed. With the icing."

"Ah," she said, and cut me a slice of the cake. I gave her a loonie tip and went to the small outside porch, propped myself facing out among the crowds of people who were still cutting through the Byward Market on their way to work, and sipped. All around me, people in suits with ID badges on little strings were rushing back and forth, some of them already chatting on their earpieces. Ottawa is a government town, and government jobs abound. As far as I can tell, while government jobs all require boring suits and little ID badges on little strings that clip to your belt, the earpieces seem optional and tied to self-importance.

It was sunny. It was warm. The Byward Market was full of people, and some of the nearby stalls were filled with fresh-cut flowers that I could smell from where I sat.

"This is the life," I said to myself. A passing woman frowned at me, giving me that odd look people reserve for those they find speaking to themselves, and then looked the other way.

My cell phone rang. I let it ring twice, then sighed and tugged it out of my pocket and checked the display. It was the spa. I thumbed the screen.

"You've reached the voice mail of Kieran Quinn," I said, "who is so completely and utterly on vacation that he can't come to the phone right now, even if someone has the most insistent need for a massage ever known to mankind." I paused, considering. "Unless he's gay, single, and really hot."

"No emergencies," said Karen, the spa's receptionist and baker of healthy goodies. "I'm just calling to remind you not to willfully forget the blind date you agreed to."

"I'm fairly certain I didn't agree so much as I was told." I sipped my tea. Heaven.

"I'm an Aries," Karen said. She reminded me of this more often than she needed to. "When we tell you to do something, that's asking."

"What's telling, then?"

"Believe me, you'll know it if it happens," she said. "He's going to meet you at the coffee shop you always go to when you're on vacation."

"How do you know these things?" I grumbled, not delighted that my morning ritual was going to be interrupted by another one of Karen's dubious blind dates. The last one she'd set me up with was with Elliot, an accountant. Try finding something fun to talk about with an accountant, I dare you.

Though, to be fair, I did end up starting an RRSP.

"Aries," she reminded me.

"Right," I said, then thought of a second exit strategy. "How will he know who I am?"

"I told him to find the dark Irish lad with the self-contented smirk on his face, brown eyes, and hipster Buddy Holly glasses who'd be sitting on the patio and lording it over the worker drones." She paused while I groaned, then put the cherry on top. "I said you'd probably be wearing your favorite green shirt."

"You frighten me."

"As I should."

I scowled. "I'm not a hipster."

"Your glasses are hipster."

"My glasses are inanimate."

"Animate is so five months ago."

I laughed.

"Be very nice to him, he's a gentle, gentle soul," she said.

"Oh for crying out loud, what is he then, a poet?" I asked.

"Worse," she said. "A Pisces!"

"*I'm* a Pisces," I said, but she'd already hung up.

I looked down at my lemon poppy seed cake. If I ate it fast enough, then I could get a lid for my tea and be out of here before—oh for crying out loud, I didn't even remember his bloody name—showed up. I'd make it up to Karen some other way, probably with many of her favorite almond mocha lattes. I took a big hunk of the cake with my plastic fork and stuffed it into my mouth. The icing was definitely worth it.

"Kieran?" It was a hesitant voice.

I turned, mouth full, and saw my blind date.

"Mlrph." I nodded.

He was taller than me, fair-haired, and had nice green eyes. He was about my age, I guessed, or maybe just on the other side of thirty, and wearing a black T-shirt that was a little tight and showed off his trim waist well enough. The T-shirt said "I'm Beyond Your Peripheral Vision."

Ani DiFranco. I gave him a point for obscure song lyrics.

He smiled awkwardly, then said, "I'll just get myself a coffee, and I'll be right back out, okay?"

I nodded again, chewing furiously. The icing was stuck to the roof of my mouth. I made what I hoped was an apologetic face. He smiled again—he had a good smile—then ducked back into Bittersweets.

I managed to swallow and swig some chai before he returned, a steaming cup of black coffee in one hand and a bagel in the other, without cream cheese or jam or even any butter, which made me wonder if he was an alien or something and cost him a point. He put his food and coffee down, sat across from me with his back to the street, and then offered a hand.

"I'm Justin." He smiled, revealing a tiny gap between his teeth. He reclaimed the lost point for dental honesty. No veneers.

I shook his hand and managed to speak now that the lemon poppy seed cake wasn't choking me.

"Sorry, I had my mouth full," I said. "I'm Kieran."

"Karen didn't do you justice," he said. Flattery was worth another point. He was racking them up faster than Eliot the boring accountant. I must have felt generous since I was on vacation.

"Karen's an Aries, which she says is permission to live bluntly," I said. "All I got about you was my orders and a 'handle with care' warning."

He winced. "Handle with care?"

"You're a gentle, gentle soul." I tried for Karen's booming voice, and missed by miles. "And a Pisces."

"Oh God." Justin laughed. "She's mean. Though I am a Pisces."

"Me too," I said.

This wasn't so bad. We were on a safe topic, even if it was a bit vapid. Justin seemed nice enough, but I didn't want to pounce on him. It was a shame. It's not that I try to make snap judgments, it's just that I know when I'm attracted to someone in a hot and sweaty way—which usually involves me having trouble concentrating and completely humiliating myself by stuttering or babbling—and Justin wasn't invoking that feeling. To be honest, I liked men who were rougher around the edges, which was something I was never going to tell Karen, because she'd probably know the perfect ex-pro-wrestler to set me up with.

"So what are you planning for the week?" Justin asked.

I raised one eyebrow. "She gave you all the details, didn't she?"

He sipped his coffee. "I may have asked."

"Today's the pride flag raising at City Hall, and the Gay Men's Chorus will sing the anthem, which I like to go see."

Justin seemed surprised. "They raise a flag at City Hall?"

I nodded. "And the mayor reads the proclamation. It's when Pride Week officially begins." I forked off a much smaller bite of lemon poppy seed and chewed carefully.

"You're really into it." Justin bit his unbuttered, dry bagel. I watched to see if he'd implode but he seemed to survive. Weird. I guess some people have invulnerable stomachs or something.

"I love Pride," I said. "I love every second of it, the dancing, the speeches, the parade."

He smiled, but I heard two words, like Justin's voice was echoing badly through a long and crooked tunnel. *Club kid.* I kept my face from showing it, but it deflated me a bit. Most of the time, I kept the thoughts of other people out of my head. I'd go nuts if I didn't. I only really "heard" things if someone really thought something strongly, or when I was distracted from keeping my mental wall in place.

So Justin *really* thought I was a club kid. He was dismissing me as loving Pride just as an opportunity to go get drunk, dance, and hook up with random fellas.

"It's not the partying," I said. "It's the way everyone gets together. The lesbians and the gay men, the drag queens and the leather crowd, the gay pagans and the Unitarians. All of it. I just love it."

People rarely understood why I loved Pride. Sure, the parties were fun, and I loved the parade, but it wasn't the debauchery—well, fine, not *only* the debauchery—it was the sense of community and spirit and, well, *pride.* It was where normal wasn't normal. Where we're all of us freaks and all of us okay with it. I loved that for all that we were so different, it was a week celebrating that different was awesome.

Ugh. I really was a Pisces.

Justin leaned back in his chair. "I hadn't really thought of it like that. I don't even go to the parade. It always seems sort of trashy to me."

That cost him all of his points. I drank some chai.

"So when is the flag raising?" Justin asked.

For crying out loud. He was going to come with me. I forced a smile and told him.

❖

We swung by my apartment for my bus pass, as it turned out that Justin was averse to making the twenty-minute walk to get to the flag raising—minus one point—and preferred to use public transit. When I unlocked the apartment door and didn't immediately crouch down to play with him, Easter walked up and head-butted my ankle.

"Oh, a cat," Justin said, and knelt down to scoop up Easter, who dodged him with a disdainful swish of tail. "She's gorgeous—so white. Oh wow, her eyes are so pretty." Easter shot off into the bedroom and under my bed.

"He's mostly a Turkish Angora," I said. "Rescued, not bought. A lot of them have one yellow eye and one blue eye." I nabbed my bus pass and tucked it into my shirt pocket.

"What's his name?"

"Easter."

Justin raised his eyebrows. "You got him for Easter?"

I shook my head. "No, it's a song lyric." I patted my pocket and tried to muster up some enthusiasm for spending more time together. "All set."

"Fantastic." Justin smiled. "Let's go raise a flag."

Boring, he thought, though, and it came through loud and clear from his head into mine.

I took a second to redouble my efforts at screening him out. This guy was one of the most projective people I'd ever met.

That, or he had very simple, very loud thoughts. Most people I could filter out with a casual bit of mental effort I almost always make on reflex. But some people—and often not those who were on the top slope of the intelligence bell curve—were much louder and just blasted their thoughts at me like they were using a bullhorn. Perhaps Justin was a bit simple. I grinned as I locked the apartment door.

"What's so funny?" he asked me.

"Oh, I'm just thinking of my brother, Callum. When I told him I was heading to a flag raising on my vacation, he said I was the most boring person he knew."

Justin rolled his eyes as if brothers couldn't possibly know anything, but he blushed a bit. What? I never said I was a saint. You try hearing thoughts for a week and see how you manage holding your tongue.

One thing was for sure. Karen owed me a ton of baked goods.

❖

The crowd at the opening ceremonies was much larger than I'd expected. I was surprised. For all that I was mentally docking Justin for considering the flag raising boring, I knew I was in a small camp of people who'd actually found it worth coming to.

"A lot of people here," Justin said, not hiding his surprise.

I nodded. "This is more than usual." I looked around and saw the Gay Men's Chorus, in pressed white shirts and black slacks, set up in a semicircle near the stage. They were probably baking, poor guys, though the humidity at least was holding off. There was press—more press than I'd ever seen at the opening ceremonies, come to think of it. And a real, honest-to-goodness crowd of gays, lesbians, bisexuals, transgendered, a gaggle of drag queens, and—be still my heart—even a half dozen leather men in harnesses and tight little black leather shorts or chaps.

Yum. One in particular, a man probably two decades my senior with buzzed black hair that was graying just perfectly at the temples, caught my eye. He had arms like a wrestler, and his thighs looked like they could snap small tree trunks. Was there some sort of ointment they all used to make chests do that buff shiny thing, even with the chest hair? Surely it wasn't natural. Whatever it was, it was worth every penny.

There were also a half dozen police officers in their black uniforms standing about. It took me a second to notice them—they were being unobtrusive but were definitely paying attention. That was very unusual.

"I'd like to get closer to the stage," I said, and started to press my way through to where the small stage had been erected close to the front of City Hall, beside the flagpole. Justin followed, amiably enough, a look of wonder on his face. I think he was considering that this might not be a snooze-fest after all.

As we broke through near the front, my eyes fell on a group of people who made the Gay Men's Chorus look frumpy in comparison. They all wore gleaming white shirts and plain navy trousers or skirts, and each carried a sign that said "Repent!" or "It is not too late to know the love of Jesus!" or "God Saves!" At the front, standing beside a slim man in a blue suit with mirror shades and two very muscular buzz-cut types in black suits with necks as thick as my thighs, was a man holding both his hands to the sky, his eyes closed, swaying back and forth like he was about to break out a tambourine at any moment. He, too, wore a white shirt, but his pants, socks, and shoes were also white. His hair, long and tied back in a ponytail, was a blond so painfully pale you wondered if he was an albino, though I knew if he opened his eyes, they'd be a piercing, deep blue.

"Oh crap," I said. That explained the press. And the crowd. It also explained the police.

I must have missed an e-mail or something. I was on the

Pride events mailing list so that I'd hear about last-minute events or schedule changes, but between the bad dream and being anxious to start my sugar-breakfast, I hadn't checked my e-mail this morning.

"Who's that?" Justin asked.

"That," I said, "is Stigmatic Jack."

Justin laughed. "Who?"

"Wyatt Jackson," I said. "He's a preacher from Toronto. He's old-school. Came down from somewhere up north because God apparently told him to. His church is a whole lot of scary. He bleeds from the hands and tells people they're going to hell." I looked behind me, a chill running up my spine despite the building heat of the day. "He protested at the Pride events in Toronto, I think." I couldn't really remember all the details, given that I'd not managed to get enough time off at all during the Toronto pride week to have made the five-hour trip worthwhile, but I remembered reading e-mails about it. Wyatt Jackson and his Church of the Testifying Prophet—which would be Jackson himself—had been loud, and there'd been a few minor yelling matches. I thought, but wasn't sure, that nothing had really come of it. "That explains the press and the crowd."

"The mayor doesn't look too happy." Justin nodded to the stage, where the mayor was whispering to her two aides with a strained face. One of the aides had just finished tying the flag in place, ready to be raised once she gave the word. She said something else, then the two men nodded and split up, one by the flagpole, one by her side.

I heard a single loud tone, like the sound of someone giving a wineglass a really hard smack with a fork. I froze, the chill sensation now replaced by outright shivers snaking up and down my spine.

Something was *wrong*. For some reason, I remembered sitting in the hospital room with my mother. I shivered again.

"Are you okay?" Justin asked.

I managed a nod. It was obvious no one else had heard the jangled note, which meant...*something*. I frowned. My heart was racing.

The mayor got up onstage to loud applause from the audience and an eerie quiet from Stigmatic Jack and his Church of the Testifying Pigheads. I glanced around, nervous.

What was wrong with me?

I took a deep breath and tried to listen to the mayor. Her cadence was perfect, as always, and her speech reminded me why it was I came to these events.

"As the mayor of Ottawa, it is a great honor to stand here today to speak to you on this, the opening day of Capital Pride Week." The mayor beamed, apparently as relieved as I was that Stigmatic Jack and his crew were staying quiet. I could handle a peaceful demonstration—I even agreed with their right to have one.

I was feeling more enlightened by the second.

"As a mother of a gay child, however, it is with great pride that I stand here in the capital of a country that recognizes love as love, family as family, and marriage as marriage. My daughter and my daughter-in-law are a constant source of joy in my life, and standing here before you today is an absolute pleasure. To the mothers and fathers of our gay, lesbian, bisexual, and transgendered children celebrating today, I say welcome. You're going to have a great time. We've come such a long way—but as always, we have a way to go. Transgendered rights are still often neglected from the laws of even our great country, but every step we take is a step forward. Every day I wake up in this city I am proud. I am proud of my country. I am proud of my children. I am proud of you." The crowd roared, and she smiled wide, raising her arms and waving.

"Maybe I should have voted for her," Justin said. I forced myself to smile at him while I was clapping and whistling and yelling support for the mayor—who I'd voted for. I docked him one more point.

"And on that note," the mayor said, laughing as the applause once again died down, "I'd like to declare this year's Pride Week open!" She raised her hands to applaud and turned to the left, where the aide tugged the rope and the rainbow flag began to ride its way up the flagpole.

I grinned at Justin, who nodded with a small smile. He seemed to be getting why this was cool. I gave him his point back.

"You are an abomination in the eyes of the Lord!" yelled a voice, and as one, the audience turned and looked at Stigmatic Jack, who was now swaying back and forth, lost in one of his so-called "raptures." I preferred to think of them as hate-spews, but I guess that didn't have the same ring to it that his Church of Testiculars preferred.

The Gay Men's Chorus broke out into the bilingual version of the national anthem, their rich baritones a stark contrast to Jack's declarations of our unworthiness, and easily drowning out his voice.

I heard three tones, like clashing rising notes from three broken tuning forks, and shook my head. What *was* that? *Abomination. He...you....hope...*

"Only He can save you!" yelled Jack. "God is hope!"

I shuddered. The last thing I wanted was to get into Stigmatic Jack's head. Though I was surprised that the voice of his thoughts didn't sound like his speaking voice—most thoughts, I've found, sound more or less like the spoken voice of their owner. I didn't care enough to keep listening, though, and tried to shut my telepathy down to its lowest setting. I pictured a brick wall in my mind. The vague whispers—and the odd chiming like broken music—stopped.

Success. I closed my eyes. I really needed to practice my telepathy more, probably with someone other than my cat.

"Oh my God," Justin said. I opened my eyes again and saw he was pointing. Wyatt Jackson's palms had begun to bleed, two red lines that trickled down his arms and stained his sleeves.

"Yeah," I said, feeling somewhat sick myself. "He does that."

Flashes of light went off as the press captured the moment. The mayor's aide had stopped raising the flag until the mayor shot him a look that would have curdled milk at one hundred paces. Hopefully no one caught a picture of that particular glance. My respect for her grew, and the flag began to rise again, nearly at the top.

One of the drag queens dolled up as a Southern belle flipped open a lacy fan and began fanning herself, and cried out, "Preacher Jackson, y'all are being rude and you're getting your pretty shirt all dirty! Mister Clean here is gonna have to come on over there and clean you up!" She pointed to a buff, bald daddy type beside her, who happened to be wearing a tight white T-shirt and a gold hoop earring. Jeers and laughter surrounded her. In return, the church group got louder in their protestations of our misguided souls.

Wyatt Jackson raised his voice again. "You will burn in the hell fires for all of eternity if you do not renounce your sinful ways!"

"Oh, fuck you," a man called back.

The flag reached the apex, and the Gay Men's Chorus finished the anthem. In the quiet that followed, the church's chanting seemed so much louder.

"In God trust, repent your lust!"

"Don't knock it till you try it," a younger man in a yellow T-shirt shouted.

This wasn't going well. The mayor had stepped back, and Wyatt Jackson's handler and two bodyguards stepped closer to him. Then one of the lesbians leveled a Super Soaker their way and let loose with a stream of water.

Laughter followed.

The police moved toward the edge of the crowd; Stigmatic Jack's newly wet bodyguards and handler closed in tighter around him, though Jack himself didn't seem to notice he'd been sprayed with water and raised his bloody hands high.

"You will be punished!" he yelled. Trickles of blood ran down his arms. My head filled with the clashing sounds of discordant notes. I pushed my hands against my forehead. The echoing cacophony almost hurt.

"Are you okay?" Justin asked me.

"Headache," I managed to say through gritted teeth. "I get migraines."

Someone screamed.

The lesbian with the Super Soaker had dropped it and was staring at her arms in horror. Two short red cuts had opened along her forearms and were bleeding freely. Beside her, the young man in the yellow T-shirt yelped as the fabric of the shirt, and the flesh beneath, sliced open along his left shoulder.

It happened again—the Southern belle drag queen with the fan had a gash open on her forehead.

And again—the man who'd yelled "Fuck you!" staggered, a long slash opening on his leg.

"Oh my God," Justin said, barely audible over the sounds of the panicking crowd. People started to shove and push, and it devolved quickly. I saw Justin step back once, then twice, and then other people were pushing between us, moving toward the front to see what was going on, or away, having seen the blood.

Justin was gone.

I didn't know what to do. Flashes of light from the cameras punctuated the screams, and as Stigmatic Jack ranted on and on about the punishment from God, more people were screaming, and some were even falling. Most of the people were trying to get away from Jack's group, but some were beside the figures who had fallen or were trying to walk the wounded away from the area. From where I was in the press of the crowd, I could see the police were trying to get to Stigmatic Jack, but his church of followers crowded around him like a human shield. His thick-necked bodyguards were locked around Stigmatic Jack and his handler.

Hide. I shook my head. *Hide.* The word felt old, and for the first time in my life, inadequate. I could handle this.

"No," I said. My mental brick wall crumbled, and I heard the tones again, and caught bits of a voice.

Punish. Yes! Punish...all. Blood is...God alone...them.

A ringing note in the tones was louder than the underlying song. There was a bellow just behind me. I turned and saw one of the leather men—who'd been trying to shove his way toward where the people were getting hurt—fall to his knees as a large and very deep gash opened up along his arm, all the way down to his wrist. Blood flowed.

Hide. The word was barely registering.

No. This had to stop.

I couldn't see Justin anywhere; I'd lost him to the shoving and heaving crowd. People were running, the crowd was thinning out, and I had a line of sight to Wyatt Jackson. I really hoped no one was bothering to look at me.

I took a deep breath and lit up.

❖

I have been psychic since I was ten.

It started when my mother and I, in what became her deathbed in a hospital in Hamilton, watched a live show with a supposed American telekinetic. The man's name was Thomas Wright, and while my mother and I watched him, a man with a history of mental illness shot Wright in the head. It was the first publicly aired example of telekinetic ability. It was the first time psychokinesis was captured on television by a named and known individual—and it ended in bloodshed and murder.

In the hospital room with my mother, I passed out, gave myself a really good bump on the head, and when I woke up, I was just *different*. Thank God I'd been with my mom. At first my telekinesis was unconscious and I had a hard time not doing it by accident. I'd reach for something and it would topple over or slide into my hand. When it happened in front of her—only hours after I woke up from my blackout—she sat me on her bed and said, "Kieran, this is a wonderful, wonderful gift. What you can do is a marvelous thing. And it will scare people. I want you to promise me that you'll keep this to yourself. It'll be our secret. We'll figure it out together, all right?"

I knew what she'd meant. I'd just seen Wright get shot, after all. I remembered a woman's voice—it must have been my mother—telling me to hide. Seemed like very good advice. But my mother was right. To hide what I could do from the people I might scare, I needed to figure out how to do it. If I knew how to do it, I'd know how not to.

We would figure it out.

"Every problem has a solution," she'd said, and smiled at me. For a moment it was like she was back in her classroom, teaching math.

The last five months of her life, my mom helped me find the solutions. We didn't even tell my father.

When her pain started, I would make stuffed animals dance around on her bed, and she'd laugh. When her pain grew worse, I realized I could feel it, and sometimes even catch words that she was thinking. I told her, and she attacked this new development with a fresh passion. I learned how to keep her thoughts out of my head, and later I even realized I could send a thought to her.

Telepathy became a second game, just like telekinesis.

Looking back now with the eyes of an adult, I think it was something for her to focus on that wasn't her cancer. It was a problem with a concrete solution, unlike the disease that was killing her. But to me, my telekinesis and telepathy were wonderful things I had with my mom that I didn't want to share with anyone else.

I held her hand as she died, my father and brother on the other side of her, our priest beside me. I could hear her final thoughts.

"She loves us very much," I said, even as I watched my father cry—something I'd never witnessed before.

For all that I was different and had these so-called "gifts," the greatest one of them was knowing, without a shadow of a doubt, that I was a loved and cherished child. Thoughts, you see, don't lie.

The first few times I used my telekinesis my mother noticed that whatever I moved would glow. It wasn't bright, but if I nudged things, they would sort of light up. Much discussion with my mother—and later experimentation and reading on my own—led me to accept that though I could tone it down, my telekinesis, for better or for worse, almost always came with a light show.

Over time—including one very boring summer when I was sixteen and had pneumonia—I learned how to bend the light on purpose, forming thin "lenses" out of my telekinesis by projecting pressure into the air that bent light a certain way. Twisting my attempt just so would produce a green glow, or a yellow if I tweaked it slightly less. I also learned how to reflect and redirect light and aim the ambient light wherever I wanted it to go, or send it bending at odd angles, making it seem like mirrors floated in the air above me, or distorting the path of light to warp the view.

At night I would take the moonlight or a streetlight and try to reflect and redirect the light in my room until it was bright enough to read my comic books. It had become a game, just like trying to move objects without looking at them or trying to hover more and more objects at the same time.

My current record is seven.

But on the other end of the equation, it didn't take long to hit my limit with weight. I could, if I really worked at it, manage about twenty-five to thirty pounds. After that, I started to feel a strange tightness around my head, like my skull was a bit too small, and the teke—what I called the sensation of using telekinesis, sort of like feeling the pressure of using a mental hand—would start to ache. It felt like if I want any further, I'd pass out.

Using telekinesis to mess with the light, however, was much easier, and something I got very good at.

❖

Forming telekinetic lenses in a band all around me except for my eyes, I reflected and refracted the bright sunlight, trying to aim it back out directly from me in every direction. The result—I hoped—was to make me a bright shiny object and none too pleasant to look at. Especially, I prayed, a bright blob impossible to identify later. Almost immediately, there were yelps and cries, and people threw up their hands to cover their eyes from the sudden glare that was me.

For a moment the tones stopped, and though people were still yelling and moving, it didn't seem like anyone was being slashed at anymore.

Stigmatic Jack and his crew were looking at me, most with their hands raised to cover their eyes, though Jackson himself was looking at me with a strange wide-eyed wonder. Bathed in sunlight both from above and reflected from me, he looked even more ghostly, and his blood seemed even redder.

"Metatron?" he cried.

I frowned behind my light. Did he think I was a robot?

There was another note, and another cry from a young woman who was trying to get away from City Hall. I needed to handle this, now.

"That's enough!" I yelled, and then with as much effort as I could manage, I created more lenses behind and above me, making three of them in series with space between. All the sunlight around me bent directly upon Stigmatic Jack and his church of lunatics. I reflected and rebounded the light against the telekinetic lenses three times over. The effect was like a dozen mirrors with magnifying glasses all aimed their way on an extremely bright day. Looking at them made my eyes water.

They yelled and threw their hands over their eyes, even the blue-suited handler in the expensive sunglasses. The tones stopped mid-chime and everyone turned away from the light. One of the women screamed. I stopped reflecting light all around myself and dove to the left, leaving the bigger lenses above in place a few seconds longer, turning them to swing beams of light all around the field. I lay flat on the grass and covered my eyes, took a deep breath, then let the lenses go, too. No one grabbed me or yelled at me. I uncovered my eyes like I was just one of many who'd just seen the light show.

No one was so much as looking my way. Success. I looked back at Stigmatic Jack and his crew.

"I can't see!" one of the bodyguards yelled in a surprisingly high-pitched voice.

I trembled. Shit. Did I *blind* them? Like, permanently?

I rose to my knees, shaking. *Hide.* The old voice was back, and this time I didn't feel the urge to argue with it. I had to get out of here. What if someone had managed to see me light up, or realized I'd been the one just a few feet over those seconds ago, when I flipped the lenses off? There was no way my luck would hold forever. I shook, adrenaline burning through me.

There was a moan, and I looked to the left, my mind still racing for a way out. The leather man was on his side and he

LIGHT

was covered in blood. I realized with a start that the gash on his arm had gone deep. I crawled over to him as fast as I could and looked for something to stop the bleeding. I gripped his arm. Blood seeped between my fingers. This was bad. My favorite green shirt bit the bullet. I tied it around the man's wrist so tight he swore at me in a thick French accent and then I added insult to injury by pressing my hands against it as hard as I could. He continued to swear but he was glassy-eyed and barely awake.

"Stay with me," I said, shivering. He met my gaze and nodded. My teeth were chattering, even in the heat. At one time, I'd wanted to do this sort of thing for a living. I must have been insane.

He grimaced, and his eyes rolled in his head.

"Oh no, you don't," I said.

I gingerly reached out with my mind and felt the man's pain in front of me like a pool of churning frigid water. I swayed, getting caught in the icy pain of his thoughts. The sensation was something akin to diving into a lake just after the spring thaw. I gasped as his mind grabbed at mine. It felt like I was going to drown in him, but I managed, barely, to get back mostly in my own head. Holding myself together against the pain and confusion in his mind, I made a second attempt to touch his thoughts.

He was in a lot of pain. All down his arm, and especially his wrist. He was afraid, too, though there was a kind of bravery to his fear that touched me—I could feel he was worried about everyone else as much as himself. His actual thoughts I couldn't make out—they were rapid, and in French, and I was on the edge of passing out with him.

I found the pain and tried to dilute it. I did something similar when I massaged my clients, finding the stresses and frustrations that led to the forming of their knots and tight muscles. People came to massages expecting to relax, and the opportunity to practice telepathy didn't come often, so I'd sometimes dip into

• 25 •

their thoughts and feel where they hurt to give myself a better map of what I was trying to accomplish. I could even nudge at their mind to relax a bit, tell the parts of the brain in charge of the tense muscles to calm down and unwind.

This was nothing like that. Aches and pains I could handle, but this flood of deep pain was something else entirely. I didn't flatter myself to think I was erasing his pain, but as I found the parts of his mind that were crying out over the deep cut, I told them to lay off, and he seemed to breathe much easier, and met my gaze with clearer eyes.

"You're going to be fine," I told him. My own voice sounded far away to my ears, and echoed funny.

"*Merci,*" he said, and closed his eyes. He was still awake, though. I swallowed, my throat dry.

I'd barely heard the sirens, but when two paramedics arrived and took over, I just sat there on the ground, light-headed. I kept catching what other people were thinking, and I just couldn't muster enough effort to screen it all out. A policeman who didn't look a day over nineteen came and asked me my name, which I gave with a kind of stunned, clipped speech. While I was speaking to him, another paramedic showed up, and she asked me if I was hurt, and I realized my forearms and hands were covered in blood.

"It's not mine," I said, "There was a man. He was cut." I touched my forearm. "He was bleeding pretty badly, so I did some first aid."

The paramedic smiled at me. "Good job. Do you need him still? He should go home, drink some juice, and sleep."

The police officer, whose name I'd missed, frowned, but shook his head. He was nervous and a bit unsure of himself. I wasn't far off on his age assessment—he'd barely been at the job two months.

I rose unsteadily, realizing I was reading the cop's mind and trying to pull back out. The paramedic handed me an oversized wet-nap and I wiped myself down awkwardly. She told me I should schedule a blood test. I stared at her in confusion, until I realized she meant I'd exposed myself to unknown blood. Silly me, I should have asked the leather man for a name and full medical history. It struck me as insanely funny. I giggled.

"You really should go home," she said, frowning. *Shock*, she was thinking, though not unkindly. I just couldn't seem to find the off switch for my telepathy.

"Are you okay to get home?" the policeman asked. *Can we spare a car*, he wondered.

"I have a bus pass." Both watched me a moment longer, obviously unsure, but I nodded, pulling myself together, and finally found the strength to force my mental wall back into place. Their thoughts faded from my mind. "I'm fine. Really. Sorry. It was just a lot of blood."

The police officer moved off to the next person who was waiting. I hadn't realized they'd stopped everyone. I looked for Justin in the crowd, but I couldn't see him. All things considered, it was okay for him to ditch me.

"You did a good thing." The paramedic patted my arm and left.

I made it all the way to the bus stop before I realized my bus pass was in my shirt pocket, which was last seen tied around the arm of a bleeding leather man.

I walked home.

❖

Easter skidded to a halt on the wood floor inches from my feet. His mismatched eyes grew wide, and then he shot off into my bedroom and hid under my bed. I tried not to take it personally and went straight to the bathroom.

I showered off the blood, then lathered, rinsed, and repeated. Twice. My head felt light, like it was full of cotton, and I knew it was only a matter of time before I crashed. I hadn't used a teke or my telepathy to that level in a long time. Ever, actually. Even though I hadn't actually moved or lifted anything and had only been messing with the light, my head felt like I used to feel once I'd pushed myself past lifting one of my brother Callum's twenty-five-pound weights. I dried off, tugged on a pair of boxers and a T-shirt, and went to my couch, where I sprawled unceremoniously.

Easter reappeared on the arm of the chair and eyed me suspiciously.

"I'm all clean now," I said to him.

He squinted.

I pictured myself stroking Easter under the chin and then risked pushing the mental image gently into Easter's mind. I still felt pretty tapped out but it didn't make me feel faint at all. I wasn't sure what that meant—was I getting better at this? I took a few deep breaths and repeated projecting the image into my cat's mind.

Easter purred and walked over, nudging his head at my fingers. I started rubbing his chin. In his mind, I could feel a kind of soft, warm happiness like the kind I sensed from my clients when I was massaging their worries and stresses from their bodies. I smiled and let myself revel in the simple happiness of my cat for a little while, until the sense of faintness lightened and faded completely.

With my free hand, I grabbed the remote and turned on the TV. There was no use denying it. *Hide.* For the first time in my life, I'd not taken my mother's advice. I'd need to scope out potential damage.

What if I'd been seen? No one had pointed fingers at City Hall, but there had been plenty of cameras.

The local news had interrupted their broadcast, apparently, when the strange events at City Hall had happened, but were now back to regular scheduling. As it turned on the hour, however, they updated.

I watched, absently stroking Easter, waiting for my world to end.

❖

An hour later, it hadn't.

The news coverage was good, well reported, structured, and correct. I was in nearly every photo, of course. But even with a dozen cell phone shots, and about half a dozen reporters and bystanders with their digital cameras, I wasn't recorded in any way that actually resembled me. There was one picture taken by someone where I could make myself out, but it was taken after my light show. My shirt was already off, pressed against the leather guy's arm. I looked sort of scary, actually, with streaks of blood and a very focused look on my face while I pressed the man's arm. I made a mental note for the future. I was no gladiator. The Spartacus effect was not a good look for me.

But in the other photos…

Though I've done it once or twice before for my own amusement, I've never really seen myself when I worked the light so dramatically. I had no frame of reference to imagine at all what I looked like when I had bent the light all around myself— something I'd only ever done a couple of times on my own when I was sure no one was around to see it except my cat.

I was a walking figure of mirror-bright reflected sunlight, with a blue shift on my leading edge and a red shift behind me. Lens flare in all of the shots broke into rainbows and spheres of white light as the digital cameras tried to figure out what to do with me. You couldn't see my face—*thank God!*—but the effect was…

Well, if I do say so myself, it was brilliant. Pretty. Glittery.

And really, really *gay*.

They kept the best image of me on the screen while the news reporter spoke. I was walking and there was an obvious human shape to me. I wasn't even listening.

It was overwhelming. Lit, on the screen, I was incandescent. Luminous.

Beautiful.

"Huh," I said, and for some reason, I thought about my mother. My eyes filled with tears.

The reporter's words caught me then.

"No casualties, though two people were taken to the hospital, and one is still listed in serious condition."

No casualties. Good. Easter batted his head against my palm, his usual subtle request for more head pats. I returned my attention to his head enough to make him content and looked back at the screen.

"The phenomenon reportedly ceased when the glowing figure released a sort of burst of light at the protesters led by Wyatt Jackson. Wyatt Jackson is the Toronto-born evangelist who has declared that he and his Church of the Testifying Prophet will protest all of the events in Ottawa's pride week, and do the same in Montreal as well. His protesters were at most events in the Toronto Pride in June and July of this year, but none of those protests turned violent. There is still confusion over who began the altercation, although witnesses report the attacks began when the protestors were loudly jeered. Once again, today at the opening for Capital Pride, more than a dozen people were wounded, two critically…"

My cell rang. I muted the television.

"Hello?" I said, not checking the call display.

"Kieran!" Karen's voice was tight. "I just got a call from Justin. I watched the news…Jesus! Are you okay?"

I flinched. "I'm fine, I'm sorry. I had to walk back, and I had to talk to the police…Is Justin okay?"

"Yes. He said he lost you, and he didn't know your number."

"We got split up once it got ugly."

"What happened?"

That was a good question. "I don't know. There was a guy who got hurt, and I was sort of taking care of him." I felt a bit guilty over the lie of omission. Karen was my best friend. I told her everything.

Hide.

Well, almost everything.

"Are you sure you're okay?" Her voice had lost its edge.

"Karen, I'm fine, but I really just want to go and be quiet for a while."

"Of course," she said. She was completely calm now. If there was anyone I'd ever want on my side in an emergency, it was Karen. I felt guilty all over again about not telling her the truth. "I'll see you tomorrow?"

"Daily swim," I agreed.

"I'm glad you're okay," she said.

I smiled. "Me too."

I hung up and noticed that they seemed to be interviewing people who'd been at the flag raising. I thumbed the volume back on and heard the tail end of an interview with a young man who hadn't seen much but said, "The glowing guy was awesome."

"I have a fan," I said to Easter. Easter smacked my wrist with one paw. I resumed his head rubs.

Then the screen changed to a picture of the leather guy I'd helped. He had strips of white bandage wrapped around his forearm and wrist, and he was in a hospital bed. No sign of the leather harness.

He was actually nice-looking, once you cleaned the blood off. He wasn't handsome in a classical way—he'd obviously had his nose broken at some point, and there was a scar that cut his left eyebrow in half—but definitely masculine. Dark hair, brown eyes, great chin.

And massive pecs, of course. He apparently used the same ointment as the older guy. It was probably a trade secret.

"Pride Week is still going forward," he was saying.

The name at the bottom of the screen was Sebastien LaRoche, which explained the dark, swarthy French Canadian look, and the swear words and thoughts in French. His title was "Pride Week Organizer." Underneath, in smaller writing, it said, "Victim of the City Hall Attack."

Really? The best word they'd come up with was "attack"?

"We're an indomitable people," Sebastien was saying, and I gave him two points for using multiple syllable words in a second language, even though we weren't on a date. "Even in the midst of the attack, people ran toward the chaos, to help. Someone gave me first aid until ambulances arrived. *That's* community."

I smiled. *You're welcome*, I thought.

Someone off-camera asked if he knew who'd helped him.

"No." Sebastien smiled. "Which goes to my point. I don't know who it was. I'm told he might have saved my life. I owe him a beer."

He had a great smile.

I allowed myself a brief fantasy of contacting LaRoche and claiming my beer and a complimentary bottle of chest ointment, then turned off the TV and dragged myself up off the couch. I walked into my bedroom, feeling unsteady on my feet, and crawled into bed. Easter hopped up with me and took his usual place in the crook of my arm. He purred. I closed my eyes and let the day go.

"This is not the vacation I was looking for," I said, waving my free hand in the air over Easter's head, but he didn't answer.

ORANGE

I'd had this dream before, and I liked it.

I was floating above the earth, like a satellite in orbit, stretched out lazily. It was not a realistic dream, by which I mean I wasn't freezing, explosively decompressing, gasping for breath in the silence, or any of the other horrible things that happen to a human being exposed to the vacuum of space. It was quite the opposite. I felt warm, bathed in the glorious orange light of the sun setting over the Earth. I could breathe. In my mind I could hear a kind of song, gentle notes like that of a delicate crystal wind chime stirred by the faintest of breezes.

Far below me, Earth turned. White clouds, rich blue oceans, and all the greens and browns of the continents moved past. Before, when I'd dreamed this "above it all" dream, I'd been above the clouds high enough to see the curvature of the planet but still within its grasp. This time, I was farther from the Earth than I'd ever been. I could look down at the whole of the planet. I felt an incredible sense of peace.

I wondered if I'd recognize the Ottawa valley from here.

"I love this dream," I said, audible in the false vacuum.

"Me too," said a woman's voice.

I turned. I wasn't alarmed, only curious. On some level the awareness of being in a dream gave me an out—even if this shifted into a nightmare, I'd just tell myself to wake up.

Beside me in space floated a beautiful black woman. Her hair was done in long, tight braids, which floated out from where they were collected at the base of her neck. She was curvy, not slender. She was, like me, wearing night clothes, which in her case was a long flowing shirt that probably belonged to a boyfriend or a husband, and bare legs that were strong with muscle. She looked to be my age, or maybe a bit older, and something about the way she regarded me made me feel a little bit on display. One of her eyebrows arched, and a sly smile twisted the corner of her lips.

This girl is whipcrack smart, I thought. *And she looks like freaking Beyoncé.*

"Well, thank you," she said, with her smirky little smile. "But she doesn't have my rack."

I blushed. "I know you," I said. "Don't I?" She was familiar, somehow.

"I should think so." She nodded, and some of her braided hair looped past her face for a moment. "You've been here before once or twice, though never this high. Don't you remember your dreams?"

It hit me.

"You're her. You're Miracle Woman," I breathed.

She smiled and raised her arms wide. "In the astral flesh. But no makeup. Don't judge my resting state."

"But…You're my age."

Her eyebrow crept up again. "You sayin' I'm old?"

I laughed. I liked her. "No, I just thought you'd be older. I remember hearing about you, seeing the pictures on television."

"Ah." She nodded, amused. "People see what they want to see. A tall black girl who can lift a bus? Definitely must be an adult. No one wants to think of a preteen doing that shit."

"Wow," I said, humbled. "This is like meeting a rock star or something."

"Oh, you can stay." She laughed, a rich, wonderful laugh that was more or less free of mockery.

I grinned. "This isn't quite dreaming, is it?"

She shook her head. "Not really."

The music grew louder and became far more complex. New notes interwove in counterpoint, creating a cadence that rose and fell in a gentle rhythm. I flowed with it for a moment, just listening.

"What's that music?" I asked.

"You don't ask the easy questions first, do you?"

I shrugged. "I heard it today, just before some bad things happened." Though it was nowhere near as lovely. This was lyrical. What I'd heard while people were being sliced up sounded like an angry toddler bashing at a xylophone with a rubber mallet.

Her amused smile returned, and the eyebrow rose again. "I saw you on the news. The Rainbow Man."

I blinked. "Rainbow Man?"

"That's what they're calling you on the news. Didn't your mother teach you to stay off the news?"

I winced. Rainbow Man? Then I realized what she had just said. "How did you know it was me?"

She just closed her eyes and listened to the music, that smile still tucked on the corner of her lips.

You're really tuned in, aren't you? I thought.

Hell yes, she thought back.

"What happened?" I asked, eager. "To you, I mean. It started with you, didn't it?"

She opened her eyes again and turned to face me, pointing over my shoulder.

My cell phone rang. I woke with the sudden sensation of falling and grabbed both sides of the bed in a jerk that made Easter leap to the floor and shoot out into the living room. A row of books on my shelves tipped onto the floor in a flare of golden light.

"Jesus," I breathed.

My cell phone rang again.

I sat up, held out my hand, and teked the phone. It flipped from my chest of drawers into my hand with a bluish blur. It came easier and faster than I'd intended, and I stared at it in my hand. The caller display said "Quinn, C."

I cringed, but thumbed the screen.

"Callum, I'll have you know you just interrupted a great dream," I said.

"Da just called me. Apparently, he saw you all covered in blood on the news. What the feck, man?" My older brother never was one to mince his words, and his Irish was showing. We'd come to Canada when I was still young enough to lose my accent, but Callum seemed to recover his whenever he was mad. I shifted up in bed.

"Dad saw me on the news?" My voice was raw.

"Covered in blood, he said." Callum ground out each word angrily.

For crying out loud. I could be such an idiot. I knew my father watched the news every night—it wasn't like he hadn't been doing so for years. I couldn't believe I'd been so stupid to just go to bed. I wondered if I'd slept through other calls. I rubbed my eyes. What had I been thinking?

"Kieran?" Callum prompted.

"It wasn't my blood. I was doing first aid," I said, hoping that would help.

It didn't.

"Some maniac is running about chopping people up and you stick around to do first aid? I thought you got out of nursing."

"It wasn't a maniac," I sighed, dropping back against my pillows. "And I'm fine, thanks for asking."

"Of course you're fine," Callum snapped. "You'd be in a hospital if you weren't fine. Jesus, Kieran. You could have at least called Da."

I felt a wash of guilt. "I didn't think. I just came home and sort of passed out."

"Did they catch the guy?"

"What guy?" I wasn't following.

"The one with the knife."

I frowned. "What knife?"

"What knife? Jesus." I could almost hear Callum counting to ten. "News said people were being cut up."

"Oh," I said. Right. Well, that usually required a knife. "No one got caught. It happened too fast." The words felt weak in my mouth. They certainly didn't convey the absolute fear all around me. Nor the chaos. Or the blood.

"I don't understand," Callum said.

"Yeah, well, me neither, and I was there," I said. I stretched. I felt amazing this morning. My head was clear, and for some reason, I had the sensation I'd never slept better in my life, even with strange dreams.

"And then Jesus showed up?" Callum asked. "Da said Jesus was there, or something? A pillar of light? Was it, like, one of them drag queens?"

I laughed. I couldn't help it. Me. The drag Jesus. "Uh. No."

"Well, what the feck was it, then?" He was back to angry. Callum wasn't the patient one in the family. Actually, I was the only patient one in the family. I took after my mom, who should have been sainted for dealing with my father's moods. I loved our dad, I truly did, but I really hoped he wasn't going to call.

"I don't know," I lied. "I really don't. Somebody did something with some lights. Maybe a floodlight or something?"

There was silence on the line for a moment.

"Are you all right?" Callum asked me. His voice had dropped to a tone of real concern. It made me smile. For all his bluster, Callum took his role as older brother seriously. When I'd been outed my last year in high school, Callum had been like a bodyguard, picking me up after school every night in his Mustang and daring anyone to shove me around with a look of murder in his eye. No one had bothered me, not after it was known Callum Quinn was on watch. I loved him.

Most of the time.

"I'm fine, Cal. Really. It was scary, but I can handle it."

He chuckled. "I'm sure you can. Your mantra, that."

"There are worse mantras."

"Indeed." He sighed. "What'll I tell Da?"

"Maybe you could tell him he should stop watching those awful tabloid news shows and stick with CNN or something?"

Callum laughed. "You tell him. Give him a call, okay?"

"Sure," I lied.

"Liar," he said.

"Crap. My battery is dying," I said.

"Bloody liar!" He laughed. "You're the worst, you ungrateful—!"

I tapped off and then powered down the phone completely for good measure.

I loved modern electronics.

❖

News said there were people being cut.

What Callum had said had sunk in, and with a night's rest and the echoes of that soft dream in my memory, I had a much clearer mind and desire to think about what exactly had happened. Whatever it was that had happened.

News said there were people being cut.

How?

I got out of bed and went into the kitchen. I filled Easter's dish with kitty kibble and put the teakettle on. While Easter munched and my water boiled I kept replaying the scene from the flag raising. The news had it right. People were cut. But the cuts had just *happened*. Like invisible scalpels, slashed razor-fast across open flesh. And through cloth, I remembered, thinking of the guy in the yellow shirt.

I poured my tea, and while it steeped, I teked the teaspoon. Once I had it hovering in front of me, glowing softly, I tried to throw it into the living room and bring it back as fast as I could. It shot off quickly enough, and I had it back in front of me in a second or two, but by no means did it move faster than the eye could follow, especially since in my case it lit up in blues and reds while it moved.

It occurred to me I'd never really practiced speed with my telekinesis. I made a mental note, but figured that no matter how fast a telekinetic moved a knife, you'd see the knife.

Was I on the wrong track? I remembered how Stigmatic Jack had rolled off all his hateful speaking while the cuts had appeared. He'd invoked God, and people had bled. Just for a second, I caught entertaining the notion. *What if...?*

I rolled my eyes.

"It wasn't God," I said firmly. Easter paused in his kibble consumption to look at me, swished his fluffy tail, and then went back to eating.

It wasn't. God wasn't cutting people in Ottawa at the Pride Week opening ceremony. I believed in God. Even if the Catholic Church and I no longer saw eye to eye on a few things (most centrally my love of loving men and deep desire to continue to pursue carnal lust with similar men), my family had all gone Unitarian when the priest at our old church had asked my father to stop allowing me to attend. My father had calmly told the priest— the same man who'd read my mother's last rites—that his entire family would no longer be attending. I'd been overwhelmed with love for my dad—and intensely impressed at how he'd controlled his temper. By the time we'd walked out of the church, his face had been a dark red. When we'd gotten outside, I'd started to apologize, and my father had just raised his hand and said, "God is love, Kieran. He doesn't much care about what kind." Later that night I'd caught him looking at a picture of my mother, and he'd seemed so sad. I rarely managed to read my father's thoughts—they were usually buried deep in his mind unless he was angry—but that night, with the picture of my mother in his hand, I'd heard my father's thoughts loud and clear.

I miss you so much.

The following Sunday, we'd gone to the Unitarian church instead. The Unitarian version of God was quite a good deal more about the love, and so far as I believed He had much better things to do than to rain down death by a thousand cuts on a Pride event in Canada.

Surely He was more worried about the idiots invoking his name all around the world in the name of war?

I picked up my tea and sipped. Since Thomas Wright was murdered, there hadn't been another public psychokinetic willing to go on television or give public performances—or at least none that had stood up to scrutiny. Fake tekes and telepaths were a dime a dozen in the grocery-store rags, and according to the tabloids everyone from the U.S. president to the cast of daytime soaps were secretly telepaths and psychokinetics of one sort or another.

I stopped.

Miracle Woman. I'd been dreaming of her. She'd been the start of it all, as far as anyone could tell. A black woman in Detroit who'd never been identified, she'd been caught on amateur film one winter when an accident involving a school bus had left it hanging on the edge of an overpass. The bus had rocked and swayed halfway off the bridge, the children inside screaming.

A woman in a toque, who'd obviously tugged it down over her face before stepping out of the crowd, walked to the bottom of the overpass and raised her arms. The bus rose in time with her hands. She gracefully turned to her right, the bus sailing out, defying gravity, the children's screams slowly dying down.

Later, the children and the driver all agreed that a woman's voice had told them to be calm, that it would all be okay and they should sit still.

This woman, dubbed Miracle Woman by the press over the days that followed, lowered her arms with a soft, gentle motion, and the bus followed suit, coming to rest on the snow below.

Then she'd run off, and the debates had begun.

Nearly eight months later, she showed up again—also in Detroit—at a fire. A grandfather had been trapped near the top of a building and was out on his balcony frantically waving and calling for help. He'd suddenly calmed down, held his arms against his chest, and then floated off the balcony, coming to a rest at the bottom of the building a few moments later.

He'd told the press that he'd felt Miracle Woman in his mind, and she'd told him she'd help him. Experts scouring the photos and news coverage of the fire eventually found a black woman with a baseball cap pulled low over her eyes and the collar of her coat turned up high. She held a hand pointing directly at the old man during his descent, but even with computers all that was seen of her face was her chin. No identification of Miracle Woman had been possible.

I shook my head. She hadn't been a woman at the time. Just a tall girl, it seemed. People had been chasing the wrong idea from step one.

After that, there was nothing for more for a year.

Then the others began to pop up.

A twenty-year-old man in New Zealand who could reportedly lift up to about five pounds with only his mind. An octogenarian woman in China who could tell what number a person was thinking or what symbol they were thinking of on those Zener cards. A nine-year-old in Glasgow who could lift himself a foot off the ground—and his puppy, too—but reportedly refused to lift anything else.

Then Thomas Wright.

Then me. And likely dozens of others, none of whom, so far as I knew, were willing to put themselves forward after the death of Wright. There were rumors of those known psychokinetics and telepaths being rounded up and "made safe" by various governments of various nations, but that was more tabloid tripe, I figured. Experts claimed to have access, and papers and discussions abounded on the nature of the abilities, the reason they had appeared—especially worldwide—and a pulse of theories evolved arguing over what was going to happen next.

But nothing really did. There was a game I played with myself, to see how many days it was between the first of the month and how long I could go without bumping into the word "psychokinesis" in print or on the news. The best I'd yet to see was fifteen days, but it seemed to grow longer every year.

In the absence of excitement, we were becoming old news. Every day nothing happened that could be blamed on a psychokinetic, the word—and the concept itself—drifted further out of the public eye, and Thomas Wright became a strange footnote relegated to conspiracy theorists.

How long it would be before someone thought to consider whether the "attack" at City Hall was something psychokinetic? Not to mention me, the "Rainbow Man."

"And could that name possibly suck any more?"

Easter looked up at me again, licking his lips. I was pretty sure he agreed. On a scale of one to weak, "Rainbow Man" was at least a nine.

I rubbed my eyes.

There was a paper I read, back when I was first trying to find out everything I could about psychokinesis. It had the most chilling question that I have ever read about the topic. It was worded simply enough.

What will we do, the paper posed, *when the wrong person gains these abilities?*

I took my tea to my desk and booted up my laptop.

❖

Do yourself a favor. Never do an Internet search for "stigmata." Especially not with the image search results enabled.

My thinking was this: the only unusual things about the opening ceremonies at City Hall compared to every other year I'd been there were the bolstered attendance and the presence of Stigmatic Jack and his cadre of loonies. I'd checked my in-box, and sure enough there'd been an "Action Alert!" e-mail from the Pride Week organizers telling people to come to the flag raising as a show of solidarity in the light of being targeted by Wyatt Jackson and his followers, as well as a reminder not to physically interact with any of the protestors who might be present. I remembered the lesbian with the Super Soaker and grimaced. Spraying someone with water was one thing. Ending up sliced up because of it?

I leaned back in my chair, tapping my thumbs on the edge of the table. I wasn't going to completely discount the notion that maybe there was a psychokinetic self-hating gay man or woman who was lashing out somehow, but it seemed like a man who could bleed on command was as good a place to start as any when looking to blame someone for the bloodshed I'd witnessed.

Hence the Internet search.

It took a few dozen clicks to track down Wyatt Jackson and his so-called "church." There were many groups—many of them religious—that decried what Jackson stood for. His views were—to say the very least—unsettling.

Jackson believed he had a direct line to heaven and seemed to receive calls with alarming regularity telling him to hate people and protest their happiness. Personally, I figured the operator messed up and his calls were coming from somewhere farther down and much hotter.

That image gave me pause. A devil-possessed psychic. Wouldn't that be just peachy?

Jackson's church also believed in not having much in the way of material possessions. Which worked out well, as far as I could tell from the articles, for the church itself, which seemed to be taking those material possessions out of the hands of its followers and buying fleets of white vans, setting up funds for the end times, and building up its already lavish church building located in a walled-in compound outside of Toronto. Nothing like the word "compound" to make you think of balanced and healthy minds.

It made me sick.

An hour and a half later, I'd printed a few dozen pages and read so much ultra-right-wing dogma my eyes *and* my soul hurt. I had, however, found the website of the Church of the Testifying Prophet and knew that tomorrow, Wyatt Jackson—the "Prophet" himself—would be hosting a sermon in a local hotel meeting room. The site had already been updated with the "miraculous events" at City Hall, including the appearance of the "Metatron" and the "light of righteousness." That light had apparently required that Wyatt Jackson and his entourage visit a hospital. Prayers offered on behalf of the Prophet warmly accepted, as were donations. There was an address to send cash or checks to, as well as an online donation form.

After, I did an Internet search for "Metatron," then turned off my computer in disgust. My father thought I was some sort of drag-queen Jesus, and the Church of the Testifying Prophet thought I was the equivalent of God's cell phone. It was enough to drive me mental. I half wanted to phone a local paper and tell them the truth: no voice of God, no messenger. Just a gay massage therapist with a few light tricks.

Right. Not likely.

My stomach rumbled. I was nearly an hour past the time I should have been having my sugar-breakfast and well into the hours I wanted to be out of my apartment. I grabbed my Pride events flyer and walked out the door.

❖

My barista gave me my tea and something she called a "maple pastry," which tasted like sugar wrapped in a croissant with some more sugar on it. I shot her a thumbs up through the window, and she nodded back sagely. Once I was vibrating down to my atoms things seemed brighter, if a little blurry.

I unfolded my Pride flyer and found that today wasn't filled to the brim with fun activities. There'd been a breakfast at one of the gay pubs, which I'd already missed, and after supper there was going to be a reading at the national library with about a half dozen gay and lesbian authors, most of whom were from Toronto or Montreal. I always went to the author readings and always vowed not to buy everything, but caved once I got there. I supposed my credit card could handle it, even if my bookshelves couldn't.

This year I decided I'd go to the reading, but only pick up the book of the author who inspired me the most. I'd likely end up with books from all seven authors, but at least I could delude myself until eight tonight.

I thumbed my phone on and it blinked at me that I had three messages. I waited for the screen to turn back off, deciding.

I looked around, but all the business suits had come and gone already, so there was nobody to feel superior to. My tea was down to the dregs, and the maple whatsit was now only a few crumbs on my napkin.

There was no avoiding it.

I tapped the cell phone back on and keyed in to my messages.

The first was Callum, telling me he'd called our dad, and that I owed him big. I owed him a little.

The second was from Karen, who said I needed to drop by her desk as soon as I finished my swim, which she reminded me I would be having today. I smiled, happy to have something to move me forward. I hoped the pool was quiet.

The third message was from a Detective Brian Stone, who asked me if I could call him back at my earliest convenience as he had some questions for me. He left his number, which he repeated twice, and asked me to call him back today, or tomorrow at the latest.

The cops wanted to talk to me?

"Crap," I said aloud, and my mug of tea skittered a half inch to the left with a flash of red light. I turned off my phone.

Time for a swim.

❖

Now & Zen was located just a block off Bank Street, past where the Glebe began and where remodeled buildings were trying to enhance the reach of that trendy strip of the city. Being built for the purpose, it had a fully stocked gym and a great pool. All the staff members are entitled to use both at their leisure. I tended to go for a swim every other day and used the gym treadmills in the winter when it wasn't nice enough to run outdoors.

I walked in the front doors and saw that Karen was on the phone with a client. I waved merrily while she chatted, but she held up a hand and made the rolling fingers gesture I knew meant she wouldn't be able to extricate herself from the phone any time soon. I ducked into the back.

It wasn't busy in the change room—late weekday mornings aren't exactly our peak times—and I changed into my orange trunks, locked my clothes in a locker, showered, and walked across the tiled floor to the pool.

It was empty. Glorious. I slipped into the water and swam at an easy pace to the far end, glad to have the whole pool to myself and feeling my arms and legs stretch and grow loose. Reaching the far end, I tucked, braced my feet against the wall, and pushed off, swimming hard against the water in a front crawl. I felt my teke building around me and smiled when my face was in the water, deciding to let myself "cheat."

When I reached the far side of the pool I tucked, flipped, and when I pushed off again, I pushed with my teke, too, which flashed with light in the water, shining prismatic bursts of color onto the bottom of the pool below me.

Unbidden, the image of Sebastien LaRoche's blood on my hands returned to me. I grimaced and swam harder. It didn't help. With every lap, it was becoming more and more difficult to stop thinking about the attacks.

I swam for nearly half an hour, back and forth, each push a mental effort as well as a physical one. In my head, I saw the blood. I'd push off—with a brief flash of light—and I'd hear one of the yells as one of the watchers at City Hall was slashed. I'd push off again, and I'd remember that awful noise, wind chimes hurled against a wall. I'd push off again, and I'd recall how hot the blood was against my hands as I tried to tie my shirt around Sebastien LaRoche's arm.

My teke kept me going longer than I should have, and I dragged myself to the edge of the pool one last time, pulling myself out with trembling arms and legs.

Karen was watching me from the pool room door, arms crossed. I had no idea how long she'd been watching. I tried to rise without shaking, and failed miserably.

"If you pushed a little harder, I'm sure you could really hurt yourself," she said sharply. Her red hair was loose today. It looked nice.

"I'm fine, love," I said, but I was panting hard from the swim. I tried not to tremble.

She looked at me, eyes softening. "Did you sleep last night?"

I shrugged. "Well enough, considering. Did you speak with Justin again?"

Her lips turned up at the corners. "Apparently, you're the worst date he's ever had."

I held a hand to my chest. "Surely not! I mean, after I arranged all that carnage and mayhem."

She shook her head. "You're impossible."

"He thinks the Pride Parade is trashy," I said.

She sighed. "How many points did that cost him?"

"All the ones he had, and a few years' worth." I shook my head, and she yelped as pool water sprayed on her blouse.

"I should stop trying to set you up," she threatened.

I pumped a fist into the air. "Yes! Yes!"

She flipped her hair over her shoulder, using only her middle finger. "I have to get back to work."

"No more blind dates," I said. "You just gave up."

"Aren't you on vacation?" she called over her shoulder, and stepped through the door.

I went to the showers, grinning.

❖

The ache in my arms and legs was a bit better after a hot shower, and I dressed and stuffed my things into my bag. I popped out to the closest coffee shop, which wasn't as good as the one with my perky barista, but had the convenience of being almost next door to Now & Zen, and brought Karen back an almond mocha latte by way of apology for snubbing yet another one of her blind dates. Once she'd inhaled her first sip, her smile turned something closer to kind, and I leaned on her desk.

"So what did happen?" she asked me. "The news was a bit unclear."

"At City Hall?" I said. "I think that bloke set it up somehow. He—or one of his cronies—cut some people pretty bad. It's just lucky no one was killed. I did some first aid." I shrugged, but Karen likely saw right through me. "He probably rigged the light show, too. His website says it was the Metatron."

"The voice of God?" Karen smirked.

"How did you know what the Metatron was?" I asked, annoyed. "I didn't know what the Metatron was and my dad is an Irish Catholic."

Karen raised her eyebrows. "Aries."

"Right." I smirked.

"Okay, fine. *Dogma*." She sighed. "I have a thing for Alan Rickman."

"What?" I asked.

She rolled her eyes at me. "Alan Rickman played the Metatron in *Dogma*. It's a movie. You may have heard of them. Images that move on a white screen at the front of a big room."

"It's not too late to take that coffee back, love."

She wrapped her hand around the cup tightly, narrowing her eyes.

"You really think it was that church guy?" she asked.

I nodded. "Yeah. He really had a hate on for gay people. Especially after this dyke hosed him down with a Super Soaker."

"That sort of sucks."

"It does indeed," I agreed.

"I read he's planning to protest every event all week long."

"I heard that."

"You're still going to go to things, aren't you?"

I smiled. "Maybe."

She gave me a sour expression and looked ready to launch into a smothering mother tirade. I tried to head it off.

"You don't think Stigmatic Jack and his lot would go to a book reading, do you?"

"'Stigmatic Jack,'" she snorted. "Nice." Then she stared at me. "Why would *anyone* purposely go to a book reading?"

I narrowed my eyes, and she laughed.

"I'm kidding," she said. "I don't know. Is it a formal Pride Week event?"

I thought about that. "It's on the Pride Week website. So I guess it is."

"Well then," she said, "I think he'll be there. Assuming he didn't blind himself with his pyrotechnics."

I leaned in and kissed her cheek. "I love it when you go polysyllabic."

She laughed. "This means you're not going to the reading, right?"

"I'm not going to miss it just because some religious nuts might be there."

"They're not just religious nuts, honey," Karen said. "They hurt people."

"I'm sure the police are all over it," I said. I pushed myself off the counter. "Keep the place sane." I waved.

"I'm lining up all the nastiest customers for you for next week," she promised.

"Bitch."

"Snob!"

"Love you."

"Love you more!"

Sheesh. Aries are so freaking competitive.

❖

I went back home, made a quick chicken stir fry and rice, and ate it while dancing the mouse toy around the room for Easter, who joyfully leaped and danced about trying to catch it. I cleaned Easter's litter box and then had a shower. I changed into a nice pair of khakis and my second-favorite red shirt, which I realized with a pang was now my favorite shirt.

I'd just sat down to read for the hour or so I had until I

needed to leave for the author readings when there was a buzz on my apartment intercom.

"Hello?" I pressed the button, surprised.

"Delivery," a voice answered, and I rolled my eyes. Probably wasn't even for me. This was the problem with being in the first apartment. I buzzed the delivery guy in and then went back to the couch.

Someone knocked at my door. Easter scrambled into my bedroom.

I answered the door to find myself face to fabulous chest with Sebastien LaRoche. I'm not short, but when he wasn't lying in the grass, he was freaking tall. He looked just as masculine in a T-shirt as he did in a leather harness, I was pleased to note.

"Uh," I said. I let my mind open slightly, without thinking. *Joli*, he was thinking. His thoughts were clear. Focused. Sexy as hell. And entirely in French, which hadn't been my strongest subject at school. Was *joli* jolly? Was I jolly?

Was jolly good?

I felt my face grow warm. I was staring.

"Hello, again." He smiled. *Très mignon quand il rougit.*

"Uh," I said. That seemed to be the extent of my language skills. I tried to close of my mind, but his thoughts were very focused, and it took some effort.

"Your shirt was ruined," he said, his French Canadian accent not as thick as it had sounded on the news, "but this was in the pocket."

In his hand, which was bandaged all the way from the wrist to the bulge of his biceps, he held my bus pass.

"Oh," I said, doubling my vocabulary, if not my expressiveness. I stared at the bus pass. I felt like I should thank it or something.

"Would you like it back?" He was smiling again. Great smile.

I wanted to touch him. A lot.

I snapped out of it.

"Of course," I said. "Sorry, come in." I stepped aside, and he came into my apartment. "Sit down," I said. "I can't believe you're out and about."

"Pft." He sat down, albeit gingerly with his right arm. "They gave me blood, stitched up my arm. Not major surgery." He held up the offending arm. "I'm healing. The doctors don't think the scar will be bad. It was a very clean cut."

I realized I was standing at my door, just staring at said amazing arm. "Can I get you something?" I asked, trying not to hyperventilate. He wasn't gorgeous or anything, but he had that rough-around-the-edges thing that was definitely clicking. There was just something about him. He face was all angles, and his body was all muscles, and...

He was staring at me with an amused smile on his face.

"Sorry, what?" I blushed, realizing he'd answered me and I'd missed it. *You're acting like a total flake*, I berated myself.

"Water?" he repeated, frowning. "Are you okay?"

"A-okay," I said, then quickly shot past him to the kitchen. *A-okay?* For crying out loud, I was acting like a complete and total loser! I grabbed a glass from my cupboard and frowned. I wasn't normally like this. Yes, he was hot, but I'd met hot people. Hell, I massaged hot people. Indeed, hot people paid me to touch them, when they weren't even wearing clothes.

Except he had something else. *His mind...*

I rolled my eyes. Yeah, I was into his *mind*. Ha.

I brought him the glass of water and then sat down beside him. I'd never in my life wanted a second chair before. If he smelled as good as he looked, I'd probably end up losing the power of speech entirely.

My bus pass sat on the table.

"I make you nervous," he said.

"What?" I said, confused. Nervous wasn't the right word

for it. It was like he had his own gravity. I wanted to lean against him. What was up with that?

"A lot of guys are nervous." He shrugged, and drank with his left hand. "The leather thing is a bit too much for a lot of people. They don't get it. It's okay."

I shook my head. "Oh no. No. I think it's hot."

I froze.

He grinned.

"You do, however, make me babble like an idiot," I said, stunned. Did I really just say he was hot? Oh. My. God.

"You're cute when you babble," he said, kindly.

Or was he teasing? It felt like teasing.

I felt my face go red. Super. I briefly considered lighting up, just to distract him. His gaze made me feel naked. And naughty.

"Thank you for the bus pass," I said, breaking eye contact to look at it.

"Thank you for holding my insides in," he countered.

"Well, they're pretty insides, but the outside doesn't need any help," I said. Satisfaction rushed through me. My brain had finally decided to re-engage. I was back, baby.

He flashed that smile again. "You've got a silver tongue, don't you?"

"Irish," I agreed. "On my father's side."

He laughed.

"Well, as much as I'd like to explore your tongue," he rose slowly, grunting with pain as his arm obviously twinged, "I'm late for a bunch of meetings."

Did he just say he wanted to explore my tongue? Oh, baby.

I pulled my mind back together, then rose, managing to speak. "That's right. You're one of the Pride Week organizers."

He tilted his head.

"You were on the news." I pointed at my television. "I saw you." Shirtless. Twice in one day. It was good. Then I put my arm down. He probably knew what a television was. I was such a loser.

He nodded. "I guess I won't be competing, but there's still a lot to do."

"Competing?"

"Mr. Pride Leather." He grinned and puffed out his chest with enough self-mockery that it was endearing. He didn't seem stuck up. I gave him a couple of thousand points. "The competition is on Friday. But I don't think this would go with the harness?" He lifted his bandaged arm, and his biceps bulged.

Oh my. "Oh. That's too bad." I managed an only half-false sadness. The world—and by world, I meant me—deserved more of that leather harness.

He lowered his arm with a wince and a philosophical shrug of his good shoulder.

"Do you need help?" It was out of my mouth before I could stop it. "I always take this week off work. It's my vacation at home. If you guys need another volunteer?" I was babbling again. "Or, since you're one-armed, I could give you a hand."

Ha. Points for a pun.

"I'd rather you just got to enjoy Pride Week," he said.

"You don't think I'd enjoy giving you a hand?"

Oh my God. Did I just say that?

He blushed. It looked good on him.

We stood there awkwardly.

Easter came racing out of the bedroom and launched himself at the open door. I caught him in a practiced scoop and tucked him into one arm. He purred, delighted at the play.

"Your cat is quick, too."

I nodded. "Easter just likes to pretend he can escape."

"You have a cat named Easter?" Sebastien laughed. "Will you ever learn?"

I blinked. He got the reference? I was astounded. Were

French leather men allowed to listen to Tori Amos? Someone was messing with my paradigms.

"I'll see you around, Irish," he said.

"I hope so," I said, and winked.

He stopped and tugged his wallet out from his back pocket with his good hand. He flipped it open and pulled out a white business card. He handed it to me, and I looked at it. "Sebastien LaRoche," it said. "Pride Week Organizer." It had a phone number and an e-mail address.

"I might call," I warned him.

"I might answer." He laughed and left.

Damn him, he had a great ass, too.

"Should have asked him for the beer," I muttered, closing the door.

I gave Easter a couple of treats for his timely arrival and then tried to read my book. I couldn't get into it, since I was replaying every second of my conversation with Sebastien LaRoche. Had he been flirting? That crack about my tongue...

And his arms. Oh my. Forget about the chest ointment, what did he do to his biceps?

I eventually put my book away, shaking my head at my own pathetic state, and watched television for a while instead. The scene at City Hall was mentioned twice more, as a news item for the six o'clock news, but I'd be out of the house by then. I set my DVR to record the news for the first time in my life. I tucked my wallet into my pocket for potential book purchases and set off.

❖

Stigmatic Jack didn't come to the author readings. About six of his church members did, but without him to whip them up into a frenzy, they merely stood outside the National Library and held signs protesting the event. One of them said "The Only

Good Book is the Good Book!" which I thought was clever, if completely wrong.

I mean, come on. Jacqueline Susann? Armistead Maupin? Just to name two.

I heard the authors speak, bought three of their books, and walked home with my autographed purchases happily in hand. When I got home, I told my DVR to play back the news for me and learned why Stigmatic Jack and his flunkies hadn't been there.

They'd been sent to the hospital yesterday after the events at City Hall, which I'd already known, but apparently, the doctors had been worried that there could have been damage to their eyes from the bright light that they encountered.

My mouth opened as the reporter went on, explaining how Wyatt Jackson, his bodyguards, his manager, and many of his congregation were exposed to an intense burst of light that left some of them temporarily blind. A doctor explained that the light didn't do permanent damage, but that some of the people needed eye drops and some time in the dark, just to be safe.

I felt sick to my stomach.

When the news reporter ended by saying that all the individuals had been released from the hospital this evening, I let out a shaky breath.

I could have *blinded* someone.

"Wyatt Jackson is calling the strange events at City Hall a miracle. He maintains that he was doing God's work and that God will punish those who turn from his light." There was a slight twist to the reporter's lips as she said this. "Many local churches have decried the attacks on the spectators at the City Hall flag raising, and police are investigating. Of the nearly two dozen spectators harmed, two were hospitalized for observation, but both have been released as of today. Eyewitnesses say that the blinding light came after a brightly glowing figure appeared"— here the reporter paused with an obvious smile of bemusement, and her thin eyebrows rose high—"and that the beam of light this figure seemingly conjured ended the attacks on those present."

"Damn right it did," I muttered.

"The directors of the Pride Week celebration here in Ottawa say that all the events will go on, including the parade on Saturday. A spokesperson for Wyatt Jackson said that he will be protesting as many of the Pride Week events as possible, as well as holding special prayer services at his hotel."

The story changed to City Council's move to expand the collection of composting boxes to a different schedule affecting many areas of the city, and I turned the television off.

"Tomorrow," I said to Easter, "I need to find a way to get closer to Stigmatic Jack."

Easter blinked and then jumped off the couch and went to my bedroom.

"Some help you are," I sighed, and picked up the first of my new books, losing myself to the joys and plights of a gay man who was getting himself messed up with the mafia by falling for a mafia don's son.

YELLOW

I woke and stretched, and sent a mental call to Easter that I was awake. I heard him pad into the room and leap up onto the bed for a head scratching. While he purred, I sent him the image of his mouse toy dancing around the room, and his purrs grew to a thundering rumble, and he jumped back off the bed. I slid out from under the covers and scanned the room for one of the little gray fuzzy things, but Easter beat me to it, bringing me one of them in his mouth. He dropped it at my feet and blinked his mismatched eyes at me.

I wrapped my teke around the toy and sent it skittering off under the bed. Easter pounced. I practiced like this with Easter as often as I could convince him to play. He would dance and chase after the toy, and I'd pick something to work on—like suppressing the light that always formed when I teked things, or teking something without actually keeping my eyes on it, which I was doing now. Holding the mouse with my mind without actually looking at it was something I'd been working on for years, and it was an odd sensation to bump it up against something solid—it was like pressure behind my eyes. I nudged the little mouse out from under Easter's paws and made it wiggle out from under the bed and dart behind my bedroom door. Easter was after it in a flash, only to see it hop over his head and float out into the living room.

My cat gave chase, and I walked after, weaving the toy between the legs of the two chairs at my kitchen table and under the couch—all while looking in another direction. I bumped a table leg with the toy and felt the disconcerting feedback in my mind. I nearly lost my grip and had to pause and adjust my mental hold. Easter prowled, crouched, jumped, and leapt about, purring all the while, and I played with him for another ten minutes before letting him catch the toy and run off with it in his mouth.

"Hail the conquering hero," I said after him. He swished his tail as he went into my bedroom to hide the mouse somewhere I wouldn't find it until he wanted me to.

Whistling to myself, I booted up my laptop to make sure that Wyatt Jackson's so-called "church" was still meeting, and to see if there were any Pride events I wanted to hit today.

According to the Church of the Testifying Prophet's website, the Prophet was still going to be holding a "faith gathering" at a rented hotel boardroom, and the Prophet himself had recovered from his "visitation with the Metatron." I figured that meant his eyes were feeling better, and surprised myself by having a hard time feeling bad about it. Any trace of guilt or sadness I felt over my role in sending him and his followers to the hospital was lost when I saw the giant "click here to donate" box at the bottom of the website.

Disgusted, I swapped over to the Pride Week web page and leaned away from the computer in shock.

"Name the Flag Raising Hero!" screamed a banner with rainbow-colored lettering. Beneath it was a photograph of me, all lit up. It was one of the ones from the news. And below, while Bonnie Tyler belted out her need for a hero, radio buttons began to appear, asking me to select my choice for naming the hero in question. Which was me.

They were *naming* me?

I read the list, horrified.

"Prism." Okay, well, that wasn't so bad.

"Lens" was next. Huh. Neat idea, and oddly accurate given what I figured I did with my teke.

"Refraction" was the next one, which was true enough, but was "Refraction" really a name to strike terror into the hearts of evildoers?

"Rainbow Man" was the one after that. I pretended it didn't exist.

"Strobe." "Spotlight." "Radiance."

Suddenly, "Refraction" sounded positively macho.

"Disco."

"Disco?" I felt sick to my stomach. That was even worse than Metatron!

"Captain Light." For crying out loud, that sounded like a microbrew. A *bad, low-fat* microbrew.

"Arc du Ciel" was there, representing the French.

And, lastly, "Glow."

I sighed. You couldn't see which name was winning unless you voted. I tapped my fingers beside the mouse.

This was stupid. It was *my* name. No one else got to vote. And besides, I wasn't about to go traipsing around the city fighting crime in a cape and tights, was I?

Then why are you going to see Stigmatic Jack?

I bit my lip. Oh, who was I kidding? I clicked "Prism," which seemed to be the least offensive of the bunch, and watched the screen load.

"Rainbow Man" was winning.

By a landslide.

❖

My barista gave me my tea and my lemon tart to go, and I thanked her and tipped her a couple of loonies. I ate the tart as I walked toward the hotel I'd researched yesterday and tried to figure out what I'd do if I was right.

The lemon tart hit my system and helped me think, as sugar usually did. If Stigmatic Jack was a telepath or a telekinetic, then I'd have to do something. But what was the something? It wasn't like there were psychokinetic police or anything.

That stopped me. Police. Crap! I hadn't phoned back that detective yesterday. I sighed, adding "call the police" to my mental to-do list.

I wondered if the police were thinking about the psychokinesis angle. I doubted it. Hell, according to the newspapers a good chunk of the population thought that Thomas Wright and his psychokinetic display—and even his murder—was a televised hoax.

I ate the last of the lemon tart with a regretful sigh. All I'd wanted was a vacation, to enjoy Pride Week, and to maybe have a completely meaningless fling with someone—preferably someone Karen hadn't set me up with. When had this turned into a game of hunt the religious nut? I sipped my tea through the plastic cover.

Fifteen minutes later, instead of going to the LesBiGay Brunch and enjoying scrambled eggs and bacon with a bunch of my kindred spirits, I was outside the hotel where the so-called church was listed as having its meeting. I was surprised to see that the place was jumping. There were three white vans in the lot beside the hotel, with the words "Church of the Testifying Prophet" written on the sides, along with the website URL and a gruesome icon of bleeding hands. Lovely.

I also saw a local news van parked outside and walked up closer as the woman started speaking into her cell phone.

"No," she said. "No, they won't let us inside the meeting room. Little officious shit in a blue suit told us that he appreciated our attention, but this morning is for a religious service, not a media event. Asked me to call back for an appointment with the prophet and gave me a list of "suggested interview questions" to memorize. We'll shoot something in front of the hotel, and then we'll try for an interview sometime tomorrow. But his people are like brick walls. I don't think they'll really schedule us in unless we agree to their terms. I'll try to see if we can lock down a time for tomorrow, but I'm going to head out soon."

I breathed out. Damn. I guessed the events at City Hall had had a boost on Stigmatic Jack's newsworthiness, but I hadn't expected this. I stuffed my hands into my pockets and walked across the road to the hotel. As I crossed the road, I pulled out the cross my father had given me on my confirmation and let it hang loosely out the front of my shirt.

It felt like an albatross instead of the loving gift it had been.

At the front desk, I asked which room "the Prophet" was going to be speaking in, and the tired woman at the desk pointed down a hall after taking a quick glance at me. I hoped my choice of wardrobe—white button-down shirt and khakis—made me look like a religious nut. Or at least, I really hoped I didn't look like a gay massage therapist. I'd even skipped using any hair product.

I headed down the hallway and was surprised to see a few people already lined up at the doorway. I stared at the floor, hoping not to show off my face and to avoid having to have a discussion.

Why did this seem like such a bad idea all of a sudden?

A few minutes later, the doors opened.

I walked into the meeting room with trepidation. I didn't want to be here, and I sure didn't want to be recognized here. I felt my stomach churn, but kept moving. I could handle this.

"If you have any cell phones, please power them off before you sit down," a woman in a white blouse and navy pants was saying as people entered. I pulled out my phone and powered it down.

Chairs had been arranged in rows like pews, halving the room and leaving a narrow walkway between the two. By the time I'd sat down, almost all of the chairs were full. At the front, a simple lectern waited; no microphone, but an embroidered cloth hung on the back wall, showing a cross with two hands, palm out, beneath, dripping blood, just like the picture on the vans.

It didn't calm my nerves.

I'd sat in the empty chair closest to the exit—just like in school, people had started sitting in the back and working their way forward. The man beside me smiled at me, nodding. I nodded back and then stared straight ahead, waiting.

Behind me, the woman repeated her message about the cell phones over and over. She never varied her sentence and never seemed to tire of sounding genuinely happy to be telling people they should turn off their mobiles.

It was a good thing I'd been early. I no longer had any doubt the news about Stigmatic Jack being at City Hall had increased his fame among the nut-job crowd over the past couple of days. People began to arrive in droves, and soon there was standing room only. A few people had brought cameras, but they were told in no uncertain terms to leave them with the woman at the door. I was pleased enough about that—I didn't need to be caught on film. A tray was passed around, and I shivered as I watched people dropping real money onto it. All I had in my pocket was a couple of quarters, and I felt like the whole room was staring when I added them to the pile—people were dropping fives and twenties on this show, and it hadn't even started yet.

What had I been thinking, coming here?

It got even worse when the thick-necked security guards I'd seen at City Hall arrived. They walked around the room, just staring at people, and it took every bit of courage I had to meet their gaze. I wanted to get up and go, but held myself firm. They went back to the doors again and opened them.

The room erupted into cheers and "hallelujahs!" when Stigmatic Jack and his ever-present blue-suited handler entered through the doors and walked down the aisle, with the two thicknecks on either side. He passed by me without even looking, but others threw their arms out, asking him to bless them, which he did with a touch and a quick nod.

Everyone was rising, applauding, cheering. I did, too, not wanting to stick out.

Holy hell.

He reached the front and then asked everyone to sit. Everyone sat quickly, rapt and quiet, staring straight at him.

It was fucking creepy.

He took a deep breath, then began.

"The first time I heard God speak to me, I was weak," Wyatt Jackson said, his voice rich and strong and filling the small room without need of a microphone. "I asked that this be taken from me."

Shocked noises from the crowd. I caught myself just short of rolling my eyes and made my face smooth into a mask of worry. Golly gee, you didn't want to hear voices? How sane!

"No, it's true, my flock. I did not want this gift, this joy that God had visited upon me." He shook his head, as though amused at his own stupidity.

Fought the gift until I proved it to you.

I shivered in my chair. There was that voice again. I'd kept myself as open as I could without drowning in the voices of the adulating crowd, but Jackson's "Voice of God" boomed in my skull. Powerful voice, that God.

It felt oily.

"I fought the gift. I did, my flock. I fought the gift, until God proved it to me." His voice cracked a little on the last syllable. He actually sounded scared.

Raise your hands, prophet.

I winced, knowing what came next. For crying out loud, this was disturbing.

Jackson raised his hands and said, "But God's proof was what I needed to see the truth of His love!"

Love? I thought.

Three jangled notes toned out in a terrible reverberating cacophony. I forced myself not to flinch—no one else reacted. Jackson's hands split open, and the crowd began to cheer their hallelujahs and amens. I felt sick to my stomach. Blood trickled from his open palms.

You love this, the voice of God said, booming in Jackson's—and my—skull. *You love God's touch.* Oily, black, and cold—the thoughts were like brackish water.

I tried hard not to vomit.

"God shows me what to do, and tells me His word, and I have learned to listen. He does not accept the wicked, nor the deniers! Nor does God allow those who just pretend to hear the word! God cares for our eternal souls, my flock, not such petty things as the flesh!"

Almost every word he was saying was just echoing what had already been said in his head. My stomach roiled at the sick, viscous edge to Wyatt Jackson's "God" voice.

This was all kinds of wrong.

"I hear God, and He is not happy with us right now!"

We must teach the homosexuals the righteousness of My path! They must learn to turn to Me, they must renounce their sin! I hate their sin! Only their sin! They must respect My word, and not belittle your faith in the eyes of others!

If I was hearing "God," too, then there was a problem. God was acting like a bigoted jerk, and he seemed to have had his feelings hurt by the whole taunts and Super Soaker thing. This didn't quite jibe with my understanding of the big guy. But the voice…I bit my lip.

I was used to people's thoughts pretty much matching their voices, and Wyatt Jackson's voice was lyrical. Or, I guess, evangelical. The voice he heard in his head was a fire-and-brimstone growling James Earl Jones sort of voice, heavy on the dark side.

It hit me: Wyatt Jackson had a kind of multiple personality

disorder. He was hearing voices in his head, *literally*. I was tuning in on his mental illness with my telepathy and hearing an ill man who was mistaking a voice in his head for the freaking voice of God.

Worse, it seemed Wyatt Jackson was a psychokinetic, like me. When his palms had opened, I'd heard the tones I remembered from the City Hall attacks—no one else had reacted. It was definitely some sort of "mental" sound that I was picking up. Wyatt Jackson had the same gifts I had.

Except he could *cut* people with his mind. And believed he was supposed to, thanks to his "God" voice.

Jackson was still talking.

"I have trodden off the path of righteousness, my people," he was saying. "Your Prophet has strayed from the path." There were nays from the crowd, but he shook his head and held up one dripping hand. Gross. "No, I did, I did. God punishes the wicked, and I am a messenger of God, but I gloried in his punishments. I forgot to hate the sin, and I hated the sinner. I was tested and I broke from my faith. I hated the homosexuals, the fornicators of sin, not their deviancy. I hated the people, who have souls, not their lustful wrongness, which is a temptation visited upon their souls. And thus the Almighty sent to me the Metatron, to show me how I had seen wrong. God blinded me with his light that I might once again see clearly on my way to righteousness."

I groaned quietly amidst the hallelujahs. *I* was the freaking Metatron. Or the Drag Jesus. Or the Rainbow Man. Or Prism.

Bloody hell, my nicknames sucked.

I had to handle this. But how?

I closed my eyes, working to tune out both of Stigmatic Jack's voices, trying to think. The issue here was pretty straightforward. Multiple personalities or not, if Wyatt Jackson was a psychokinetic, could he cut people? I mean, was that an actual application of telekinesis?

I looked down at my own palm, trying to picture in my mind

how to do such a thing. I tried to pinch myself. A yellow flicker flashed in my palm, and I saw my flesh wrinkle. Yep, I could teke my own skin. Neat. I tried to tighten the hold, to see if I could pinch…

"Ow," I muttered. A red mark appeared, like a cat scratch.

Okay, so you could pinch. I suppose you could cut, too, not that I had any intention of trying it out for myself. What kind of mind takes telekinesis and considers using it to cut people open?

Jesus. Sick or not, Wyatt Jackson was a complete freak.

"Let's rise and sing the praises!" Wyatt Jackson cried out.

I'd had enough. When everyone rose, I ducked into the narrow aisle and started weaving my way through the crowd to get out. It wasn't far, but the crush of late arrivers had left little room to move.

"You!" Jackson's voice called out, loud. "Don't turn your back on God!"

Oh crap, I thought.

The crowd shuffled slightly around me, but the place was so cramped they couldn't quite make an open circle to truly outcast me, though they probably would have denied me three times with ease. I took one more step, hoping it wasn't me Jackson was speaking to.

"Don't turn your back on God! Don't walk out on Him!"

No such luck. I turned around but kept my face tucked low, aimed at the ground. The people between me and Jackson shuffled, but they couldn't quite clear out of the way.

"I'm not," I said calmly. "I'm turning my back on you." As soon as I said it, I did a mental head slap. Now was not the time to be honest.

Silence fell. People jostled, trying to get a view, though I couldn't tell if they were trying to make sure they could see Jackson or look back at me. Thank God the place was so packed. I ducked my head even lower.

"Brother," Stigmatic Jack said. "Come back to the fold."

I heard the tones again. Brutal and cold compared to the music of my dream. And in my head, I caught again the ugly dark voice that Stigmatic Jack was listening to.

He must be brought back. The others mustn't see you lose a member of your flock. You must always appear strong. I resisted the urge to glow. Not that anyone here knew me, but a lot of people sure were looking at me.

Police sketches could be wonderful things.

"I'm sorry," I said politely. "But I'm afraid I do not believe in a God that hateful."

Teach him. Show him his doubt is blasphemy, came the thought as a hot slice of pain opened up on my right forearm, where I'd rolled up my sleeve. Blood welled. I swore, threw up my hands, and pulled together my teke. It came together quickly, to my surprise.

"Don't you dare!" I yelled, and tilted and twisted the lens of the teke behind me. It warped light randomly throughout the room. I made more telekinetic lenses and did the same all around myself, warping the panes and making light travel in curves, not lines. It turned the meeting room into a funhouse-mirror experience for everyone. I sent up a prayer that it would work, feeling a familiar tightness in my head as I handled five lenses at once.

People screamed as—it seemed to them—everything elongated or shrank, twisted and warped in front of their eyes, and the whole room began to glow with traces of yellow light.

"Demon!" thundered Stigmatic Jack to my retreating back. But he sounded nauseous.

Geez. First I'm the voice of God, now I'm a devil? Make up your bloody mind...

I made for the exit, trying to keep a path of normal light between my face and the door, but warping everything else at the same time. It was hard work, and I nearly lost my footing, but most people were either hanging on to their seats with both hands or just trying to stay upright. More than a few clued in enough to just close their eyes—that was also fine by me. I shoved through.

Behind me, more than one person retched. Must have been motion sickness, or maybe vertigo. It was probably a sin to make someone throw up in a church, whether or not the church was actually a hotel meeting room.

Once I made it to the door, I hit the hallway, turned, and ran, leaving little drops of blood behind me for the first few steps, until I thought enough to press my arm against my shirt. I burst through the lobby. The woman who'd looked at me on the way in raised her head, surprised. I slowed down to a normal walk and kept my head down. I made it to the front doors of the hotel just in time to hear running footsteps from the hallway. Both of the thicknecks had made it out of the impromptu church once the light show had ended, I figured. Opening door to the hotel, I worked the light one more time, flooding all the sunlight through the front windows, then shot off down the street.

I walked toward downtown, head down, arm gripped tight. When I caught my breath, I looked down at my arm. It wasn't too bad—the cut was smaller than I'd thought, and very clean, though the blood was vivid where I'd pressed it against my white shirt. I could tell people it was an accident of some kind. I stopped in a pharmacy on Rideau and politely asked where the bandages were while pressing on the cut. The woman at the counter blinked, but showed me to the aisle and even helped me wrap it up.

"Looks like it was sharp," she said.

"I cut myself on a bigot," I said, feeling a bit punchy and light-headed. "He was actually pretty dull."

She frowned. "I hope you called the police."

"I think I will," I said, remembering the detective who'd called earlier.

"Good," she said. "People can't just go around hurting each other."

"Thank you," I said again. "Really." I scooped up the rest of the package of oversized bandages and started for home. I checked my watch and winced. The morning had completely run away from me, and it was moving past noon. I needed to see the news—to make sure I wasn't on it. And as much as I didn't want to, I needed to make a phone call and make an appointment to talk to the police.

I can handle this, I thought, and tried to ignore the blood on my shirt and the pain under the large bandage.

❖

I washed my arm, replaced the Band-Aid, and then changed clothes. I made a quick lunch for myself, then hopped onto the couch with it. Easter purred in my lap while I waited for the news to come on and tried to eat some mac and cheese without spilling any on his white fur. I sent him an image of his stuffed mouse toy dancing around the room, but he showed no interest, preferring to curl up on my legs and make it awkward for me to eat. I guess he wasn't in the mood to play.

The local news described the service that the Prophet Wyatt Jackson delivered in a local hotel meeting room as a "loud religious observance that caused some consternation" among the rest of the hotel guests. But there was no description of any demon warping the light. Even my last-ditch effort that had showered the front hall of the hotel with sunlight wasn't mentioned. I was surprised and pleased, but then grew nervous. I wondered if the hotel clerk had been asked not to say anything. Or maybe paid off? It could just be Jackson wasn't looking for bad press. That showed some savvy. I wasn't sure him having savvy was a good thing. Either way, I'd dodged the media bullet a second time.

Next up, potential incarceration. I pulled out my phone, replayed the message, memorizing the number, and then I called.

"Detective Stone," came the detective's voice.

"Hello," I said, aiming for the voice of a conscientious citizen and coming off a bit more like a cheerleader. "This is Kieran Quinn. You left a message saying you wanted to speak to me?"

I heard some papers shuffling.

"Yes, you were at City Hall two days ago, correct?"

I shivered. "Yes."

"I have a few questions about things you might have seen. I'm wondering if you have some free time at the moment?"

I frowned. This wasn't good. He had a way of asking if I had free time that sounded a whole lot more like an order than a question. I wondered if he was an Aries.

"Mr. Quinn?"

I bit my lip. I could handle this.

"Could we meet tomorrow, perhaps? I'm on vacation this week, but I'm on my way somewhere right now. If it's easier, I can drop by your...uh, office?"

He seemed taken aback that I wanted a face-to-face. "That would be good, yes. Do you know the police station downtown? I'm in there."

"I know the building. It's near the museum, right?"

"Yes. Just ask for me at the front desk."

"I'll see you tomorrow, then," I said chirpily, still channeling my inner cooperative citizen. I politely thanked him for being flexible, then thumbed off my phone and stuffed it into my pocket. I nodded to myself.

If I had to talk to the police, I at least wanted to have an advantage. Face-to-face, I could do my best to hear what he was thinking. At the very least, I needed to know if I was a suspect.

"I've got it under control," I said to Easter.

He yawned and rolled onto his back for belly rubs.

Not wanting to be a liar, I scooped Easter off my lap and went to my computer. There was a Pride event this afternoon—an art and photography showing at a small gallery—and I wanted to go. I didn't think that Wyatt Jackson would go to the gallery. He was due, according to his website, to be having more of his gatherings at the rented hotel meeting room.

Assuming they'd cleaned up the vomit.

"Screw it," I said, and scooped up my bus pass. "Let's get some culture."

❖

On the painting side of the exhibition, there was a wide variety of abstracts, and I was in heaven. It amazed me that people could smush paint around on a canvas and make something that actually looked good—having maxed out my artistic talent as a finger-painting kindergartener, I was in genuine awe of my betters.

I stood in front of one, where the clever artist—J. Cochrane, according to the label—had affixed smaller mini-canvases painted in a variety of bright abstracts overtop each other on a larger canvas done in more muted tones. The effect was three-dimensional and strikingly vivid.

"What do you think?"

I turned, surprised. Justin smiled gamely at me. He was dressed up—a black collared shirt, nice gray pants, and shiny shoes. He'd gelled his hair a bit too much, but overall, he looked pretty slick.

"Oh, hey!" I said, mustering up some goodwill. He was a nice guy. It wasn't his fault that the last time we'd hung out people had nearly died. "How are you?"

"Well, I've been better," he said. He looked like he was going to barf.

I flinched. I guess the poor guy was still thinking about City Hall. I imagined I wasn't high on his list of people to see.

"Don't worry," I said, awkwardly. "Everything will be fine.

It's good to see you again." I turned back to the painting. "It's great, don't you think? I love abstracts. I love the little paintings layered on top. It's neat. I could see it in my apartment, that's for sure. Don't you love it?"

When he didn't reply, I looked at him. "What?"

"I painted that," he said.

I blinked. "You did?"

"I thought Karen told you," Justin said. "I thought that's maybe why you'd come? It's my first showing."

"No," I said. "I didn't know. I just like art."

"Oh," he said. His shoulders dropped visibly. In my head, I heard him think: *I'm such an idiot.* I flinched again.

"It's really good," I said.

He smiled, recovering a little. "Thanks."

There. We'd gone on a date that ended in disaster, but here we were, being polite and friendly to each other. This didn't have to be awkward.

"Hello, Irish," someone said, and gave my shoulder a squeeze. Before I looked, I knew it was Sebastien by the way my tongue tied itself into a knot and my brain slowed down.

"Uh," I said, looking at the big man. His milk-chocolate eyes made my brain melt. He truly had a great jaw. I realized the silence had gone on a bit too long.

"Sorry," I said. "Sebastien, this is…" My mind blanked. "Uh. This is…" I stared at the man I'd gone on a date with. Who I'd just been talking to. Whose name I'd known a few moments ago.

Oh Jesus, help me.

"Justin," Justin said, his voice tense, and they shook hands.

"Justin's the artist," I said, feeling my face burn.

"Just the paintings on this pillar," Justin clarified. "There are six artists showing work tonight." He frowned at me while Sebastien looked at his work.

I tried not to stare at Sebastien. He had on a red T-shirt that was very snug. He had really good shoulders. I felt pain up and down my arm and realized I was picking up Sebastien's thoughts. I tried to shut my mind tighter.

"I like the little ones," Sebastien said, pointing at the piece I'd liked.

"Thank you." Justin still sounded like he was going to hurl.

"Your boyfriend is very talented," Sebastien said to me with a big smile.

"What?" I said. I was having trouble keeping Sebastien's pain from registering. I was impressed he was up and about.

"He means me," Justin said. His smile was brittle.

I frowned. "You're not my boyfriend."

"Yeah." Justin nodded. "I'm gonna go get a drink."

We watched him go.

"I didn't mean to upset him," Sebastien said.

"Sadly, that was still better than our first date." I sighed.

"You're dating?" Sebastien asked.

I shook my head. "No. We got set up by my friend Karen. Bad idea."

"But you came to his show? That's nice." He shifted his shoulder, raising and lowering his wounded arm. It jolted him, and he winced. I could feel the pain.

"No," I said. "Well, yes. But…" I shook my head, distracted. "What brings you here?"

He smiled, and I realized how that sounded.

"Not that you can't be interested in abstract art," I added.

He shook his head. "I'm not. I'm manning the volunteer table. I just saw you and thought I'd say hello. And thank you, again."

I looked at the bandages on his arm.

"Is it hurting?" I asked, knowing full well it was.

He gave a half shrug. "I'll manage. I should get back to the table."

I smiled. "I still have your card."

"I still might answer."

He left.

I turned back to the painting and looked at the price tag. If I revisited my college days and had some noodle dinners...

My phone vibrated. I tugged it out and thumbed the screen. There was a text message from Karen.

Coffee. Coffee. Coffee.

I texted her back. *Rough day?*

COFFEE, came the response.

I laughed and turned to go, stopping to ask the gallery owner if the J. Cochrane painting on the pillar I admired had sold yet. It hadn't, and I gave her my name and credit card before I could change my mind.

❖

I put the almond mocha latte on the front desk, and Karen's smile was full of love and caffeine-deprived thankfulness. Then she frowned.

"What happened to your arm?"

I made a mental note to add "eagle-eyed" to the list of Aries traits. I wasn't about to tell her I'd gone to visit Wyatt Jackson.

"Remember how you said I'd hurt myself if I pushed myself too hard in the pool?" I asked.

She narrowed her eyes.

"I was all wobbly-armed and I managed to slice myself on the locker after." I felt bad for lying, but at least I'd given Karen an opportunity to say the three words she treasured most.

"Told you so."

I nodded. "You'd think I'd learn. Busy day?"

"Not so bad. I'll be off in five minutes," Karen said. "Listen, there's this guy I know."

I raised my hand. "No. Honey, I love you. I love you to bits. But in case you're not keeping score, the last blind date was a new low. I just bought some of his art to make myself feel better about scarring him for life and stepping all over his ego."

Karen frowned. "Justin's an artist?"

"See? You don't even know these guys you set me up with. This new guy is probably some sort of poet. With a clown fetish."

She sighed. "Michael's a doctor. No clown fetishes." She paused. "I don't think."

"Double no. Do you know what self-absorbed, arrogant pricks medical professionals are?"

"Didn't you train to be a nurse?"

"I rest my case." I smiled at her. "I'm going to be single forever. With my cat."

Karen smirked. "Uh-huh. I'll find someone."

"Why do you do this to me?"

She regarded me for a moment. "Because you won't. You deserve to be happy with someone. You keep guys at a distance, and I don't get it." She sipped her latte. "Also, I'm a meddling bitch who can't stand it when I'm not allowed to be a matchmaker."

"I could point out that you're single."

"But you'd never make a lady feel bad," she said. "And the world does that job already. I have all the reminders I need that I'm not a size two blonde with a perky tits and perfect skin, thank you very much."

"You're pretty," I said, meaning it. "And I like your boobs."

"Said the gay man."

"Callum thinks you're hot." I grinned.

She laughed. "Your brother? Wasn't he drunk when he met me?"

"It was a Christmas party. But he thought you were hot."

"He's dating that bimbo."

I shook my head. "They broke up. Finally."

"Good for him. But I'd destroy him," she said.

"I don't know. He's pretty tough."

"Destroy." Karen snapped her fingers. "Like that."

"Maybe I'll find the right guys someday—for both of us," I said. For a moment, I thought about telling her how hard it was to be with a guy—really be with a guy—when you could hear what he was thinking. Karen was incredibly strong-willed. I almost never heard her voice in my mind, not even when I was tired. But the usual urge to hide returned, and I said nothing.

"Well, if you shut your eyes every time, you won't see either of them," she said.

And with that sage advice, the phone rang. She answered, and I pointed to the door to let her know I'd wait outside. She nodded.

Standing in the sun, I closed my eyes and enjoyed the warmth. Cracking my mind open a bit, I caught snatches from the minds of people as they walked past me, and even a few random bits from drivers as they drove by on Bank Street. It was a susurrus, not loud enough to really make most of it out, and was mildly soothing. People were, for the most part, just going about their usual day.

I opened my eyes, putting the mental walls back in place, just as Karen came outside. She smiled.

"Not super hot," she said. "What did you do today?"

"There was a LesBiGay Brunch this morning," I said, which wasn't a lie. I shrugged to make it look like it wasn't worth talking about. "Then I went to the gallery where your good friend Justin was selling his art."

She rolled her eyes. "Any religious crazies?"

"Nope."

She took my non-injured arm. I smiled, and we walked down the street together.

"So Justin is an artist?"

"Yep. Painter. They're really good. Abstracts."

"Must be a Pisces thing."

"Keep talking, woman, and there will be no more mocha deliveries this week."

"Do you want to get Chinese tonight?" she asked.

"Sure," I said. I dropped my voice as low as it would go. "Your place or mine?"

She laughed. "Mine."

We walked a few blocks in silence.

"Callum *is* pretty cute," she said.

"I was kidding."

"But he is cute."

"He's my brother. I can't think of him that way."

"Nice eyes, decent fashion sense."

"Once more: he's my brother."

"No one's perfect."

GREEN

S itting at my desk, I stared at my closed laptop and frowned. I couldn't help myself. I had to look.

"I'm just going to see what's winning," I said to Easter, who paused in crunching his kitty kibble to give me his disdainful look of long suffering.

"Oh shut up," I muttered. "I clean your freaking litter box."

I booted up my laptop and went to the Capital Pride page. It wasn't Bonnie Tyler this morning, alas, but Mariah Carey. *For crying out loud.* I shivered, once again selected "Prism" as the least offensive name for my super alter-ego, and clicked the "vote" button to see how things were going on the naming front.

The upside was that "Rainbow Man" wasn't winning by a landslide any more. The downside was that "Disco" was the name coming up from behind quite quickly. I rubbed my temples and wondered if it was too late to retire from the world of superheroics. Especially given my inability to do much more than run away quickly. Bleeding.

There were three Pride events listed for the day. The AIDS Benefit Dinner and the Drag-Off Competition to elect Miss Ottawa Pride were tonight, as was a comedy night at the lesbian bar. None of them started until the evening. Unfortunately, the dinner and the Drag-Off happened at the same time, at seven thirty, and the comedy night was starting an hour later—which also overlapped. I tapped my finger on the desk. I was lost.

I was pretty sure Stigmatic Jack was a psychic. I knew that he was also off his nut. I was pretty sure he'd lost it and had decided to listen to the voice in his head that was telling him that bad people—meaning anyone not a part of his church—deserved to be punished. With excessive cutting.

Were there going to be repeat performances now that Stigmatic Jack's eyes were all better? Had my visit to his hotel boardroom "church" warned him off or made things worse? I loaded up the Church of the Testifying Prophet web page, but it hadn't been updated.

If I went to every Pride event there was, and Jack and his group showed up, what would I do? The Drag-Off was probably the more "damning our souls to hell" in the eyes of Stigmatic Jack's whacked-out inner voice, but the AIDS Benefit Dinner had a pretty high price tag and usually had press and some local politicians present—and the lesbian comedy hour probably rankled on about a thousand different levels. Which would he go for? For that matter, if he did go to an event and went psychokinetic on everyone's ass, what was I supposed to do?

"Seriously, I don't think I have enough shirts," I said aloud. I'd already ruined two. Easter stopped eating and padded to my feet. He gave me a cheek rub of ownership, so I knelt down and scooped him up. Holding his face in front of mine, I pressed my forehead to his and let my cat's thoughts come inside.

Cat thoughts weren't words exactly, they were more like images and feelings. Warmth and sunlight. Happiness and sitting on a pile of newspaper. Purring and being rubbed.

Easter was so comfortable. Happy and loved. I smiled, suddenly remembering my mother with an ache that brought tears to my eyes. I pressed my face into his furry forehead, and listened to him purr until he started to wiggle to be let down. I put him on the ground and took a deep breath.

Okay, the benefit dinner and the Drag-Off were at the same time. This meant Stigmatic Jack couldn't be at both events, right? Plus, if he showed at either of those, he probably wouldn't go to the comedy show after. So which event was going to be awarded the Bigoted Choice of the Year Award? I thought about it for a bit and decided on the Drag-Off. You needed to buy tickets for the dinner. Surely a group of non-materialist bigots wouldn't cough up money to get tickets to picket something? Would they?

I snapped my fingers. Easter jumped.

It took me a few minutes to find Sebastien's business card. I'd tacked it to my cork board, where I always intend to put business cards but normally never actually do. It took me a few more to get up the nerve to dial the number.

"Sebastien LaRoche," he answered, with his rich rumbly French Canadian voice. I felt my legs go all wobbly.

"Uh," I said, then smacked myself in the head. "Hi. It's me. Kieran. Uh, Kieran Quinn."

"Hello, Irish," he said, and I could hear his smile.

"Hi." I took a breath. "Listen, do you have anything to do with the AIDS Benefit Dinner tonight?"

He laughed. "That sold out. I can't get you tickets."

"Sold out? Good," I said, relieved. "No bigots invited, right?"

"What?" Sebastien sounded a bit lost.

"Sorry. I was just thinking about those church people. The ones from City Hall."

"Ah," Sebastien said. "No, there will be security there. They won't be let inside without a ticket, and when we went over security again, we looked at all the names on the list. I don't think they'll be there."

"So they'll be at the Drag-Off, then."

Sebastien paused. "Probably."

"Any chance you're sending security to it?"

"We have it covered," Sebastien said. "I think the police have spoken with those people."

I thought about the meeting. Stigmatic Jack hadn't seemed very "spoken with" to me.

"Thanks, Sebastien." I was grinning like an idiot.

"Will I see you at the Drag-Off?" he asked.

"You're going?" My voice rose an octave or two.

"Yes," he said. "I got a new dress for it."

My mouth moved, but nothing came out.

"I'm kidding," he said.

"You're mean." I laughed.

"Will I see you there?" he repeated. I liked that he really wanted to know.

"Oh, well...I suppose I could squeeze it in." See more of Sebastien? Yes, please!

"Are you bringing your friend?"

"Who?" I blanked. What friend? "Oh! Justin. No. I don't think he wants to be my friend, actually."

"That's too bad," Sebastien said—and he didn't sound even slightly sincere. Huh. "If you come early, it turns out I could use a hand."

"What with only having one," I pointed out.

"Yes."

"So really, you're just using me. It's nothing to do with seeing me." I sighed theatrically.

He laughed. "If you can be there by six? I promise a good time."

"Well, if you promise," I said.

"See you later, Irish," he said, and hung up.

I stared at my phone and tried not to melt into a puddle.

"Okay, Easter. Now I've got to figure out how to stop the Drag-Off from being another bloodbath."

Every problem had a solution. I could figure this out. I could handle this.

Who else was going to? Was anyone else even trying? My cell phone rang. I looked down at the display. "Oh, right. The police."

❖

"Hi," I said to the man at the front desk of the police station. "I'm looking for Detective Brian Stone? He's expecting me." The man nodded and directed me down a hallway marked "Hate and Bias Crime Unit." Every officer I saw at every occupied desk in the area was a white man. I chuckled at the irony. Stone's office, which had his name on the door, had glass walls, and I could see a man in a simple gray suit talking on the telephone. His shirt was blue, unbuttoned at the collar, and his blond hair was sticking up all down one side, as though he'd run his hand through it a few too many times today.

He looked very frustrated as he hung up the phone.

I knocked. He looked up and then made a quick "come in" gesture.

I stepped inside, closing the door behind me, and sat down in the chair opposite Detective Stone.

"You're Kieran Quinn?" he asked abruptly, flipping pages on a pad on his desk and stopping when he apparently found my name.

"Yes, sorry I'm a bit late. Fell behind," I said, and opened my mind to Brian Stone's thoughts. They were warm, and very still. Like a lake at the height of summer.

One of the ones not in the picture, he thought.

Not in the picture? What picture?

"Thank you for coming here," he said, smiling affably. His thoughts were tired but focused. He was pretty sure I was a waste of time, but was being methodical and doing his job. That was good. I just needed to give him no reason to keep looking at me.

"It's no trouble. Like I said, I'm on vacation."

"Quite the vacation," Stone said, a wry smile on his face. He was thinking about the attacks.

"City Hall." I shivered. I didn't have to fake it.

"I have to ask you a couple of questions," he said.

"Shoot."

"First, if you wouldn't mind, could you tell me everything you saw that day, what happened, everything you remember?" His eyes, a soft blue, were sharp and intelligent. His tone was casual, but his thoughts weren't. He was probably very good at making people slip up.

"Okay," I said, and thought back. "I arrived about ten minutes before the mayor was going to make her speech, with Justin."

Stone said, "Justin Cochrane. He said it was a first date."

"A last one, too, given the results." I cracked a smile, and Stone mirrored it. "Um, so, normally I walk, but we took the bus, so we were a little early. I noticed how crowded it was and that there were police and press there. I was surprised, because it's not normally quite so full of people, and I've never seen police there before. I found out later that the Pride Week organizers had sent out an e-mail to everyone to show solidarity, given that Stigmatic Jack was going to be there." I flinched. Crap. "Uh, I mean, Wyatt Jackson, the uh, priest."

Stone's lips twitched. He was amused, slightly, by the appellation. Also, he had an aching pain in the small of his back. I tried to ignore it, like he was trying. I worked too much to get his discomfort out of my head and lost track of his thoughts entirely.

Damn, but he had a very quiet mind.

"We were pretty close to the front, the mayor was speaking, and then Stig—um, Wyatt Jackson started to spout off his religious intolerance. They raised the flag anyway, the Gay Men's Chorus started to sing, and then…" I shivered again, in spite of myself, and tried to get back into Stone's thoughts. What was he looking for?

I looked at him. Eye contact restored the connection. The warm still sensation of his mind washed into mine. *Did he see an attacker?* Stone was thinking. "I heard screams," I said. "People were being cut or something. I didn't really see anyone getting attacked. The crowd started moving around, a bit panicked, honestly, and I'm not short or anything, but I couldn't really see what was going on. I found this one guy, and he was really badly cut—"

"Sebastien LaRoche," Stone said. He'd really done his homework. I suppose police did that. I wanted to find that comforting, but instead it made me nervous.

"Yeah. Sebastien. He was bleeding a lot, so I started doing first aid on him. I'm afraid I didn't really look up after that, I didn't see anything, like I told the policeman who was there. I was sort of busy keeping the man from bleeding to death."

Nursing school, Stone thought, and I gave him even more points for thoroughness. "You stuck around to do first aid?" He shifted in the chair, trying to alleviate the ache in his back.

"I was in school to be a nurse," I said, as though confiding. "I switched halfway to be a registered massage therapist instead."

"Why the switch?" he asked casually, but in his head, there was a sharp focus. He was watching me, looking for something. *If he flunked, could be bitter. Angry.* I didn't get the sense he believed that, just that he was being thorough. I wondered what it would be like to have to think the worst of people all the time.

Probably tiring.

"I didn't like the death," I said, surprising myself by being completely honest. "My supervisor said I was a bit too empathic. I got too wound up in the patient, especially if they were really ill, or dying. She said I'd probably burn out in no time since I didn't have a good way of not taking it home with me at night. So I switched to something where I could still help people, but wouldn't get too deep." I shrugged. "Also, the hours at the spa are way better and I'm not constantly run off my feet."

He nodded, apparently satisfied. I'd missed what it was exactly he was looking for, but his mind had drawn a mental line through my name on his list. I was not a suspect, not that he'd ever really seriously considered me to be.

Except for the picture, he thought, and I felt myself tense. What freaking picture?

"Did you stay with the wounded man the entire time?" he asked me.

I paused, as if replaying it in my mind, but really I was listening to his thoughts, trying to figure out what he was after. *Where did you go?* He was thinking, *Why aren't you in the pictures once the light show starts?* Oh crap. Suddenly I got it. The police were trying to find all the people who weren't visible in the photos after the appearance of Rainbow Man. Which definitely included me. I needed an alibi.

I said, "Well, when there was that big flash? I, uh..." I looked down, as if embarrassed. When in doubt, tell a lie that makes you look bad. "I kind of, well, hit the deck. I didn't want to leave the patient or anything, but I didn't want to be a target, either."

Of course, he thought, satisfied. My name all but left his mind. He was trying to think of a polite way to say good-bye and get me out of his office. His back throbbed, and he was nowhere near done for the day with tracking down people to talk to about these incredibly confusing assaults.

"Thanks for your time," he said.

I felt a surge of relief and let his thoughts fade from my mind, rebuilding my mental wall. The ache in his back dimmed to my senses. I offered him my hand. "I wish I could have been more helpful."

He looked down at my arm. "You get that at City Hall?" He was looking at the extra-large bandage.

I froze and tried to retract my hand at a normal pace. I attempted to get back into his thoughts as I spoke.

"No. I cut it at the gym," I lied. He was listening carefully, watching me. He knew damned well I'd told them at City Hall I hadn't been hurt. "I swim. It's sort of my outlet. I went for a swim, and, to be honest, I pushed myself. I kept thinking about the blood and stuff." I grimaced, again not really having to fake it. "By the time I got out of the pool, I was all rubber-limbed, like you get after working out too hard?" I looked up at him, and he nodded, once. "I sliced my arm on the edge of the locker when I was pulling my bag down."

It was the same fib I'd given Karen. At least I was keeping my stories straight.

In his mind, I felt my name restored to the list, but faintly. Damn. He wanted to believe me, but he was too good a police officer not to consider it odd that I had a wound.

"Does it hurt?" he asked.

I shook my head. "Not really. I just didn't want it to get infected or anything." I smiled.

"And this was yesterday?" he asked. Bloody hell. I really didn't like how he was fixating on this. He was thinking about something else as well, and after a second I caught the name of the hotel where I'd visited Stigmatic Jack and gotten sliced. Damn it! Had someone reported what had happened? That someone—namely me—had been cut again? I remembered the blood I'd dripped on my way out the door. Could they do some magic CSI stuff with that? I'd seen TV shows about this stuff. Someone could probably do a blood test and then they'd know it was me.

Don't panic. I cleared my throat. "My coworker, Karen, gave me grief over pushing myself," I said. "I swim at the gym where I work."

"Well, thanks for coming. If I have any other questions, I can call you?"

I nodded and rose. He did as well, and grimaced when his back ached.

"It's the way you're sitting," I said.

He looked puzzled. "Pardon?"

"You lean forward all the time." I pointed to him. "I can tell your back is hurting you. You need to sit up straighter and keep your shoulders back. Move your chair closer to the table when you're on the phone."

He smiled. "I'll keep that in mind."

I tugged a business card out of my wallet. "Here," I said, and handed it to him. "I'm back at work next week. Come by and I'll see if I can help you out some meaningful way."

He took the card, and as I left, I heard him wondering, with a slight amusement, if I was hitting on him, and if he'd come across as somehow interested in me. He was worried that he might have seemed unprofessional—and although I was cute, it wasn't his intention. I had to stifle my laugh at that last bit.

The cop investigating the attacks at City Hall thought I was cute. Apparently not every policeman in the Hate and Bias Crime Unit was a straight white man. That was what I got for making assumptions. It made me grin.

I sobered quickly, though.

I wasn't sure, but I thought I might still be a suspect.

My phone buzzed. I fished it out of my pocket and blinked in surprise.

❖

"Is it wrong that my first thought was that you're dying of a rare blood disease?"

Callum rolled his eyes. "Har."

"Seriously," I said, holding up my phone. "Invited to lunch by my brother. His treat." I sat down in the booth across from him. "Is it your kidneys? Do you need one of mine or something?"

"Keep talking and I'll give you the bill after all."

I smiled. "Sorry. It's nice. How's work?"

Callum shrugged. "It's work. I've got a crapload of papers waiting at home, but it's a nice day." Looking at my brother was like looking at a slightly older version of myself. A slightly older version of myself that didn't believe in hair product or in having a more-than-passing acquaintance with a razor.

"So you thought you'd come spend time with your little brother?" I wasn't buying that for a second. I wondered if Dad had put him up to this. Was he following up on me after City Hall?

He toyed with his fork. "Remember when I went to your Christmas party?"

I blinked. "What?"

"Your Christmas party." He looked up from playing with his utensils. "Your tree-trimming thing?"

"You showed up late and didn't bring an ornament."

"Right." He nodded. "Well, you introduced me to everyone, and..." His voice trailed off. "Thing is...I had some eggnog..."

"You had a lot of eggnog and you slept on my couch."

"Right." He bit his bottom lip. "Which one's Karen?"

I leaned back in the booth. "No. Fecking. Way."

"She's the redhead, right? Not the blond. Because the blond was horrible. I'm ninety-nine percent sure Karen's the redhead, and I said yes, but now I'm second-guessing myself, and I'm afraid she's the blonde..."

"Said yes?" My voice rose. "What did you say yes to?"

"A date."

"You're going out with Karen?" I was shaking my head. "That was a joke!"

Callum frowned. "A joke?"

I leaned forward. "She's my best friend. I adore her."

"I'm your brother."

"I adore her more."

He scowled. "Y'know, you can be a kind of an asshole."

"Please," I said, leaning forward. "Please. I'm begging. Don't date my best friend."

"Why not?" He crossed his arms. *Am I such a big loser?*

I paused. Ouch. I hadn't meant to catch his thoughts, but that one had come through loud and clear. Despite his bravado, Callum could be way too hard on himself. I reminded myself that he sometimes didn't realize how smart he was—he had two and a half degrees from university, for crying out loud. But my brother's ex—the Bimbo—had done a real number on his self-confidence, dumping him and then marrying another guy in less than six months. Also, despite my earlier denials with Karen, he was indeed a good-looking guy. When he shaved. I cleared my throat.

"I'm sorry," I said. "I'm overreacting."

He smiled.

"But…" His smile vanished, and I leaned forward, speaking quickly. "Imagine if I wanted to date your best friend."

"Robbie's straight."

"Okay, well, imagine I was your sister and I wanted to date your best friend."

Callum didn't budge. "That'd be fine. Robbie could really use the shag."

I rubbed my forehead. "Okay. Fine. I'd rock Robbie's world with your blessing. Multiple orgasms abounding in an endless stream of bliss. And then, after a month or three of incredible sex I'd get tired of his terrible sense of humor and his hideous addiction to puns and dump him."

"Multiple orgasms?" Callum smirked.

"God, you're such a guy. Yes. Multiple orgasms. Look it up online. It's a real thing."

Callum smiled.

I leaned in. "And then when we'd broken up and you had to decide if you could keep talking to both of us…?"

Callum leaned back. "Oh."

"Oh," I agreed.

"It's just one date." Callum picked up his menu. "It's not like it's serious."

I picked up mine. "Fine." I started scanning the prices for the most expensive lunch item.

"But," Callum said, "she is the redhead, right?"

I was definitely going to order a dessert.

❖

"One almond mocha latte," I said, handing Karen the cup. "Oh, but they were out of my freaking brother, so you'll have to order something else to go."

Karen rolled her eyes. "So you're going to be mature about this, then."

"You're seriously going out on a date with my brother?" My voice was approaching hysterical. I cleared my throat.

Karen looked up at me. "It's just a date. He's a nice guy. You said it yourself, lots of times. Didn't he used to pick you up from school every day so no one would bother you?"

I flinched. "Yes."

Karen laughed. "It's going to be fine. Really." She reached out and patted my arm. "You're acting like I'm going to break him in half."

I gave her a look.

"I won't break him." She laughed. "I might spank him if he asks nicely, but—"

"For crying out loud." I held up my hand. "Don't. Please. I beg you."

"Maybe a little bit of role playing…"

"Stop. Begging."

"Do you think he'd look cute in just a fireman's helmet and boots?"

"I have to go swim now," I said, and walked away while she laughed at me. The mental images would scar me for life.

❖

Chances was floor-to-ceiling pink. The walls had been covered with pink beaded curtains, and the stage was backed with an eye-straining art deco flamingo backdrop with sequins and faux feathers. Onstage, Mizz Anne Thrope, the winner of last year's Drag-Off, was aiming a long pink wand at the open concept ceiling where a guy at the top of a very tall ladder was tying pink streamers that dangled down to just higher than a tall person could reach if he stood on tiptoe. Three other volunteers were inflating fuchsia balloons with helium from a tank and tying them off with pink ribbons. Beside them, weighted pink plastic stars were waiting for three balloons each. A small pile was already ballooned up, but the larger pile wasn't.

The bar staff were busy setting up the tables, including white plastic tablecloths with—of course—pink stenciled letters that screamed "Drag-Off!"

As I walked in, one of the bar staff, a tall buff guy in a ribbed white tank top and tight jeans, said, "We're not open yet."

I tried my best smile. "I know. I'm a friend of Sebastien's. He asked if I could come early and help out?"

The bar guy gave me a look up and down and apparently found me wanting, since he sniffed and went back to the bar, where he began unloading bottles of beer and sliding them into the many fridges I assumed here hidden beneath.

"Kieran?" came a voice from behind. I leaned around the corridor where the coat-check was and saw that Sebastien was sitting at a table just around the corner from the entrance, where he had three boxes, still taped closed, and two shopping bags from the Dollar It.

"Hi," I said, and walked over. "How's your arm?"

He shrugged. *"Pas mal."*

He was lying. I'd be chugging vodka and aspirin if my wrist was throbbing like his was, and his shoulder felt bad, too. I had to work harder than usual to build my mental walls up again. What was it about this guy that broke down all my barriers? Y'know, beyond the whole "I'm a leather stud" effect. He rose, and I got a great view of his chest as he stretched his arms out. He wore a black T-shirt that said "Volunteer" on it in white blocky writing. Little bits of chest hair were escaping the top of the neckline.

I tried not to salivate. It would be tacky.

"Want to make help a drag queen's dream come true?" he asked.

I looked around at the overwhelming pinks, "Apparently, the dream is to be smothered in Barbie's Dream House?"

Sebastien laughed, and I felt his shoulder jolt him with a pain. He winced.

I really couldn't seem to keep him out of my head.

"You haven't been taking it easy, have you?" I said, and nodded at his shoulder.

He gave me a grim smile. "I have been on the phone with the press, with the police, and then I came here and have been trying to help. A couple of volunteers couldn't make it..."

I held up a hand. "How do I make a drag queen's dream come true? And make you sit down and relax?"

He laughed. "The ballots need to be put at all the tables," he motioned to the boxes, "with pencils, and we need to set up the ballot box for the competition."

I pointed at the chair. "You sit. I'll do it."

He sat, and I realized that he really was feeling bad. He didn't strike me as the type to do as he was told. The bar guy who'd found me unworthy walked by and gave Sebastien a look that I couldn't read. Sebastien ignored him, but I couldn't help myself. I opened my thoughts to the bar guy.

Never gives me the time of day, and this twink gets his attention? Typical.

I bristled. I am not a twink. I have black hair, and there's scruff on my chest, and quite frankly, twinks don't have thighs or calves like mine. So there. I glared at the bar guy, who had no idea we were having an argument and didn't seem to care that I was winning.

Instead, I worked out my ire by tearing open the boxes and spent a good half hour mind-numbingly cutting the sheets into individual ballots and then placing those at every table, with pencils from the dollar store (which I had to sharpen with the pencil sharpener also bought at the dollar store), and then I started to put together the ballot box, which should have come with a warning that it required an engineering degree and three shots of tequila to assemble.

On my second attempt to "insert the tab into the proper slot" Sebastien started to laugh at me.

"What?" I looked up, trying to be annoyed with him, but failing in light of the way he was smiling and how stoically he was holding through his pain, which I still couldn't quite block out.

"When you're working, you stick out your tongue, like this," he said, and mimicked me. There was a flash of silver.

"You have a pierced tongue," I noted. All the hairs stood up on the back of my neck, and I felt my toes tingle.

He nodded.

"For your information," I said, trying not to think about the many interesting things that a tongue stud might do, "I only stick my tongue out like that on special occasions. Like when I'm putting together something designed by NASA." I held up the offending box, which wasn't yet remotely box shaped, and sighed.

"Do you want me to try?"

"No, I want you to relax," I said. "Your arm is killing you. I can handle it."

I attacked the box for a while and finally figured out which slot was for which tab, and with a small flourish, snapped the last bit of cardboard into the appropriate place and held up a completed ballot box.

"Ta-da. For every problem there is a solution."

He smiled at me, but his eyes were tired.

"You should take some Tylenol or something," I said.

"It's fine," he said.

"Liar," I said.

He narrowed his eyes. "How would you know?"

"I'm an RMT, a massage therapist," I said. "I know pain when I see it." It was a small fib.

He seemed to consider. "It hurts," he admitted.

I put the ballot box down. "I can try to work on your neck and shoulder a bit, if you'd like."

He grunted agreement, and I stepped around behind him. I hesitated before touching his neck for the first time—it seemed like a moment I should savor and potentially memorize so I could replay it later in every possible detail—and then set to work. His neck, not surprisingly, was a mess of knotted muscle and tension. He'd obviously been doing everything with his left arm, and barely moving his right unless he had to.

I slid into the barest edge of his mind, just enough to feel where the tensions were. It was like dipping my feet into a pool of warm and bubbling water after a long day of standing. I shook myself, then worked methodically with my thumbs to undo some of the knots. He groaned with pleasure, and I felt my face grow very red.

Bar guy was watching. I winked at him. Take that, twink-hater.

I kept at it for about ten minutes, lost in the zone like I am when I've got someone on my table at the spa. His mind continued to push into my thoughts louder than I needed it to, and I had to keep nudging my mental walls to let him keep his actual thoughts to himself. A few words snuck through, all in French, and I let them drift by without trying to translate.

He smelled wonderful. I caught myself wanting to breathe in deeply whenever I leaned a bit forward, and tried to remember how to be professional, so as to not lick him.

I didn't numb the pain telepathically, not wanting to try when we were surrounded by people and my concentration wasn't at its best. Also, he seemed like the type who would push himself if he didn't have the pain to hold him back.

"If getting a rubdown is part of the volunteer work," a voice cracked over the speakers, "then I'm next in line!" I jumped and glanced over at the stage, where a pink body-suited Mizz Anne was grinning, holding the microphone.

"I mean, check. Check. One, two, three," she said, all innocence.

I laughed and called out, "Special rate for the walking wounded."

"Honey, we're all wounded. Have you seen these heels?" she said back. Then handed the microphone off to one of the volunteers, nodding.

Sebastien stirred. "Thank you. You're very good with your hands."

"Told you," I said. "What's next?"

❖

By the time seven thirty rolled around, I'd hung beaded curtains, prepared door prize baskets, set up a donation table and the ballot box table, helped the bar staff carry in seemingly endless boxes of plastic cups, and become the proud owner of a black T-shirt that said "Volunteer." I tugged it on over the shirt I was wearing.

"Twins," I said, smiling at Sebastien. He nodded. I'd convinced him to take a couple of his prescribed painkillers, and he seemed in much better spirits.

We were sitting at the ballot-box table, where Sebastien said we'd have a good view of the stage and the shows and could direct people to fill in their ballots. I was going to help count them, which delighted me in some mildly demented way I couldn't put my finger on.

Better, there was no sign of Stigmatic Jack or his crew, which made me happy. It was a large bar, and I'd realized that you had to pay a twoney to get in tonight, which maybe would deter the Church of the Testifying Prophet from coming inside. If they wanted to yell and scream outdoors, that seemed fine by me.

The security that Sebastien had organized arrived, and they were an intimidating group of five men (and one woman) in black shirts that mirrored my own, except that their shirts weren't a size too big, and said "Security." I wondered if all the men were leather men like Sebastien.

Were there leather women? It occurred to me I'd never seen one.

The music began, and people started to show up around eight or so, a full half hour after the listed starting time. I had to smile. Gay Standard Time was alive and well.

By the time the bar was nearly full, I'd all but given up worrying about Stigmatic Jack. Mizz Anne took the stage and did her classic opening stage routine of explaining how much she hated everyone (especially you) and then explained the contest.

All the drag queens were going to do one song routine, and then they'd all take the stage for a brief comedic routine. After that, everyone would vote, I'd count the ballots while Mizz Anne Thrope did her swan song for being Miss Ottawa Pride, and then we'd announce the winner, who'd inherit the pink scepter and rainbow tiara until next year's Drag-Off.

I loved every second of it.

With a flourish, Mizz Anne called the first drag queen, Brenda Over, to the stage.

Brenda Over was a view. She was a tall Asian done up in black dress slit up to the thigh, a white feather boa, and a short choppy platinum wig. She performed "I Don't Know How to Love Him," from *Jesus Christ Superstar* with a classy sort of air that really worked for her tall, leggy appearance. The applause was genuine and warm, and she blew a kiss to the crowd.

I clapped loudly and grinned at Sebastien. He smiled back.

Then I saw them. The Church had arrived, in their white shirts and tan slacks. They were lined at the door, each holding a twoney in their hand with a determined look in their eyes.

I nudged Sebastien and nodded over to the entrance. He looked, and frowned darkly.

"Tyson!" he called. One of the big guys in the Security shirt turned and then saw what Sebastien was pointing at. Tyson nodded and slipped down the hallway, where two of the other Security people were already going to meet the protesters halfway. At the back of the crowd of white-shirted folks, I saw the two thicknecks, though I couldn't see Wyatt Jackson himself.

"Are they going to let them in?" I asked Sebastien.

He shook his head, "No. Private Property and Trespass Act of Ontario."

I blinked.

"You don't have to let anyone in if you don't want to. You don't even have to say why."

I relaxed a little.

On stage Mizz Anne had spotted the protestors.

"Ooh, everyone, the Church is here!"

I winced.

As one, the crowd turned and looked. A few catcalls started.

"Now, now," Mizz Anne said, wagging one gloved finger. "People, people. Behave. You know I hate everyone equally, but let's not judge!" A few people laughed. "After all, if God had wanted men to fuck other men, he'd have given them dicks and shoved a G-spot up their assholes!"

The crowd roared, and I found myself smiling, even though I was worried.

I heard tones. Those awful notes, rising jangled and off-key.

I looked around but couldn't see anything happening.

Sebastien glanced at me. "Are you okay?"

"And God knows, I loved the church!" Mizz Anne was saying. "All those frocks! And you know there's just no better place outside of NAMBLA for a boy to learn about man-boy love than with his priest!"

Laughter and groans all around, and scattered applause. Some of the church protesters were turning red, but Security seemed to be handling getting them away from the doorway. The one Sebastien had called Tyson was shaking his head and talking with the guy in the blue suit who had been standing with Stigmatic Jack at City Hall. Behind the two thicknecks, I could now see Wyatt Jackson himself, looking serene in his all-white ensemble.

Dressed...Babylon.

I barely heard the thoughts, but recognized the dark oily sensation of them immediately. Same as in the church, same as at City Hall. Damnit, Stigmatic Jack was about to go off on a rant.

"You worship this icon dressed as the Whore of Babylon and expect to be greeted at the gates of heaven?" Wyatt Jackson didn't have a microphone, but he didn't need one. He could project. Just my luck—we had a bigot trained for the stage.

"Honey," Mizz Anne countered, now facing down to the entrance, "this is a Chanel. And whores get paid." She deep-throated the microphone for a moment, then added in a manly, gravelly voice, "I go down for free!"

The room exploded into laughter and applause. Sebastien was grinning, beside me.

I bit my lip.

Punish...I heard, and tensed.

"God will punish you for your sins!" Wyatt Jackson yelled, and with a single clashing note, his palms opened up, bleeding. He hissed at the pain of it, but raised them high.

"Baby, that's gross." Mizz Anne sighed. "You don't get to spank me with your hands like that. Now get lost. You might have missed it, but none of us want to talk with you."

There was a blast of notes in my head, and I saw one of the heavy speakers behind the stage shove itself forward, tipping toward Mizz Anne.

"Look out!" I yelled, one of many voices. I rose and tried to shove back with my own teke. The speaker was too heavy for me, but I tried to slow it as it tipped, and the flickering green light my teke made caught Mizz Anne's eye and she jumped back. The speaker made a loud crash as it slammed over. I'd only barely slowed it down.

Stigmatic Jack was a much stronger psychokinetic than I was.

A couple of people were starting to mutter and more than a few had risen, but Mizz Anne stood regally on the stage and smoothed her tresses with one fuchsia fingernail. It shook, but she kept her smile in place.

"You see?" Stigmatic Jack yelled. "You see God punishing you?"

Mizz Anne turned back to the hallway. "Honey, the word 'killjoy' was made for people like you. Get your scrawny ass out of my soiree. Mizz Anne Thrope didn't invite you."

"God shall punish all of you!" Stigmatic Jack was all but foaming at the mouth, and I saw Tyson and the other security people starting to force the issue, bodily blocking the entrance completely and gesturing behind them at the doors.

The church members began singing some sort of hymn. I rubbed my temples.

"Maestro, if you could fix the speaker here, I daresay we could use a different tune?" Mizz Anne asked into the floodlights. Two of the bar staff came out and righted the speakers, checking the wires and looking puzzled at where the speaker had fallen.

I kept staring down the entrance corridor, waiting.

"Just go..." I muttered under my breath, still standing. Sebastien's jaw was clenched.

"You are all damned!" Stigmatic Jack yelled.

Cacophony blared in my mind, and I took a step away just as the donation table at the front entrance hall flipped up and slammed into Tyson and another security guard, who went down with grunts and lost breath. The church members surged forward, but two other guards linked arms and shoved back into them, including the woman, who, it seemed, could definitely take care of herself.

"Sinners! Fornicators!" Wyatt Jackson yelled. Drops of his blood had streamed down his wrists and into his shirt. The guy in the blue suit beside him gripped one of Jackson's elbows, glaring out at the room, the thicknecks taking up positions on either side of them.

Another table, one of the ones at the front near the stage, launched itself at Mizz Anne, scattering drinks onto the floor and knocking one of the people sitting at the table to the ground. Mizz Anne tried to dodge, but the table caught her calf, and she tumbled off her stilettos.

People started to panic and yell. The security people shoved at the church protesters, who were still singing, and I saw Tyson slide the table aside, but he lay on the ground, not rising.

Enough, I thought.

I made a lens by the floodlights aimed at the stage and bent the beams down the entrance hallway. They lit the backs of the security guards, but shined directly into the eyes of Stigmatic Jack and his crew. Someone gasped.

"The light!" someone said. I suppose seeing the bright beams turn themselves at a forty-five-degree angle was a bit unusual.

"I'm going to see if Tyson is hurt," I said to Sebastien, who was rising. "Stay put."

He gave me a stunned expression, and I threw myself down the hallway, trying to keep concentrating on the light.

As soon as I was through the light, I triggered another lens and magnified the spots that were already streaming down the hallway. Two tekes were harder than one, but I'd practiced this so much it was second nature—though usually I was using the light to read.

"Rainbow Man is here!" someone yelled.

Oh for crying out loud, I thought. I tried hard to keep the lenses in place without looking at them, worried I'd need to do more. But the strange jangling notes had silenced, and Security was managing to heave the protesters back. I caught a glance of the two thicknecks leading Stigmatic Jack into the stairwell, the blue suit with them, and smiled to myself.

I let the lenses drop and fell to my knees beside Tyson.

"You okay?" I asked him.

He bobbed his head. "Just winded."

I smiled. Thank God. The other guy that had been hit by the table was also fine. I rose and saw that most of the church members had been shoved out now, still singing.

Sebastien was standing beside me. He obviously hadn't stayed put.

"Should we call the police?" I asked.

"Has anyone else noticed," came Mizz Anne's voice, once again on the microphone, "that his God has lousy fucking aim?"

People laughed, though nervously.

"And did anyone else notice that once again, the light seemed to be on our side?"

I looked down the hallway. Mizz Anne was standing, though favoring the leg that had been clipped by the table.

There was applause to this pronouncement.

"Rainbow Man?" Mizz Anne glanced around the room. "You here?"

I looked all around, just like everyone else. Gee. Who could he be?

Mizz Anne looked around. "Well, it looks like I've got an angel on my shoulder tonight." She paused and smiled, turning her head to regard her shoulder. Then she scowled and made a flicking motion with her bright fingernails. "Now fuck off, Clarence. My ankle hurts like a son of a bitch, and I've got a show to finish."

The audience laughed.

"I don't think we need the police," Sebastien said.

❖

One ballot revelation, melodramatic crown-and-scepter ceremony, and three hours later, Sebastien told me our work was done and we could head out. He was holding himself stiffly while we walked, and I asked if he was sore again. He nodded.

"Where do you live?" I asked, once we were outside.

He pointed with his left hand. "I'm a couple of blocks that way."

"Do you have an early start tomorrow?"

"Yeah, there's a brunch for the Capital Leather Crew. I'll be fine," Sebastien said. "I'm just not sleeping well."

I weakened my mental barrier and could feel the ache in his wrist and forearm. It wasn't as bad as before, but it would have kept me up at night, if it was me.

"They gave you painkillers, though, right?"

He shook his head. "I don't like taking pills."

Ah. One of those. He'd been reluctant to take them earlier, too. I bit my lip. I'm not a pill popper by any means—mostly because they make it nearly impossible for me to filter out the thoughts of other people—but it seems to me that when a doctor hands you pills to help you cope with pain, that you should take the pills to help you cope with the pain. They're probably right; they have those degrees and everything.

"I'm pretty sure I could get you to sleep. At least you'd have a good night." I was half-fibbing. I was sure I could help get him to sleep, but what I was intending was a lot more telepathic than therapeutic.

Sebastien gave me a crooked grin. "I'm not really up for it."

I frowned, then realized. "Oh. Oh, no. I didn't mean sex." I felt my face grow hot.

He laughed. "You're cute when you blush."

He thinks I'm cute. I forced myself to change the subject. "Ever heard of acupressure?" I asked.

"More massage?" he asked, but didn't sound disinterested.

I nodded. "It deals with pressure points. Sort of like what I did before, but a bit more intense." And psychic. And telepathically invasive. Surely my motives were pure.

He seemed to be considering. The ache in his wrist was a palpable hiccup in his thoughts. Poor guy. I just wanted him to feel better. Yep. My intentions were as pure as the driven snow.

"I swear I'm not hitting on you," I said, as much to myself as to him.

He curled his lips in a crooked grin. "That's too bad."

"You are the king of mixed messages, buddy." I shook my head.

"No, I'm just the walking wounded," he quoted me. "But when I feel better, will you hit on me then?"

I shrugged. "You'll just have to wait and see."

He laughed and wrapped his good arm around my shoulders in a quick, affectionate tug. Every nerve ending I had fired off happily.

"Gluh," I said.

"Come on," he said. "I'm this way."

We walked in silence until we got to his apartment building, which was nice and had a great view of the river. It must have cost him a fortune in rent. It occurred to me I didn't know what he did for a living.

"So when you're not organizing Pride, what do you do?" I asked, once we were in the elevator. I felt butterflies flickering around in my stomach. It felt like a date. I was going to see his place. I almost never made it this far in my dating life. Usually I found a reason *not* to get this far on my dates, unless seeing where the bloke lived was more or less just a speed bump on enjoying a carnal evening with a one-night stand.

That put images in my mind of a carnal one-night stand with Sebastien. I tried to focus on what he was saying, instead.

"I'm a woodworker," he said.

I'll bet. "A woodworker," I repeated, not quite sure what that meant.

"I restore antiques."

"That must be different every day," I said. He'd have strong hands and a firm touch. I was willing to bet that would translate well to other endeavors.

He shook his head. "Mostly sanding, varnishing, buying, and selling."

"Ah," I said. God, he had great arms, bandaged or not.

The elevator pinged, and we stepped out onto his floor. He was the third door on the left.

"Don't let Pilot intimidate you," Sebastien said.

"What?" I asked, but he'd already opened the door to his apartment, and a huge black hairy beast was barreling out into the hallway and slamming into his legs. I may have squealed and stepped back.

Sebastien rubbed the thing with his good hand. "Okay, buddy. Okay. I missed you, too."

"Why do you have a horse in your apartment?"

Sebastien smiled at me. "It's a dog. He's a Russian terrier."

I frowned. "Aren't terriers supposed to be small?" I took another step back. This was a problem. Because pretty soon the dog was going to get over being enthusiastic about Sebastien's return, and...

The horse-dog stopped, tilted its head, and looked at me.

"I think he likes you," Sebastien said.

"Oh shit," I muttered.

More than a hundred pounds of animal leapt at me, tongue first. I bounced off the hallway wall and had to grab the dog's collar to keep him from jumping up onto me. The thoughts radiating from the dog were like the beat of a train on railway tracks.

Friend, friend, play? Friend, friend, play? Friend...

"Uh, sit!" I tried. The beast's tongue slathered my hands and forearms.

Sebastien laughed. "He likes you."

"Dogs always do," I said ruefully. I tried to fend off the dog's advances and could barely hold the giant beast back. "He's... really...strong."

"Pilot," Sebastien said, "Sit."

Pilot sat, but his giant brown eyes never left mine, and his whole body was trembling. *Friend, friend, play!*

"I'll take him out. You can wait here if you want." He gestured to the inside of his apartment. He stepped inside for a second, and Pilot whined low in his throat, looking at me. His tail started to thump against the carpet, hard. His whole body was tensed, waiting to leap at me again.

"Stay," I said, nervous. Any second now his urge to play with me was going to outdo Sebastien's command to sit. This was always a problem.

Sebastien returned with a lead and clicked it onto Pilot's collar. He looked up at me. "Big dogs make you nervous."

I shook my head. "I'm not afraid of dogs. They just... really...like me."

"They have good taste." There was that sly smile again.

Pilot barked. I stepped back.

"Hush," Sebastien said. "He's normally better behaved. I'll take him out and be right back."

I nodded. He had a dog. Well, that would help keep me on the purer path, wouldn't it? Dogs went nuts around me. Had done ever since I'd first started picking up thoughts. It was like they knew, somehow, that I was open for business. I'd never had any luck whatsoever shielding out the thoughts of a dog. Not that there was a great variety of thoughts going on in the minds of most dogs. Food, the urge to go outside, food, chasing something, food, playing, food, scratches, and food were pretty much their entire repertoire. But boy, did they love letting me know about it.

The two went back toward the elevator. I rubbed my forehead as Pilot's litany of joy faded, and stepped inside Sebastien's apartment.

It astonished me.

It was beautifully—and tastefully—decorated with wonderful wooden pieces, which made sense now that I knew what he did for a living. The kitchen was also lovely, if small, and had beautiful cabinets I assumed he'd done himself. I went to the sink to wash some of the dog slobber from my arms and hands, and dried my hands on a plain blue towel. I'd barely dried off before the door opened again and the barrage of energetic thoughts returned.

"He didn't take long," Sebastien said, putting a baggie of what I assumed would be dog poop into a steel trash can. It looked huge.

Pilot was thumping his tail and looking at me again. *Play? Friend. Treat?*

"Would you like a drink?" Sebastien asked. He looked exhausted.

"No," I said. "I shouldn't keep you."

"Let me just get Pilot into his crate," Sebastien said.

I watched him lead the horse-dog down the hallway, and the two went inside what I assumed was the second bedroom. Pilot's thoughts reduced in volume, with a vague disappointment, but a genuine thrill that he was going to bed. He liked going to bed. In fact, everything was wonderful in his crate. I rubbed my temples again, smiling to myself. Pilot was certainly a positive creature.

"He's big, but he's a baby," Sebastien said, coming back in a moment later.

"You trained him in English," I said. The horse-dog's limited repertoire of thoughts was in English.

Sebastien nodded. "My ex and I got him together. But Pilot outlasted the ex."

"Ah," I said.

"You sure you don't want a drink?"

I shook my head. "Go get changed for bed, and then I'll come in."

He laughed. "I sleep naked." He went into his bedroom, awkwardly tugging off his shirt. The view of his back was as nice as his front, I realized, then purposely turned around to regard the bookshelves he'd set up in his living room, trying to restore my thoughts to a G-rating. He had quite a book collection, many of them nicely bound. I itched to go read the titles, but thought it might be snooping.

There were also photographs along the dividing arch between the kitchen and the living room, and I looked closer.

They were sepia tones, and all of Sebastien himself. They were tasteful nudes, with careful lighting and shadow that kept them from being openly erotic, but they definitely still managed to be alluring. The man was the poster child for masculinity, and I caught myself smiling.

Karen would say he was obviously self-involved, but somehow, I didn't see that in the photographs. It made me proud of him, somehow. I couldn't quite put my finger on it.

"I'm ready," Sebastien called. My heart fluttered, and I told it to calm down. I was aiming to put him into a restful sleep. That was all. Farther down the hallway, a low-pitched "woof" came from Pilot.

I walked into his bedroom and saw that he'd lain, facedown, on the bed, with his second pillow supporting his right arm. He'd tugged a sheet up to the small of his back, and I resisted the urge to figure out if he was nude beneath it.

"Actually, if you could lie on your back?" I asked. "It's mostly a face massage."

He rolled over, and I kept my eyes strictly on his face. I moved the pillow for him, and he settled, his head back on the other pillow, eyes closed. He was obviously exhausted, and I felt so bad for him. Poor guy.

I got onto the bed awkwardly, on my knees, and positioned myself without jostling him too much. He had a beautiful four-poster bed, obviously a restored antique, and the chest of drawers matched.

I placed my fingertips on either side of his forehead and rubbed lightly.

"That's nice," he said, and opened his eyes. Our gaze locked, and I felt my chest tighten.

"It's supposed to be," I said.

He smiled and closed his eyes again. "You have the touch."

"Hush," I said, and then went to work.

I massaged his temples and face and neck while I

telepathically brushed his mind. Dipping into his mind this way was gentle, like slowly wading into a warm pool. I started looking for the parts of his mind that were focusing on the pains and aches. I nudged them away, one by one, while my fingers traced lines on his face, neck, shoulders, forehead, and chest. Every time his brain thought of the ache, I told it to ignore it, just for a while. One by one, the little hot points dimmed. His breathing became more and more regular, and I smiled to myself, moving deeper into his mind and gently urging his thoughts to slow down as well.

Finally, when he was barely awake, I sent a brief thought into his mind.

Sleep.

He slept.

I gingerly got off the bed and pulled the sheet up higher onto his chest, without peeking, though I really *really* wanted to. His skin was warm, and I allowed myself to touch his chest hair again, once, before turning out the light and leaving his bedroom.

In the living room, I stopped for a moment to look at the photographs again. They were masculine, and strong, and yet gentle at the same time. I really did like them. They body matched the mind, so to speak.

Friend? Play?

Pilot wasn't asleep yet. I smiled, trying to keep quiet. I let myself out, happy that Sebastien's door had an auto-lock as well as a dead bolt, and trusting that he'd be fine one night without the dead bolt thrown.

I went home, picked up Easter—who immediately smelled Pilot and twisted out of my grip in a huff—and then I fell into bed, exhausted, my cat glaring at me from the end of the bed.

My phone buzzed.

Groaning, I picked it up, still trying to mollify Easter by wiggling the fingers on my free hand. He wasn't buying it. There was a text from Callum.

She was the redhead.

I sighed and was about to turn off my phone when it buzzed again, this time from Karen.

No spanking tonight. But your brother is a good kisser. Coffee tomorrow, please—getting home so late!

"This is such a bad idea," I said to Easter, who squinted at me, still not in a forgiving mood. "Mark my words."

BLUE

I was floating again.

I smiled and stretched myself out, tumbling head over heels without vertigo in my boxers and T-shirt. The Earth was between me and the sun, and yet I was warm. The music was as lovely as ever, cadence and rhythm and those wonderful crystalline tones. Everything seemed so much more possible when I dreamed this dream. Even normalcy.

"Welcome back, Rainbow Man," Miracle Woman said, when I flipped back upright—though it occurred to me that the idea of upright was rather moot in the zero gravity of this dream space.

"Thanks," I said. "You know, if we're going to keep having these midnight trysts, you should probably call me Kieran." I don't know why I trusted her with my name, but anything was preferable to Rainbow Man.

Hell, Disco was winning out over Rainbow Man.

She nodded almost warily. "Okay. Kieran."

"You don't have to tell me your name," I said. "Don't worry."

She relaxed. "It's not that I don't trust you," she said. "It's just…Well, I don't trust you."

"And you just moved and you don't want to have to move again," I said, without thinking. I knew I was right even as I said it, but I hadn't really processed it.

She didn't look happy that I'd pegged it. She tapped her forehead. "Who's in tune now?"

"Wow," I said, and blushed. "Sorry."

She shook her head. "Don't be. But you're right. I don't tell anyone, and I stay safe."

I got that. I floated for a while with her, in companionable silence.

"Does your boyfriend know?" I asked.

"What makes you think I got a boyfriend?"

"You're too hot to be single."

"Flatterer," she said, but she smiled. A few seconds later, she nodded. "Yeah. But he doesn't know the whole deal, or that I'm Miracle Woman—and hell, isn't that a stupid name."

"Hello," I objected. "Rainbow Man. Way more stupid."

She snorted. "True fact."

Her boyfriend knew. I'd never told anyone. I'd never dated anyone seriously, either, and the two weren't unrelated. My eyes stung. I forced myself to get a grip.

"You can have as much fun as anyone else," she said. "You really can. Just because you can read minds and toss shit around, it doesn't mean you don't get to have fun."

I nodded, not trusting myself to speak. Time to change the subject.

"Last time, you were going to show me something," I said.

"Ah." She smiled and pointed behind us.

I rotated in the effortless way of the dream and looked out behind us, leaving the Earth to my back.

There was a star—or maybe it was a galaxy, who knew?—and it was shining and glittering, even though there was no atmosphere between us to make it twinkle. It was blue, not white. As I watched, I realized it flickered in time to the tones of the music.

It was the music.

Or the source of it.

"That's where it comes from?" I said.

She nodded.

"Wow." It was all I could think of to say.

She laughed. "Yes. Wow."

"That's how it started?"

She got a kind of mischievous grin on her face. She looked at me as if assessing and then gave a kind of mental shrug—it felt a lot like the "oh, what the hell!" you think before you do something fun and potentially embarrassing.

"I was maybe a teeny bit stoned at the time," she confessed.

I burst out laughing.

"Oh, like you've never smoked up?" she asked, scorn plain on her face.

"I'm sorry," I said, chuckling. "It's just...you got psychic powers from smoking pot?"

She laughed with me. "No. I think..." She laughed again. "God, I can't believe I'm telling you this. I think that the pot opened my mind just enough to hear them. And after that, I knew what to listen for, and found it all around me."

I didn't get it. She picked up on my confusion before I could speak it.

"It's like this, I think," she explained. "You know what blue is, right?"

"Sure. A color."

"But how did you learn what blue was?"

I shrugged. "My parents, I guess. A book, maybe? Like a kid's book. This is blue."

She nodded. "Exactly. You can't learn what blue is unless someone points to something blue and says so. This is blue, that's yellow, this is red."

"Okay."

"I think that a lot of us can do what you and I and a few

others are doing, but that until you've done it once, or until you've heard the music, you don't even know what it is, let alone how to do it." She was excited, and her eyes were full of energy. She'd thought about this a long time.

"So," I said, trying to follow her train of logic, "Until you hear a thought, you don't know you can hear thoughts, so you don't hear thoughts?"

She didn't seem particularly impressed at my version, but went with it. "More or less. I think it has to be in you, I think you have to be able. But until you're exposed to it, I don't think you're aware you can."

I thought about it.

"I was watching Thomas Wright," I said. "Live. When he was shot."

She flinched. "That shit was ugly."

"That was when I heard it. I wanted it to be so real, so magical." I smiled a bit at the memory. My mother and I watching the show in her hospital room on that crappy little television set that swung out from the wall.

Miracle Woman shifted beside me, looking remarkably... guilty?

It hit me.

"You were watching, too."

She nodded. "Yes."

"It was you," I breathed. "You were the music, weren't you? When he was shot, I heard a voice in my head, telling me to hide. That was you."

She flinched. "I'm sorry. I didn't do that on purpose. When I saw him on television, I got so scared for him—for all of us. I thought, what if he pisses off the man? And then that guy in the audience started yelling, and I tried to tell Thomas Wright to hide. All the way from Detroit." She shook her head. "I passed out, trying."

"You knocked me out cold, too, I think," I said, and flipped up my hair to show her the scar from where I'd cracked my head on my mother's bedside table at the hospital.

She sighed. "Well, it didn't work. Man got shot. And I gave you—and a few others, I'm told—one hell of a headache." She looked annoyed. "Why in the world he thought he should put on a demonstration for television I will never know." She glanced at me. "Sorry about your head."

I shook my head. "No. You did a service." I tried to find the words. "I might have told the world, if I hadn't had that…urge… to hide in the back of my mind. It was good advice. It gave me time to figure out how to control what was happening, and it was something special and wonderful I had with my mom before she died."

Miracle Woman shook her head. "But I did this to you. To a lot of folks. Woke 'em up and turned on their…whatever."

I shook my head. "You didn't make the sky blue. You just showed me I could look up."

"I was pretty loud about it." She seemed truly upset. It surprised me.

"It's a beautiful sound, though. That music?" I pointed off into the light. "And yours, too."

"It's the music of thoughts," she said. "Can you hear yours?"

I'd never tried. She smiled, knowing what I was thinking, and closed her eyes for a moment. I started to hear the strong beautiful tones of her thoughts.

"That's you." I smiled. "It's beautiful."

And then there were two songs playing. I realized she was listening to my own thoughts, the music my mind made, and reflecting it back at me somehow, so I could hear it.

"Resonance," she said.

The songs together became something stronger than their own notes. Each tone reverberated against a tone in the other song, and I felt my mind widen, open, even past the point at which I normally felt the strange barrier inside my skull. Her song was freedom and willpower and the desire to live a life without being held to any limits. My song was independent. Capable.

This, I thought, *is what handling it sounds like*. I smiled.

You don't have to fix all of it yourself, you know, she thought back to me. Her voice was incredibly clear, as though I'd had her thoughts myself.

"That's amazing," I said, and pulled back. She did the same, and the music faded.

"I don't get to do that very often," she said. "I don't meet many people like us that I feel I can trust." She narrowed her eyes. "Not that I trust you."

I raised a hand in surrender. "Of course not. You've met a lot of others?" I asked.

She looked down at the Earth. "Up here, mostly. In these half-dreams. But once or twice in the waking world. It's a pretty wild thing, especially if they don't know. I've helped one or two realize, and—I hope—move on to accept themselves and keep their heads down."

I looked at her. "How are you so together?"

"You think I got it together?" she said. There was a wobble in her voice. She wiped her eyes. "Shit. I'm just me. Me is good enough, most days." She sighed and wiped her eyes again. "I'm going to wake up an emotional mess."

I grinned. "I'm sure your boyfriend will make it better."

She smiled. Nodded. Then looked at me again.

"You should take a chance with this guy."

I blinked. "Guy?"

"The one you were thinking about when you asked me if my boyfriend knew."

I balked. "I haven't known him very long."

"I don't mean telling him you're psychic. Lord, you are

stupid. No, you don't tell them that until they pretty much figured it out already. My boyfriend took a hell of a while to clue in I was catching his thoughts. Freaked him the hell out at first." She smiled at the memory. "I meant dating this guy. And all that can entail." She opened her eyes wide. "Y'know...Sex."

I blushed. She laughed. "God, you're a prude. Is he a nice guy?"

"He has a dog," I said, not quite answering the question, though to my mind people who had pets were generally better people. "Which of course, just loves me."

"Oh shit!" She laughed again. "Isn't that the worst? My man wants a dog, but as soon as they get anywhere near me..." She shook her head.

I blinked. "That happens to you, too?"

"I think all dogs can tell. They're...tuned in."

"Well, this dog is freaking huge. It's more like a pony."

She laughed louder. "Did it hump your leg? This one time I had to ward off a beagle with my purse, and that dog was bound and determined."

"This thing could hump my neck."

She laughed even louder.

I crossed my arms. "I don't think you're taking this quite seriously enough."

"Oh," she said, blinking suddenly. "Shit. Alarm clock."

She vanished.

I floated a while longer, smiling. So the dog thing wasn't just me. Huh. I guess I'd just have to stick to being a cat person. After all, Easter didn't try to molest me every waking moment. I smiled, and thinking about the way the music of our minds had been so much stronger together, I turned back to the blue light. What had she called it? Resonance? If two people could be so much stronger together, what would a whole world of people capable of telepathy be like?

Thank you for the song, I thought, as hard as I could, out into the endless night.

But I don't think they heard me.

❖

I woke up and checked the Capital Pride website, not even pretending to be doing anything else. "Disco" was now ahead of "Rainbow Man" by a narrow margin. I voted for "Prism" a third time, but it didn't seem to help much.

"I refuse to be the hero known as Disco," I muttered, and brought up the Pride events for the day.

There was a picnic lunch at Brewer's Park, across from Carleton University, being hosted by the university Gay, Lesbian, Bisexual, and Transgendered Centre. I smiled. I'd used to volunteer there, back when it had first just been the "Gay and Lesbian Centre." And there was a bar night with a band from Toronto playing at Chances tonight.

I clicked over to the website for the Church of the Testifying Prophet.

The site had been updated. They'd called for as many protesters as possible to show at the picnic. It was a public event on public ground, the Church's website declared, and therefore they could not be evicted.

I closed my laptop.

"Hey, buddy," I said to Easter. "You're on your own for lunch today."

He meowed at me and went into the kitchen to have some kibble.

I needed a better plan of attack this time, I decided. City Hall and the Drag-Off had taught me two things: one, that Stigmatic Jack was a bigoted freak with a voice in his head and a propensity for psychokinetic violence; and two, that I'd twice shut him down by shining a bright enough light in his face. It seemed he hadn't yet mastered the trick of using his teke on something he couldn't see.

Amateur.

But I also wasn't scaring him off. Maybe I needed to try something different. I'd been pretty lucky so far—a few nasty bruises were the net result of Wyatt Jackson's religious tantrum at Chances, and no one had been killed at City Hall. But if he went off at the picnic, it could be a repeat of City Hall, and I was done letting him hurt people.

I needed something new.

Easter wandered back into the living room, and I looked at him. I sent him the image of himself, sitting down.

He sat, purring. We'd worked on this for ages, and it was one of the few ways I ever practiced my telepathy. Given that I didn't want to get caught, and using telepathy on folks without them noticing is pretty hard since they could pick up on anything I thought if I wasn't careful, my cat had become the guinea pig. Easter was purring because he knew doing whatever I asked him to do with my mental images usually resulted in a treat.

Easter and I had mental images for sit, stay, come, playing with his mouse toy, being quiet, head scratches, and a host of other things. I sent an image for Easter to roll over. He did, and I rewarded him with a treat from the cupboard, which I teked open and floated out to him.

He went into the bedroom after that, probably to nap, what with how exhausting it was to be a cat.

I tapped my finger against the cardboard tube of cat treats.

I had an idea.

But first, I needed a religious education. Unfortunately, I'd mostly ignored the one I'd gotten when I was a kid, and didn't often pay attention on Sundays.

I sighed and dug out my cell phone.

❖

"Where in the Bible does it actually say I'm evil?"

"Hi, little brother, how are you?"

"Evil. You?"

"Not as much," Callum said. "Though I masturbate, so I'm probably going to hell, too."

"Too much information," I sighed.

"Karen is amazing."

"I really don't want to know why you're linking Karen with masturbation."

"I'm not. Pervert. We had our date last night. I got home pretty late."

I rubbed my eyes. "I know. Apparently you're a good kisser."

"I am?" He sounded pleased. "What else did she say?"

"Nothing. And I didn't tell you that. See, now this is why I didn't want you guys to date. I'm going to be the bloody monkey in the middle."

"Leviticus."

"Sorry?"

"Leviticus. That's the part of the Bible people usually toss about. 'You shall not lie with a male as one lies with a female; it is an abomination.'"

"Well crap. I'm going to hell." This wasn't so helpful. Wasn't God supposed to be love? I remembered that much from Sunday School.

"I doubt it," Callum said. "For perspective, shellfish, tattoos, and poly-blends are also abominations."

"Well, at least they're right about the polyester."

"The thing about Leviticus is the translation could mean 'abomination' more in an idolatry sense." Callum was moving into his professor tone. "Also, it's Old Testament, and the New Testament basically tells us that those punishments are more to be applied in the afterlife now. There's a case to be made for the scriptures intending to refer to idolaters offering prostitution, rather than two men having consensual fun."

"Ah. Well then." That was interesting. Useless, but interesting. "You really know your stuff, don't you?"

"Enough to make a living. Dare I ask why my brother suddenly cares about what the Bible says?"

"Just getting my ammunition in line for some bigots. What about cutting people? Is the Bible pro-cutting people? Throwing things at them?"

There was a long pause. "Uh, Kieran, you're worrying me."

"Not me." I sighed. "The bigots. They were the ones throwing things."

"That thing at City Hall?" Callum asked.

"On the nose," I said.

"Well..." Callum sounded evasive.

"Cal?"

"Keeping in mind what I said about the Old and New Testaments, there's actually a lot of punishment tossed about in the Bible. The Bible is sort of okay with punishment, really. But it also says things like he who is without sin is the only one who should be casting the first stone."

"It's amazing to me that anyone thinks they can use this stuff to map out their life."

"The Golden Rule is represented in most theologies. Mostly these theological writings are guides to living well, though they can be a bit dated. It's common sense to think that they need to be interpreted in the face of cultural evolution, but people who want to misread things to justify their own ideas will find a way." Callum sounded genuinely sad about that.

"Is that the professor version of 'haters gonna hate'?" I said.

"I guess so."

"So is this the first time your humanities degree has ever come in handy?" I asked him.

"Shut up," Callum growled.

"It doesn't really help much," I sighed. "I was hoping for 'O, thou shall love of the faggot as much as the straight' or something."

"Sorry. Faggots were for lighting fires." Callum laughed. "Why don't you look for it in your own Bible?"

Uh-oh.

"Um," I said.

"Didn't Dad give you a Bible for your birthday a couple of years ago?"

"Yes." I drew the word out into a hiss.

"Where is it?" He sounded mischievous now. "Should I tell Dad you need a new one?"

"No!" I yelped. "I just…misplaced it."

"Tell me you didn't throw out your Bible."

"No," I said, annoyed. Actually, I'd wrapped it up as a gag Christmas gift for Karen last year after covering it with brown paper and writing "Salacious Porn" on the cover. She'd howled. I wasn't sure if she'd given it back yet.

"I don't want to know, do I?" he asked.

"Probably safer," I agreed.

"Now you owe me twice," he said.

"I'm allowing you to go on a date with my best friend," I said. "That's worth way more than two favors."

"You're not in charge of me. Or her. See you." He hung up on me before I could hang up on him.

He was so immature.

❖

I had to give the university GLBT Centre credit, the field looked festive. They'd arranged the picnic tables into six neat rows, with barely any walking space between them, and each one had been covered with a plastic tablecloth—a row each of red, orange, yellow, green, blue, and purple. The effect was of a pride flag. With potato salad.

Rows of barbecues had also been set up, with signs offering hot dogs and burgers for a twoney each, and in metal tubs full of ice floated cold drinks for a loonie. Quite a crowd had already gathered, most of them younger, given the midday timing. It looked mostly like a university crowd, with a few others who'd either taken their lunch breaks to come here, or were playing hooky, or otherwise worked jobs that weren't nine-to-five.

It was a sedate gathering, though I did see the new Miss Ottawa Pride, resplendent in her tiara and carrying her scepter, walking arm and arm with Mizz Anne Thrope from table to table to pass along their version of callous kindness. The sun was warm on the skin, and I gave myself a second to tilt my head upward and enjoy it.

When I looked back down at the field, I saw three white vans pulling into the parking lot beyond. They had the cross and bleeding-hands logo on them that I'd come to know and dread. I moved over to the rows of barbecues to watch them disgorge from the vans.

Wyatt Jackson was third out of the first van, right after his two thicknecks. The blue suit guy followed, sticking close to Jackson, who raised his hands and said something. The other vans spilled out about a dozen people each—were they sitting on the floor in the back?—and they all gathered around Stigmatic Jack, eyes rapt.

"Is that the preacher guy?" asked one of the guys flipping the burgers, a chubby Latino with a goatee and a T-shirt that said "Bear Necessities." The guy on the next barbecue looked over, shading his eyes with his hand and spatula.

"Yeah," I said. "It's him."

They both turned and looked at me, and I offered them a

weak smile of support, then started walking toward the parking lot area.

"Never doubt you do the work of the Lord God," Jackson was saying as I got close enough to hear. The man's voice was really something. He'd be a killer salesman.

Y'know, if he wasn't totally fucked in the head.

"Hallelujah!" one of the followers said, a young woman maybe my age. She was blond and blue eyed, and really cute. It made me sad.

"Kieran?"

I jumped with surprise and turned to see Sebastien and his friend Tyson had come up behind me while I was eavesdropping.

"Just listening to the warm-up speech," I said, jerking my thumb at the group in the parking lot. "So far, it's all just rah-rah, God loves you the most."

Tyson scowled. "God don't love those folks at all."

"Hallelujah!" I crowed, and the church folk all turned to look my way with admonition.

Sebastien looked well, and there were only bandages on his wrist. The long cut on his forearm was thin and scabbed, but looked like it was healing well.

"Maybe we should get the rest of the guys?" Sebastien said.

"Yeah," Tyson said.

They looked at me. I realized they wanted me to follow them. Crap.

"I think I'll stick around, just to hear how the pep rally ends," I said lightly.

Sebastien frowned. "I don't think that's a good idea." Behind us, I heard Stigmatic Jack finish another round of spiritual masturbation, and the group exploded into hallelujahs.

"You don't want to be between them and the picnic," Tyson agreed.

Damnit. I crossed my arms. "Are you guys gonna drag me off?" I didn't want the church to even get to the field, let alone the picnic. And they were wasting my time. I should have been inside Wyatt Jackson's head by now.

Tyson raised his eyebrows and smiled, but Sebastien frowned.

"Kieran, when these people are around, people get hurt."

"I know," I snapped. It came out harshly. Sebastien's brows knit deeper, into a scowl.

"Then why would you want to be closer to them?" he asked me.

"I can handle it. Go get Security," I said.

Another chorus of hallelujahs floated to us from the parking lot.

"Fine." Sebastien shook his head, and he turned and stalked off. Tyson gave me an awkward look, but then followed.

Damn.

I turned around, facing Wyatt Jackson, and opened my mind.

They shall be punished for flaunting their wicked ways. They shall lie prostate on the ground before the glory of God. They shall bleed as my servant bleeds, to honor God.

Jesus H, Jackson's "God" voice was spouting off like a spurt of cold and oily water flooding up the wrong direction in a basement. I pulled myself together and focused. This was the first time since my mother's death I'd ever purposely tried to make myself heard in the mind of another.

The reflex to hide didn't rear its head. I smiled, realizing I hadn't heard that voice in a while. Maybe whatever Miracle Woman had done had worn off, finally. Carefully and clearly, I aimed my thought directly into Wyatt Jackson's mind.

Let he who is without sin cast the first stone.

Wyatt Jackson stopped speaking, midsentence, and everyone turned to look at him expectantly. The bodyguards glanced around, and the blue-suited guy stared at Stigmatic Jack from behind his sunglasses, taking hold of one of Jackson's arms. It looked like they were all waiting for him to faint. Given how much blood he was always leaking, I supposed that made sense.

"God speaks to me," Jackson said, but there was a note of confusion to his voice.

Wrath is a deadly sin, I thought to him. *God is love, not hate.* Every thought I sent felt easier than the last one, and I could even hear a pale echo of the way it sounded in Jackson's mind. I was much better at this than I thought.

Jackson started to look left and right, almost panicked. I nodded to myself. This was going to work. I could totally handle this.

God is righteous wrath! thundered in Jackson's head, and, by proxy, mine. I winced and actually had to take a step back. It looked like Stigmatic Jack's other voice was coming out to play. *Bring them to their knees, and show them the glory of the Lord!*

Wyatt Jackson turned, and a mix of pain and exaltation filled his face as he raised his hands to the sky. I heard the three broken notes and saw the red begin to flow from Stigmatic Jack's palms. That man's poor hands.

God is not pain and blood, I sent, louder than I'd ever tried to send something to someone before. My vision grew hazy around the edges, and my hands clenched. *God does not want you to suffer, nor anyone else.*

Wyatt Jackson's followers had begun to rally around him now and were singing a hymn. They all started to walk toward the field.

I wasn't winning. If anything, I seemed to be confusing the hell out of Wyatt Jackson, and that probably wasn't going to end up doing good for anyone. I had to back off as the group moved past me, marching and singing "Onward Christian Soldiers" with quite a bit of skill. They'd have been beautiful if they weren't terrifying bigots.

I moved along the line of barbecues, hanging back behind the row of volunteers cooking the burgers, and saw that Sebastien and Tyson and the rest of his security people had formed a line on the field between the picnic and the protesters. I could feel notes twanging and pinging all around me. Stigmatic Jack was about to let loose.

No, I sent to him. *You will not harm anyone!* And with no delicacy or softness to my touch, I tried to find the part of his mind in charge of sleeping, and pushed at it.

Wyatt Jackson stumbled and shook his head, his eyes drooping. One of the thicknecks grabbed his arm to steady him. I pressed harder, feeling a drowsiness wash through the so-called prophet's mind.

He is mine! roared the voice in Jackson's head, and I felt the sense of grogginess I'd manage to create evaporate.

Jackson grabbed his temples, leaving bloody smears on his cheeks. It wasn't a good look.

"No..." I whispered. Nobody seemed to be looking at me, everyone was transfixed with the seemingly insane prophet who was now grabbing his head and yelling, "Thy will be done!" over and over. I walked farther behind the barbecues, closer to the fence.

Sebastien and his group exchanged glances, but stood their ground.

Wyatt Jackson raised his hands and screamed out "Thy will be done!" again, at the top of his lungs. His bodyguards stepped in front of him, and the blue suit's head shot to the left. I looked in the same direction just in time to see one of the barbecues launch itself end over end into the air, toward the picnic tables, raining down burning charcoal in its wake.

People screamed. There was no way I could try to catch the barbecue with my teke—it would be way too heavy, like the speaker at the bar—but I could give it a good shove. I managed to slam it down so it hit the ground in a flash of blue light just short of the picnic tables. People leapt out of the way of the hot charcoal with yelps and screams. Wisps of smoke started to form among the grass and tablecloth.

Punish them! screamed the voice in Wyatt Jackson's head. *And drive off the demon!*

Plan B had officially failed. Time for a repeat performance of plan A.

I lit up.

❖

"It's him!" someone yelled. I warped the light in the reflecting dance and strode onto the field as Wyatt Jackson's people, bodyguards and blue suit inclusive, took a collective step back. Only Jackson didn't move.

"Lord! I have done as you commanded!" he all but frothed at the mouth, and the blood on his face and sleeves didn't help him look any saner. I'd have felt pity for him if he wasn't tossing around burning charcoal.

Don't make me blind you again, I thought to him, stunned at just how easy it was to push a thought into the man's head. *Just go. No more throwing things, no more cutting people. Just go.* Keeping the light bending and reflecting around me made me look like his walking column of light, I supposed. Maybe he'd listen to his Metatron. Hopefully before I got too tired to keep it up. I really needed to practice this more.

"Lord?" he said, confused. His face fell.

That is not me, came the angry voice in Jackson's skull. *He is a false idol!* Jackson's face screwed up in disgust.

So much for listening to the Metatron.

I heard sirens. For crying out loud. Someone had called the cops? That was all I needed.

Jackson seemed to hear it also, and his head jerked. I heard those broken tones again and looked where Jackson was looking, trying to figure out what he was grabbing with his teke.

I didn't see what cracked me across the back of my shoulders, and it sure didn't come from wherever Jackson was looking. I stumbled, dropping to one knee, and nearly lost my lenses. Whatever had just smacked me had cracked me hard and hurt like hell. My eyes watered.

The crowd booed. Actually booed.

My life is weird.

I'd had enough. I bent the light to flare in the faces of Jackson and his group and then flashed it, twice, brightly, moving the lenses back and forth behind each other into a sort of strobe. They yelped and covered their eyes, most of them turning away, Jackson included. The tones stopped again, though I wasn't sure if it was me or the sirens. Sebastien and his group jumped back from them, except for one of the security people, who came toward me.

"Are you okay?" he asked. He reached a hand out awkwardly, not sure where he should be reaching, squinting into the bands of light that surrounded me. I blinked. Neat. I had a fan.

I got to my feet again. There were cheers. The sirens were much closer now. I needed an exit. It seemed like poor taste to blind everyone just so I could slip away. Especially with the booing and the cheering.

I settled for doing the funhouse-mirror effect again, like I'd done at the church, and dropped my light at the same time. There were gasps and groans, and one or two people fell over as their eyes told them up was sideways, but it was enough that I managed to get over and behind the barbecues again while most people closed their eyes or worked hard at holding in their lunches. I knelt down behind one of the barbecues and sighed. I'd just made an entire picnic stumble and retch, my plan hadn't worked well at all, and now my back was killing me.

At least no one was getting sliced up.

The police arrived and climbed out of their cars. They were walking straight for Wyatt Jackson, and they didn't look happy. The guy in the blue suit was tending to Jackson's bleeding palms, and the thicknecks had stepped away from Sebastien's line of security.

I smiled. At least that seemed to be the end of that.

"Dude, did you see that?" the Latino guy with the goatee was saying to the other cook.

"I saw it," the other guy said, though he didn't seem to believe that he had.

"It was the Rainbow Man," the Latino guy said. "He totally shut down that freak!"

"I think he prefers Prism," I said, climbing to my feet and brushing grass of my knees.

They both looked at me.

"Instead of Rainbow Man," I said. "Prism. I think that's the name he uses."

"I heard it was Disco," said the second cook.

I sighed. There wasn't enough dignity in my life. My shoulder blades throbbed, and I winced.

"Kieran." Sebastien had arrived. "Are you okay?" He sounded more angry than concerned.

I tried to give him a confident nod. "I just had to dodge a barbecue," I said.

"It totally flew," said the cook, pointing. A couple of volunteers had dumped one of the tubs of ice on top of the smoldering grass and tablecloth while some others were standing the barbecue back upright.

"You shouldn't have been anywhere near them," Sebastien snapped.

Excuse me? If it hadn't been for me…

I got angry. "And what did you accomplish?" As soon as I

said it, I regretted it, but Sebastien just turned and walked away, joining Tyson to speak with one of the police officers.

"Shit," I said. My shoulders hurt like hell. What had Stigmatic Jack hit me with, anyway? I looked into the middle of the field, where I spotted a bicycle where it had landed on its side.

Wyatt Jackson hit me with a *bicycle*? Damn. That was going to leave a mark. I rolled my shoulders—they burned with pain.

I watched the police put Wyatt Jackson, his bodyguards, and the guy in the blue suit into their cars. The followers stood off to one side, many of them rubbing their eyes. The blond woman who was about my age looked shell-shocked.

I walked over to where Sebastien and Tyson were speaking to the police officer and heard their version of what had happened. They both called me Rainbow Man, and the police officer frowned as he wrote in his notebook. Eventually, they finished, and Sebastien and Tyson gave the officer their names and phone numbers, and he moved on.

Sebastien saw me, tightened his jaw, and then walked the other way.

I waited for my turn with the police, gave a short description and tried not to hold myself like a man in pain, then went home, pulled off my shirt, and saw the dark red bruises already appearing across my back. I got into the shower and cried like a child.

❖

The news said that Wyatt Jackson was once again at the hospital, getting a blood transfusion, and that Jackson had asked his spokesperson (who was the guy in the blue suit, and who had apparently fared better given his sunglasses) to deliver a message. I hit Mute before he could speak. I just didn't want to hear it.

I supposed that this meant there was no point in going to Chances to hear the band, given that Jackson was out of commission for the evening. Maybe this should be my new plan. Just keep blinding him until Pride Week was over.

I couldn't work up a laugh over that.

All I wanted was to enjoy my vacation. Now I was on the news websites, and people were voting on my name. The police wanted anyone knowing anything about the so-called Rainbow Man to contact them. The word "psychokinesis" had officially been used on the news, though it wasn't being taken completely seriously. I shook my head. People just didn't want to believe. I rubbed my eyes. If I hadn't deflected that barbecue, it would have been way uglier.

And maybe Sebastien wouldn't think I was a complete idiot.

What had I done wrong?

Screw it. I was going to have a good time at least once this week. My head was throbbing from overextending myself to make a field-wide light show, and my shoulders ached like the devil from the bicycle—and wasn't that just the high point of my day, getting clocked with a bike?—but I was going to go out.

Hell, maybe I'd even have a one-night stand.

So long as the lights were off and no one could see the bruises on my shoulder blades.

I moaned, but I went to get changed for a night out anyway.

❖

Tyson was one of the two people manning the door at Chances, and I paid up and went inside and had a beer right off. It wasn't long before I was feeling mellow and happy, and the band from Toronto turned out to be decent. I danced, mostly by myself but not caring at all, and once or twice with a blond guy in a blue tank top who knew how to dance, but knew he knew how to dance and couldn't stop thinking about how everyone was looking at him. Thanks to the beer, I couldn't stop hearing his self-congratulatory thoughts, so I gave up.

I sat down at the bar for the second set and just allowed myself to ride the happiness in the bar. People were out, proud, and enjoying themselves, and it felt good to be a part of it. This was what it was about, I felt. The whole week was supposed to be about this, not about trying to stop a bigoted religious nut who heard voices.

"Hey," came a voice.

I turned. Justin offered me a small smile and a wave. I smiled back.

"How you doing?" I asked.

"Good," he said. He seemed tense and a bit awkward. I felt bad for him. First the world's worst blind date, then the ego bruising at the gallery.

"Listen," I said. "I want to apologize."

His smile widened. "Don't worry about it."

"No," I said. "I feel bad about...uh, pretty much everything."

"Everything okay?" someone said from behind me.

Justin looked past me. "Yeah."

I turned. A tall, dark-haired man stood there with two open bottles of beer. He gave me a slight frown and handed one of the bottles to Justin.

"Kieran, this is Michael," Justin said.

"The doctor with the clown fetish?" I asked. It popped out before I could stop myself. I should never have had a beer. No tolerance.

Michael said, "Do I know you?" and Justin said, "Clown fetish?" and then both of them were staring at each other.

"I don't have a clown fetish," Michael said. Justin looked horrified.

"But you're a doctor," he said.

"No," I said, and they both turned to look at me, neither in a particularly friendly way. "See, Karen told me…I mean, she keeps trying to set me up, and…"

"Oh!" Michael said. "You're Karen's friend Kieran." His voice had warmed now. In fact, it was a bit too warm. I glanced at Justin, who was frowning at the doctor. Michael held out his hand. "Nice to meet you, finally."

"Uh," I said, shaking his hand.

Way more fuckable than the blond, he was thinking. Ew.

"So you guys are on a date?" I said, pulling my hand back. Justin's lips closed tightly.

Michael seemed to realize he'd been staring. He smiled. "Yeah. Karen. She's definitely a force of nature." He looped an arm around Justin, who seemed very uncomfortable with the gesture. "And I don't have a clown fetish."

"That's fantastic," I said. If either of them ever told Karen I'd said that, I was a dead man.

"Are you here with your friend from the gallery?" Justin said. His voice was icy.

"No," I said, and desperately tried to think of a way out of this conversation.

"You're welcome to join us," Michael said, and his thoughts definitely left nothing up to the imagination in which way he'd like me to join them. Ugh. I sincerely needed to have a talk with Karen about the quality of gay people she hung out with.

"I'm good," I said, raising both hands and physically stepping away. "You two have fun. I'm going to go get myself a drink, maybe dance a bit. Have a great night, Justin."

"Thanks," Justin said. There was more warmth in his beer than in his voice.

I caught sight of Tyson again when I ordered another beer, which was officially two more beers than I should have had, and thought about Sebastien. I felt bad. Worse, I felt like I'd fucked up. Sure, I'd scared off the bigoted psychokinetic with the hate on for my kind, but I'd also snapped at Sebastien and pissed him off. I couldn't quite figure out what he'd done to deserve it, too, which meant he hadn't.

I mean, he didn't know I was the one handling the problem, right?

When you thought about it, he was actually pretty fucking brave, standing between Stigmatic Jack and the rest of the crowd, with a wrecked wrist and no superpowers of his own.

I bit my lip.

After finishing my beer, I went to the door and asked Tyson if Sebastien was coming tonight.

"He took the night off," Tyson said into my ear. "He was sore."

"I pissed him off, didn't I?" I asked.

Tyson laughed. "Boy, he was just worried about you. I think he likes you."

I felt miserable. Judging my Tyson's laughter, I looked it, too.

"Think he'll speak to me again?" I asked.

"Give him a couple of days," Tyson said. "His temper runs hot, but not long."

I thought about that. I could give Sebastien time to cool off. I looked back into the crowd. Justin was dancing with Michael, who met my gaze over Justin's shoulder and winked.

I left the bar.

❖

I'd intended to apologize as soon as he opened the door, but I forgot something important.

Pilot threw himself past Sebastien the moment the door was open a crack and launched himself at me. His front paws hit my shoulders and I went down, hard. I barely had time to grunt in pain over my shoulders connecting with the far wall before I slid to the ground and a wet tongue was slobbering all over my face.

Friend, friend, friend, play!

"Help," I managed, trying to grip the huge beast's muzzle and push it away from my face. Thanks to the beers, I couldn't even begin to plug the rush of thoughts pouring onto me alongside the dog slobber.

"Pilot," Sebastien said, and I couldn't help but note some humor in his voice. "Down."

No dice. Pilot was climbing all over me. One paw went south and slammed into my crotch, and I grimaced and curled against the wall. The dog's tongue was everywhere—my face, my arms, my hands—and I tried in vain to push him off me a second time.

Play, play, play, play!

He was so damned happy to see me. I started to laugh, finally got my hand around his collar, and held his face away from mine.

"Pilot." Sebastien took the collar and pulled him back. The dog sat beside him, looking up at him with eyes full of adoration and shame, the way only a big dog could.

Play? he thought.

"I'm sorry," I said, wiping my face. My stomach hurt from laughing, and I managed to roll onto my butt. "I forgot about your dog."

"What are you doing here?" he asked. The humor wasn't entirely gone, but it was much less apparent.

Pilot made another lunge for me, and Sebastien had to yank on his collar. "Pilot!" He frowned. "He's not normally like this."

"It's me," I said. Then I looked Pilot in the eyes and projected an image of him lying down. "Hey, buddy," I said. "Take a load off."

Play? Pilot lay down. His tail thumped. Sebastien let go of his collar, then frowned at me. "I'll go put him in his crate," he said, and then went back inside his apartment.

He closed the door.

"Ouch." I got back onto my feet. I needed to think of the right way to say things. I needed to apologize, but I needed to be honest. I rubbed my face, trying to find the right words.

The door opened again, and Sebastien looked at me.

"I'm psychokinetic," I blurted it out in one breath.

For a moment, he just stared at me. I cringed. That wasn't the right way to apologize at all. What with not even including "I'm sorry" in there anywhere.

"You're psychokinetic," he repeated, accent awkward around the word. His voice was even, calm, and careful. He wasn't particularly pleased to see me—though his thoughts were in French and I couldn't catch them well enough to translate—and my proclamation wasn't helping.

I nodded and suddenly wished I was inside his apartment, or at the bar with him, or anything other than standing in a hallway. My hands had nowhere to go. I stuffed them into the front of my jeans pockets.

"That means psychic," he said.

I nodded again. "Not an especially good one. I can't flip a car over or anything. Can I come in?"

He stared at me, his angled face impossible to read. His thoughts were in and out of focus, like a radio dial being spun. Between the beer and being a nervous wreck, I couldn't get a grip on my telepathy. I had no idea what he was thinking. And it was all in French, anyway.

I couldn't believe I'd just told someone.

"Okay," he finally said, and walked toward his kitchen, where he turned and stood beside the counter. He was wearing a pair of sweatpants and a white tank top. He looked edible, which only made me feel worse.

He was still staring.

"Please say something," I said, and my voice cracked. I wanted to run away.

He leaned back onto the counter, and I flinched at even this slight movement away from me. He crossed his arms, and I couldn't help but look at the bandage on his wrist.

"Show me?" he asked.

Oh. Shit. Right. Well, in for a penny...

I looked around his apartment and saw that he had a coffee mug on his small kitchen table. I teked it. It lifted, turned around twice, and sat back down, flickering with a white-blue halo.

Sebastien's mouth was open when I looked back at him. It took him a while to process.

"It glowed," he said.

"I can't really help it," I said, "especially if I'm nervous. Something about my teke refracts light. It's hard for me to move things, especially if they're big or heavy, but it's actually easy for me to do the light thing."

I trailed off. His eyes were still on the cup.

I watched him and saw the moment he realized what I was saying. His eyes locked with mine.

"You're the Rainbow Man."

I spread my arms and summoned a slight nimbus of white light by reflecting the lamp in his living room back at him from behind me. I kept it dialed low so he could still see me through the sheen of light I wrapped around myself.

"Ta-da," I said weakly.

"Tabernac!" he swore. He was pressing back against his counter. If he could have walked through it, he would have. I felt like throwing up.

I stepped away from him. "I shouldn't have said anything." Miracle Woman had totally warned me about this. Her boyfriend hadn't known until they'd been together a good long while. What was I thinking? I turned to go.

Sebastien was shaking his head. "Wait. You blinded the people at City Hall," he said. "You stopped the cutting. And at Chances...and today, at the picnic."

"Sort of," I said. "I don't know if I stopped him or just distracted him."

"Him..."

"Wyatt Jackson," I said. "I think he's a psychic, too. And nuts."

"You stayed behind to help *me*," he said. "At the flag raising. You could have gotten caught."

"I was pretty sure no one could tell it was me. I ramped the light so high I nearly passed out," I said. When he put it like that, I sounded sort of reckless and stupid.

"Pretty sure," Sebastien repeated.

I nodded. "Yeah."

"And today at the picnic...I tried to get you to move, but..." He shook his head. "You were trying to stop that priest. You're doing this on your own."

He looked at me with such sadness that my eyes filled with tears. Crap. This was not what I wanted at all. I wanted him to understand why I had snapped at him. How I wasn't normal. But I didn't want pity...

"Come here," he said.

I wasn't going to cry. I could handle this.

"I should just go," I managed to say, though my voice wobbled. "I didn't mean to just blurt that all at you. I'm a little drunk and I was worried I'd pissed you off and then I realized it was all my fault, and—"

"If you don't let me kiss you right now, I will never forgive you," Sebastien said.

I blinked.

Wait. What?

He came at me in two steps, his good arm wrapping around the back of my neck, holding my head, and tilted my face up. He kissed me and crushed me all in one, and I lost my breath to it. The heat of him pressing against me was palpable, and I felt tears spilling down my cheeks. He pulled back.

"Why are you crying?" He looked lost.

"I don't know," I whined.

He laughed and kissed me again, just as fiercely. The tongue stud was a wonderful, wonderful thing. I felt my body respond, which was sort of embarrassing, as he was pressing against me so firmly that there was no way he couldn't tell. Then I felt him respond in kind against my stomach, and it stopped being embarrassing and started being something else completely.

Je veux... His thoughts flitted in and out of my mind. I had no idea what it meant, but the heat behind the thoughts was clear enough. I started tugging at his tank top, desperate to run my hands over his flesh, and he started leading me toward his bedroom, with only barely a break in his hot, possessive kisses. The back of my legs hit his bed.

I concentrated, forming a teke and wrapping it around the light spilling in from the living room. All the light in the room shifted to deep red. I grinned at him.

Sebastien looked up, laughed, and then pushed me over.

❖

"That was some light show," Sebastien said, stretched out beside me.

"I was inspired," I said, and rolled over onto my side. He had his good arm behind his head, and a smug smile on his face.

"You look like the cat that ate the mouse," I said.

He reached over and squeezed my thigh. *"Ma petite souris."*

I laughed. I knew that much French.

J'aime ça, he thought.

"You like what?" I asked.

He rolled onto his side, and looked at me, surprised. "When you laugh. I didn't say anything. How did you...?"

I can hear what you think. I sent the thoughts to him. His eyes widened. I bit my lip. "Sorry. It happens more when I'm relaxed. And I had a couple of beers, which is a really bad idea for me. It's harder to screen things out."

He rolled on top of me. It hurt my bruised shoulder blades, but I couldn't seem to care.

"And you're...relaxed?" He ground his hips against me.

"Yeah," I said into his neck. "Totally relaxed."

I felt myself respond to him, and he growled against my neck.

"J'aime ça," I said.

He laughed. "You have a terrible accent."

"I'm Irish." I nibbled at his neck. "You should be happy you can understand my English at all, buddy."

He bit my ear, balancing on his one good arm, which did amazing things to his biceps and chest. I pushed up enough to feel his chest hair against my own chest. I kissed him, and he flicked his tongue stud against my tongue. I shuddered.

Can you hear me now? His thoughts were awkward in English.

"Yes."

He rolled over, tugging me on top of him. His good arm snaked down my back, teasingly, while he licked and nibbled at my neck and chest.

And...hear...now? The heat of him pressing against me was making it hard to concentrate. Every time his tongue flicked my flesh, I lost more and more of his thoughts.

"A little," I said, and he rolled me again, this time leaving me chest-down on his bed, and climbed on top of me. He reached out with his bad hand for the lube.

Je vais...dans...

"It's getting harder now," I gasped, grinning. The liquid was cool between us.

"Bon," he said, and he was inside me.

Sex with telepathy, in my experience, isn't the amazing thing you'd expect it to be. Be brutally honest with yourself for a moment, and consider some of the things you've thought while having sex. I'm no gigolo, don't get me wrong. My sexcapades are pretty limited, numerically speaking. But given my particular abilities, I've had the mixed joy that is telepathic sex. I've heard the guy I've gone down on thinking about how his ex did it better, and I've had more harsh critiques than that, let me tell you. I've even been with one fellow who thought about his mother.

Yeah. His *mother*.

With Sebastien, something was different, and I didn't mean that I was limited in my ability to translate French mid-orgasm, though that was nice, to say the very least. It was that Sebastien's mind was so focused on what (or who) he was doing that his thoughts and his actions were a blend of the same thing.

Also, he was a freaking hunk with a tongue stud.

Sebastien flipped me back over, and we were face-to-face again. I stared into his eyes and redirected the light so that the room filled with a soft blue light. He grinned at me and then dove down and started doing things with his mouth that made my toes curl. I felt myself letting go as he did wonderful things to my body, and he inspired me to do all sorts of things right back. We were teasing each other, not frantic and aflame like the first time. I explored his tongue stud with my tongue and gave his fantastic nipples the attention they deserved. He seemed very taken with my calves and thighs, and his stubble left me writhing.

His thoughts were a hot liquid when they were flickering through my head, and I let myself ride them.

I heard music. Tones and notes.

I froze, remembering City Hall.

Sebastien noticed, and paused.

"Are you okay?" he asked, breathing heavy.

The notes were different. They were lyrical, musical, not harsh or discordant. It was beautiful. It was *Sebastien*, I realized with a start. Somehow, I'd gotten to the music of his thoughts.

I reached up and wrapped a hand around the back of his head.

"Even your thoughts are handsome," I said, and then we went back to lovemaking without words.

❖

"When did it start?" Sebastien asked me, much later. The room was dark, and I'd been dozing against his good shoulder, lulled into a kind of drifty half-sleep after he'd brought warm, wet towels and cleaned us both up.

"Hmm?" I rolled onto my side and brightened the room by reflecting the streetlights around a few times over. He watched with fascination as the beams of light reflected around the room.

"When did it start for you? Being psychic?"

I thought about it.

"When I was ten."

"So young."

I smiled. "It happened in front of my mother. She helped me figure it out."

"Your mother knows?" That seemed to make him happy.

"She did. My mother died when I was eleven. She had cancer."

"I'm sorry," Sebastien said. "I didn't mean to bring up bad memories."

"It's fine," I said. "One of the best things about being psychic was that last year with my mother. It was this thing we had, and it made it special. And I could read her mind, sometimes, so I knew she loved us. The very last thing she thought before she died was

I love you all. It sucked to lose my mother, don't get me wrong, but I knew—knew for sure—that she loved me. It made a world of difference."

"And you can hear what people are thinking, all the time?"

"No. Or I try not to. It takes some effort, but I haven't really done much with telepathy. It's too hard to practice without people noticing something is wrong."

"I heard what you were thinking when we were having sex," Sebastien whispered into my ear with a sly whisper. "You like my tongue stud."

I blushed. "Yes, I do. But that's what I mean. When we were having sex, I guess I let my guard down and projected thoughts into your head. It's like leaking. It's partly the beer and partly just, well...you."

"Me?"

"You're very, uh...good."

"Ah." He grinned again. "Yes, I am."

"And so modest." I shoved his good shoulder. "I'm not very good at telepathy, so I try not to use it. I shouldn't sent thoughts into people's minds. I could get caught."

He grunted.

"I practice with my cat," I admitted. "I can tell him when to come play, when it's time for dinner, that sort of thing."

Sebastien chuckled. "You can read minds, and you use this to read your cat's mind."

I bristled, a bit embarrassed. "And my clients."

"You massage people and read their minds?"

"I did it with you."

"Acupressure," he said. "I believed you. You lied to me on our first date."

"It wasn't a date." I snorted. "Besides, you slept like a baby, Mr. Snorey-pants."

"I don't snore," he said.

"Right." I smirked. "But normally I only use my telepathy on my cat. And your dog. That's how I got Pilot to lie down. But what I did with you I do with my clients. Sometimes I can tell where they're sore or stiff if I listen in a little, and I can...figure out why they're stressed, or what's bothering them. And we chat while I massage." As I spoke, I took his hand and listened enough to hear what his brain was telling him.

"Your shoulder hurts," I said, "because of the way you've been carrying your arm. I can feel it." I traced my fingers lightly from the bandages on his wrist to the skin of his forearm and up until I got to his shoulder. "When my mother was really sick, she was in a lot of pain. I could sort of get inside..."

I bit my lip, then slipped into Sebastien's mind enough to find the pain and dim it. I hadn't tried to go into someone's mind and completely erase pain since I was a kid, and I was surprised to find that it was almost as easy to do as it was to nudge down the aches and pains of my clients.

Sebastien gasped. "That's amazing..." He raised the bandaged arm, but I pressed gently on his shoulder.

"It's still healing. Don't think it's better because it isn't hurting. I just told your mind to ignore it for a while."

Sebastien nodded, but still turned his hand left and right before dropping his arm. I rolled onto my side to reach for the glass of water that Sebastien had brought me with the wet towels earlier.

"Does it hurt?" he asked, rubbing his hand across my shoulder blades.

"A little," I said. "I can't really block my own pain, but it helped to, uh, stretch."

Sebastien chuckled. His hand slid down.

"I meant to ask," he said, touching the small of my back. "What is this?"

I sipped the water and smiled. "My tattoo?"

"It looks like seven suns." He traced them with a finger.

"They're my marbles," I said, and rolled over onto my side to face him.

He frowned.

"My mom gave me a bag of marbles, when she was sick," I explained. "And I used to float them around the room and make them glow, like little stars, when she wasn't well. Spheres are easiest to teke."

"Teke?"

"Float. Telekinesis. Teke. It's just faster to say," I said. "I used to practice with the marbles and try to get as many of them in the air at the same time as I can. My record was—is—seven. When I turned eighteen, I got the tattoo."

He wrapped his good arm around me, and tugged me close. "Show me?"

I snuggled in. "Got any marbles?"

He just laughed. I thought for a moment.

"How about pennies?" I asked him. The penny had been taken out of circulation, but it seemed like everyone had a bunch of them lying around.

He nodded and extricated himself from me.

It was excellent watching him walk away, and better watching him walk back, holding something in his good hand. He slid back into the bed and held out his hand. Seven pennies were on his open palm.

I lifted the first one, lit it red, and sent it into an orbit around the bed. Once I was sure I had it patterned right, I teked the second penny, lit it orange, and did the same. As always, once I hit the fifth, the other four wobbled a bit. It took longer for me to get the fifth into place, this one glowing a soft blue color.

Sebastien had been quiet the entire time, and I hadn't looked at his face since I was concentrating so hard on the pennies.

I nabbed the sixth and lit it indigo. It wobbled into the air, and I nearly dropped the red penny and the orange penny.

"I haven't done this in a while," I muttered. I spaced the pennies out equally, breathed twice while they orbited, and then went for the last penny, which I lit a brilliant violet, and let slide in between the indigo and red penny. They all wobbled, and I felt the strange sensation in my skull I got when I pushed my teke, like my head was full and I was pressing against a shell that encased the inside of my skull.

"Ta-da," I said, and looked over at Sebastien.

He was looking at me in awe, and more than a little lust.

"You're amazing," he said. He slid his hand down and grabbed my ass.

I let the pennies drop around the edge of the bed and aimed a beam of red light at his very erect dick.

"No," I said, "that's amazing. Don't you ever get tired?"

"Not yet," he said, and proved it.

INDIGO

"I told him," I said, watching the bluish star flicker in time to the music.

"Are you insane?" said Miracle Woman.

I gaped.

"What part of 'just date the man' was unclear?" she said. "You told him? Just like that?" She snapped her fingers. "Do you have any idea what he could do? How much danger you could put everyone in?"

"Uh."

She shook her head, sending her braids out behind her hair in a wave. "Men," she said, and there was such frustration in her voice I felt like I should apologize on behalf of the gender.

"Sorry," I said.

She blew out her breath. "No. My baggage." She regarded me through narrowed eyes. "But listen, if I give you any more advice, you will follow it, understand me?"

I smiled. "Are you an Aries?"

"I don't follow that astrology shit."

"I understand," I said.

She crossed her arms. "Telling him is a big deal."

I rolled over in space, Earth looming into view below us. "Yeah."

She looked at me. "Do you regret it?"

I shook my head. "No, I don't. His mind..." I blushed.

She raised her hands high. "Uh-huh, tell me all about his *mind*." In her long yellow nightgown, she looked somehow regal. I felt like I was discussing my sex life with a queen or something.

"I swear his mind is appealing," I said. "I think he's good. Also, I can't imagine him outing me—maybe it's a gay thing, but...outing someone is just not something we do."

"Unless they're closeted Republicans?"

"We don't have Republicans in Canada."

"Lucky Canada."

"We have Conservatives." I smiled. "I don't think he'll tell anyone. Besides, I've got the police interested in me, a psychic schizophrenic hearing voices telling him to hurt people...really, it seems sort of minor to tell him the truth, lady."

Rachel.

I frowned. She glared at me.

My name is Rachel.

I held out my hand.

"It's nice to meet you, Rachel."

We shook.

"You're really in trouble, aren't you?" she said.

I sighed. "I don't know. So far it's more of a draw, though I gotta say, having a bicycle chucked at your back is very unpleasant." I grinned, but the smile faded. "I can't seem to shut him down. I tried getting into his head, but his 'voice of God' keeps drowning me out."

"It ain't God," she said dryly.

"Amen," I said. I held out my hand and waved my fingers at Italy as it went by.

"What are you going to do?" she asked.

"Well, I'm going to keep going to the events he keeps crashing," I said. "And I'm going to try to stop him from hurting anybody."

"Without the police figuring out who you are?" She raised an eyebrow. "And without telling any more goddamn people that you're the Rainbow Man?"

"Yes, that, too," I said.

"All by yourself."

"I can handle it," I said, and she shook her head, amused.

"Every problem has a solution," I said.

She paused. "Honey, I agree. But sometimes problems are bigger than one person."

I had to concede that. "Who else should I call? Unless you're going to fly in to Ottawa for me, I'm fresh out of psychics. And given that this lunatic can cut people with a glance, or throw bicycles at them without breaking much of a sweat, I'm not sure I've got many other options."

She fell silent.

"Sorry. That wasn't very smart. I just speak before I think sometimes. I'm not asking you to come to Ottawa," I said, wishing I could take it back. "This isn't your problem."

"I'm not going to get caught. If I got caught..." she said, but didn't finish the sentence.

"I'm sorry," I said. "I just meant that calling the cops wouldn't help, and really, I think they're pretty aware that something psychokinetic is going on, it's just that...well...you can detain someone for causing a disturbance, but then what? He didn't actually physically assault anyone or anything, right?"

"He threw a bike at you," she said.

"Yeah, well, but how do you prove that? He didn't touch it. And realistically speaking, I'm not likely going to come down to the police station and press charges, am I?"

She laughed mirthlessly. "I guess not."

I stretched, enjoying the sunlight. "I don't want anyone to get hurt, myself included. If I can just figure out how to shut him down...I can send people to sleep. I've done it before, but only when they're relaxed. I've never really done it when they're walking around. I tried to do it to him once already, and I think I came close, but then his psycho voice came out to play, and he went ballistic with the bike."

"You can make people sleep?" she asked, surprised.

I blinked at her. "You can't?"

"I don't think I've actually tried, though unlike some, I don't run around actively trying to get caught." She hit me with the back of her hand across my shoulder. "But I think you might be a better telepath than I am."

Well. That was something. I felt a strange pride.

Don't let it go to your head. Her thoughts filled my mind.

I sighed. "Don't worry. Stigmatic Jack has handed me my ass twice now. Overconfidence is not an issue."

"And the police?" I wasn't sure if she was asking me to reconsider, or if she was reminding me not to get them involved. It didn't matter.

"I just don't see how they can help," I admitted. "The last thing I want available is a loaded gun—he could pull the trigger with his teke."

She hissed. "Good point."

I suddenly frowned, feeling a kind of falling sensation.

"Oh," I said. "I think I'm waking—"

"—up," I muttered, and rolled over. My eyes were gritty with sleep, and I blinked a few times, rubbing them. I was staring at a wall painted a deep green. It wasn't my bedroom.

Where was I?

Sebastien let out a light snore, and I rolled over to my other side and saw his face, smoothed with sleep.

Oh. Right. I grinned and stretched, curling my toes and enjoying the way parts of me ached in ways that had nothing to do with telekinetically hurled bicycles.

My stomach growled, and I winced at the noise. Not the way to wake up a fella after he rocks your world. I gingerly slid off the bed, then teked the various bits of my clothing into my hand, quieter than I could manage wandering around. I slipped out into the living room and got dressed quickly.

My stomach growled again.

I didn't feel right raiding his fridge, but I could probably step out, grab something, and bring it back before he woke. I reached out with my mind and found him very much asleep. I fumbled for my cell phone in my pocket and tugged it out. It wasn't even six yet.

I had three messages.

Frowning, I thumbed the phone on and dialed in to my mailbox.

The first message was from Callum.

"Listen, Kieran, I really like her," he said. I groaned and rubbed my forehead. "But I need some advice. I think she likes me, but sometimes the way she talks to me she's sort of bossing me around, so I don't know if she really likes me or if I'm doing something wrong. I'd really appreciate it if you could talk to her and maybe call me?"

I deleted the message.

Karen's voice came up next.

"Your brother is so shy. It's adorable. But I don't know if he's ever going to make a move. He's a great kisser, and I'm sending signals, but I think your brother needs an engraved invitation. Oh! And Justin called. I need to talk to you about clowns, apparently?"

I deleted that message, too, and smiled to myself. At least they were getting along.

The next message began. At the sound of Detective Stone's voice, I felt my happy bubble pop. He wanted to speak to me again in regard to the events at Brewer's Park. At my earliest convenience. The picnic.

Crap.

I tapped the phone against my thigh. I sighed and looked

around. There was a notepad beside Sebastien's phone. I quickly scrawled a note saying I had to go, but that I'd call him as soon as I grabbed a free moment. Once I was done, I stared at it a while, then wrote my name beneath it.

Then I added a couple of Xs and Os.

I pondered erasing them, then realized the pencil didn't have an eraser.

"You suck," I said to myself, then decided that I could do one better and went back to the doorway. I teked all seven pennies, one by one, to my palm, and then left them in a circle around the note.

Then I left to go grab a sugar-breakfast from the closest coffee shop and to visit Detective Stone again.

❖

It was awkward sitting in Detective Stone's office in the same clothes that Sebastien had torn off me the night before, but if Stone noticed my somewhat rumpled look, he didn't seem to care. His office was on my way home, and it occurred to me that showing up as early as I could would be a good idea.

"You were at City Hall, and Chances, and the picnic," Detective Stone said, flipping through his notes. His hair was already sticking up. I wondered if he ever had a time when he hadn't messed it up in frustration. It was sort of cute. I tuned in and found that while he found my attendance at all the events interesting, he didn't quite yet find them damning. I caught the number fifteen and realized I was one of fifteen people who'd been to all the events, though I doubted many of them weren't volunteers or organizers, like Sebastien.

"Yes," I said. "I take vacation for Pride Week so I can go to everything."

He looked up. "Even with things like this happening. It must mean a lot to you."

I caught his thoughts. *Maybe enough to hurt people.*

What? He thought I was the one behind the attacks because I liked Pride Week? How did that make sense?

"It does," I said, aiming for calm. "I love the gay community, as corny as that sounds. I like what Pride stands for. The whole 'look how far we've come' and the way we celebrate our diversity, all of it." I smiled.

Scandal gives it more press, he was thinking. *More press is more money.*

Oh. I got it. He wondered if this was about getting Pride Week more attention. The funds for Pride had been dwindling for years. This was definitely getting attention. But he wasn't convinced himself. He was being a good cop and exploring all the angles.

I relaxed about a millimeter.

He nodded. "I guess it is a pretty good message. But these attacks..." He trailed off, trying to decide how far to go with me. "They're kind of unorthodox." I realized with a start that he thought I was an intelligent, informed person. And something else—that I was a good person. I'm not sure what he was basing that upon, but it made me sit a little straighter.

He was wondering whether or not to broach the psychic angle.

"Psychokinesis," I said, since he was thinking it, and I really wanted to see what he thought about the topic.

He leaned back, tapping his pen on his pad.

"You believe in P.K.?"

I made a face like I wasn't 100 percent sure, but said, "I watched the Thomas Wright thing. I was only ten, but...it left an impression."

He nodded once. "I saw that, too." His thoughts were almost blank. He was still waiting for me to speak. His mind was locked up tight. I pressed a bit harder, and his eyes flicked up like maybe he'd heard something. I pulled back.

I bit my lip and then went for it. "If it is a psychokinetic, a genuine psychic, then…what can you do?"

He looked surprised. He thought, *good question.* Yay me. I asked good questions.

"There aren't exactly laws about P.K.," he said, "But assault is assault." He didn't sound very convincing because he wasn't convinced. *No weapon,* he was thinking. *No fingerprints. No physical evidence at all. How do you prove someone flipped a table at someone else when they don't have to touch the table? How do you stop someone who can throw a bicycle across a park? Or light up like the sun?*

I didn't particularly like being lumped in with Stigmatic Jack, but I got his point.

"I bet it would be a nightmare to make something stick, though, right?" I raised my eyebrows.

He waited, thinking, then seemed to realize the conversation was in a shaky territory.

"Flat out," he asked me, "who do you think is behind all this?"

Egad. His expression was open to anything, but he was thinking Wyatt Jackson. Everyone was thinking it, according to the papers and the net. But Stigmatic Jack kept getting out of jail because religious protests really only counted as disturbing the peace, and no one had charged him with anything worse because, well…

There was no *proof.* Just a lot of finger pointing and some stories about a glowing man.

Stone was actually fully aware that Stigmatic Jack should be his target.

He just couldn't do anything.

"Wyatt Jackson," I said firmly. Stone's eyes widened, but I hadn't surprised him. I said, "He's always off on one of his religious rants when things start to go all wrong."

"Okay," Stone said. "Now what about the Rainbow Man?"

I blinked. Hadn't seen that one coming.

"Other than a really crappy name?" I asked, hedging for time.

Stone's lip twitched.

"He—or, I guess, she, since no one has gotten a picture— seems to be helping," I said, awkwardly.

Stone paused again. "Okay, but does he, or she, seem dangerous to you?"

I forced myself to pause, as if considering it, and worked very hard to keep my face blank. Dangerous? I was the only freaking person even slowing Stigmatic Jack down! What an ungrateful jerk.

"No," I said, after counting to five. "If anything, every time Rainbow Man shows up, it seems like Stigmatic Jack and his bunch of loonies are already causing trouble, and it's the light show that seems to shut them down."

Stone tapped a finger. "None of the P.K. experts"—in his head, I saw air quotes around the word "experts"—"understand the light show."

"I'm a massage therapist," I reminded him. "I know even less."

He looked at me, and in his mind, his thoughts disagreed. *No. You know something. You're just really good at not telling me, and I don't know why.*

It took everything I had not to flinch. For crying out loud, he was suspicious of me.

His face betrayed none of that, however. He just got up from his chair. "Well, thank you for coming in again, Mr. Quinn."

I rose and offered my hand. He took it, and there was a slight discomfort in his thoughts. I realized he was nervous from the first visit and my offer to massage him. He thought I wanted to touch him. I let my grip linger longer than it needed to.

"You don't make it unpleasant." I shrugged. I let him chew on that while I tried to walk out as though I wasn't a suspect in a police investigation where the head detective believed in psychokinesis.

Which is to say, not nearly as quickly as I wanted to.

❖

I stopped off at home long enough to earn the ire of Easter, who hadn't seen me since the evening before and refused to do more than swish his tail at me in passing while I cleaned his litter box and refilled his food dish. He could smell Sebastien—and, worse, Pilot—on me. I sent him a few telepathic apologies and offers of tinned treats, but he wasn't buying it.

"You know," I said to his retreating tail, "I could always get a dog. It's much more macho, anyway."

I dug out my cell phone and called Sebastien, but got his voice mail.

"Hi," I said, "It's me." Then I winced. "Uh, Kieran." Oh Jesus, now I sounded even more flighty. "Just wanted to say thank you for last night, and that I hope I see you again." Augh! Too needy! "Um, y'know, if you wanted to get together again. Uh. I'm going to go. You're having that babble effect on me again." I ended the call and rubbed at my eyelids.

It was official. I was a moron.

Instead of dwelling on the world's most pathetic voice mail, I grabbed my gym bag.

I went to Now & Zen, dropping off a coffee with Karen and offering a brief wave in passing. She was on the phone. She raised a finger to me, asking me to wait, but I mouthed "later" to her and went straight the men's changing rooms. Once inside, I waited until I was alone and then used the mirrors to take a glance at my shoulder blades. They didn't feel as bad as they looked, but they were pretty sore. I knew that bruises turned that ugly shade of purple, I'd just never seen it on myself before.

I tugged my shirt back on and sighed. There was no way

I was going to go in the pool looking like that. People would definitely notice.

Treadmill it was, then. I dug out my sneakers and changed into my running shorts.

I stretched, set the machine for a half-hour run, and then started. I didn't tax myself—it was a fairly level field on the setting I had the machine on—but by fifteen minutes into it, my shoulders were burning, and I thought better of it and turned the machine off.

Stepping down, I saw that Karen had been watching again, and she frowned when I walked up to her.

"You're stiff."

"Vacation makes a man lazy," I agreed.

"Not the one you're having," she said. "Did I mention a police officer came and talked to me about you?"

I kept my expression calm. "Detective Stone?"

She shook her head. "No, someone else, but I think that was the name on the card he gave me." She looked at me. "The officer asked me how you got that cut."

I looked down at my arm. The cut was scabbed over completely now, and on its way to healing. "I hit myself on the locker. Didn't I tell you that?" I felt like a complete ass for lying to Karen, but the last thing I needed was an Aries enraged on my behalf. Or, worse, enraged at me.

She nodded. "He seemed a little let down about it, actually."

I frowned. Did that mean they'd hoped I was a good lead? "Oh."

"Be careful, Kieran," she said. "The last thing you want to do is get all messed up in this crazy shit. Do you have to go to every event this week? Maybe you could skip the rest?"

"The parade is tomorrow," I said. "And it's the leather men tonight." I wagged my eyebrows. "Did I mention I'm kind of dating a leather man?"

She grinned. "You are?"

"Sebastien LaRoche. The guy I gave first aid to at City Hall."

She shook her head. "Ah. So it's a Florence Nightingale thing, eh?"

I frowned. I hadn't thought of that. "No. I think he likes me." I didn't sound certain. It probably meant I wasn't. Crap. Was that all it was?

"Oh, honey." Karen laughed. "I'm sorry. I'm sure he'll really be into you. I was just teasing."

I grinned at her. "He's already been into me. A few times."

"Ugh!" Karen shoved my shoulder. "Too much information."

"He has a tongue stud," I gushed, suddenly aware of how much I wanted to share this information with her. "And he's built like a brick shithouse."

"See, now why is that a compliment?" she asked, shaking her head. "Come on, I'm supposed to be on the desk. My break is almost over."

We walked back to the front room while I elaborated on all of Sebastien's generous positive qualities. She smiled at me as she sat down behind the counter again.

"He sounds really nice," she said.

"I can't wait to introduce you two."

"Maybe we could double-date," she said, regarding me uneasily.

"You, me, Sebastien, and the incredibly shy kisser?"

She had the grace to blush. "I was a little tipsy when I sent that text."

"You made out with my brother."

"Multiple times," she said. "And we're going out again tonight."

I took a deep breath. "So this is…"

"A third date," she said firmly. She seemed quite happy about it. "He seems a bit...timid about making any moves."

I rubbed my forehead. "Okay. I'll do this just once because I love you. My brother was a lot more wrecked by the Bimbo than he'll ever admit. I'm sure he likes you because he told me so. I don't think it would be a bad idea for you to set the pace if you want things to go faster. And now I need some brain bleach, because I pictured that."

Karen smiled, even though she looked massively uncomfortable. "Thank you. Seriously."

I leaned on the desk. I could read the "change the subject" subtext and was happy to oblige. "Are you coming to the Pride Week closing party?"

She leaned back in her chair and stared at me like I'd just asked her to go to a hockey game or something else that was horrible and boring. "Kieran, people have been assaulted at a lot of the Pride stuff. I don't think I'm going to the party."

I sighed. "It's that stupid Wyatt Jackson. He's off his nut."

"I thought the police kept releasing him?" she asked.

I nodded. I wasn't going to get into the whole psychokinesis thing with Karen. "Nothing sticks. They keep detaining him for disturbing the peace, shit like that."

"And that other one," Karen said.

I bristled. "Hey, the Rainbow Man seems to be doing a lot of good." I cringed. I'd just used the name. Ugh. Was it like when you named a pet? Did I have to keep it now?

"How do they know it's a man?" she asked.

"I don't think they do," I said. I did, but that wasn't exactly information I was about to share.

"This is what's wrong with the world," she said. "If the Rainbow Man turns out to be a black lesbian, how much you want to bet the world has a collective heart attack?"

"They already have the Miracle Woman," I pointed out.

"She hasn't been seen in years," Karen said, and there was real sadness in her voice. It surprised me. She caught my look. "When I was a kid, she was…I don't know. Better than Nancy Drew and Barbie, that was for sure. I loved the whole idea of her."

I smiled. "Me too." We'd never talked about psychokinesis before. I tried so hard to avoid anything that would make the topic come up. It gave me a warm feeling that we'd shared a childhood hero.

I wished I could tell Karen I'd met Miracle Woman face-to-face. Kind of.

"You're probably right, though," she said. "It's probably a guy. All those rainbows and sparkles are way too tacky for a woman."

I frowned. "I think I'm offended."

"If you're not offended, you're probably not alive." She slid her headset back on. "Seriously, though—if that nut is in jail before the closing party, then I'll be there. But if he's not…"

I nodded at her.

"He will be."

She seemed about to question me, but the phone rang. While she answered it, I went back to the changing rooms, showered quickly in one of the closed-off stalls, got dressed, and left.

❖

There was a message from Sebastien on my cell. I grinned and played it back.

"I like it when you babble," he teased. "And I am with the Pride committee all this afternoon. A detective is speaking with us over the trouble. I will be at the leather Pride event tonight. I hope you come. It's at Chances, at nine. If I don't see you there, I will call you again."

"See?" I said to myself. "That's how you leave a voice

message that says you're interested without sounding like an idiot."

A man passing on the street looked at me oddly, but kept walking.

I tucked my phone back in my bag. Nine was quite a while off. I was unsurprisingly beat.

I was on vacation, I'd had a bike thrown at me and my arm cut, and the police were interested in me, I'd had a glorious night of sweaty monkey sex, and I was fairly sure there was a schizophrenic preacher on the loose whom I'd slapped in the face no less than three times with my teke.

I deserved a nap.

My phone buzzed. It was my brother.

Does Karen like flowers?

You, I typed, *are on your own*. I hit Send.

Traitor.

Almond mocha latte, I typed. *Really bad romantic comedies. Vanilla frozen yogurt. Anything involving strawberries. No idea about her taste in flowers.*

You're the best.

"I'm a bloody saint," I said, and turned off my phone.

❖

A burly bearded man in a black leather jock strap decorated with silver studs stood in the center of the stage, arms crossed over his chest while he answered questions from the three judges. Other than the jock strap, he was wearing nothing but thick boots and a smile. The man had confidence. And a very full jock strap.

I wondered if he'd stuffed it with anything.

It was the first time I'd ever come to a leather event—I'd seen them announced, but wasn't sure if it was a bit tacky to show up if you weren't bedecked in leather gear yourself. Looking around the crowd, it was obvious I shouldn't have worried about it. The vast majority of the spectators were wearing regular clothes like me.

Which made finding Sebastien much easier.

"You know," I said, "it really is a shame you're not up there."

Sebastien turned at my voice. He was wearing his leather harness again, and it looked as fabulous as always, bandaged arm or not. No leather pants, though. He sported a plain pair of jeans and regular running shoes. No leather boots or codpieces. He probably didn't feel like getting all geared up if he wasn't going onstage. Poor guy. Also, poor me. The man had fine legs and I'd hoped to ogle them. He smiled at me.

"I missed you this morning," he said, wrapping his good arm around my waist and tugging me close.

"You were sleeping so well I didn't want to wake you," I said, blushing.

He wagged his eyebrows. "You tired me out."

I snorted, leaning against him. "You snored."

"I don't snore."

"Apparently you do when you're all tired out." I looked up at him and wagged my eyebrows.

He laughed. "You're funny."

I could live with that.

"I bought you a present," he said.

A gift, already? That surprised me. Also, it made me grin like a kid.

"Really?"

He nodded and walked with me to the front of the bar, where he reached under the counter where some back-shirted volunteers were taking donations for the local HIV/AIDS hospice and offering safe BDSM pamphlets. He tugged a small red bag out and handed it to me. I tugged open the yellow string and laughed out loud.

"Marbles," I said. "Nice."

"Because you lost yours," he said, and I laughed again at the pun. I was touched. I held them tightly for a second and then hugged him. "Thank you. I love them."

"You're welcome," he said. "Come home with me tonight?"

"You think I can be bought with marbles?" I arched an eyebrow.

He nibbled my ear. "I think you can be bought with this," he said, and flicked his tongue stud against my earlobe.

My whole body shivered, and when he pulled back, he had a sexy leer firmly in place. Confident bastard.

"I don't think I should come to your place tonight," I said.

He leaned back, surprised.

You should come to my place, I projected the words into his mind.

But my handcuffs are at my place, he thought, in his careful English. Again, I was stunned at how clear his thoughts here. Then what he said sank in, and my face went hot.

He grinned. "You were listening."

"Uh," I said. My tongue felt glued to the roof of my mouth. "I've never, uh…"

He put one heavy arm around my shoulders. It felt very good there. "It's fine. Maybe we'll work up to handcuffs. Start with some tamer stuff first, then."

Oh my. I glanced around, still blushing.

"Any sign of Stigmatic Jack?" I asked.

Sebastien shook his head. "Not yet. Do you think he'll still come?"

I opened my mind a crack, but only caught the whispers of people enjoying the show—many of the thoughts more than a little X-rated. This was a horny crowd.

I shook my head, not feeling Wyatt Jackson's awful thoughts

anywhere nearby. "I can't begin to figure him out. He's like two different people."

"The voice in his head," Sebastien said.

I sighed. "Yeah." I looked up on the stage and saw the next contestant—a muscular black man in chaps and codpiece, tight leather armbands—start to stretch and pose.

"That man is no stranger to the gym," I noted. The crowd was eating it up, and there was the barest smile on his face. "He's definitely aware of the impact he's having, too."

"Pride," Sebastien said. He winked at me. "If you want to pick up some leather, I think you could pull it off."

"Pull it off you, maybe. I dunno." I shook my head, blushing. "I don't think I'd look right."

"You've got great legs."

"You've got my attention."

He grinned. "Leather chaps. Definitely. You've got the ass for it, too."

I opened my mouth to reply, then stopped. *Den of sin*, I heard, in that loud and angry voice.

I leaned in closer to Sebastien. "He's coming." I frowned, trying to catch more. I couldn't make out words, but I felt the strange atonal chiming. It was outside. "He's outside."

Sebastien nodded, letting go of me.

"Let's go."

"No, I'll go," I said. "You get Security together, just in case. Maybe I can put him to sleep or calm him down or something." I tried to sound confident.

"You shouldn't go alone." Sebastien frowned at me.

"That's why I want you to get the security people organized," I said, and slipped away from him before he could grab me. "I can handle it," I called over my shoulder, and went for the door.

They had lined up outside, on the opposite sidewalk across from the bar, all of them in their white dress shirt and navy slacks, except for Stigmatic Jack, who had his head-to-toe white ensemble ready. His shirt was fresh and crisp—I wondered what his dry-cleaning bill must have been like. All that blood he needed to wash out of his sleeves couldn't come cheap. His bodyguards were on either side of him, and the blue suit was talking on his cell phone a step or two away.

I waited for a second at the door, nodding at the bouncer, who I didn't know.

"They don't seem to be ready to storm the gates," I said.

"I told them they couldn't come in," the bouncer replied. A moment later, two more men arrived behind me, both wearing black shirts with "Security" written across the chest. One of them was Tyson.

"Hey," I said.

He smiled at me, looking out into the street.

"There aren't as many of them as there were at the picnic," I said. I scanned Stigmatic Jack's followers and didn't see the pretty young blond woman from before. In fact, the group seemed pretty thin, and mostly middle-aged. I couldn't decide if that was a good thing or not.

"Maybe the police scared a few of them off," Tyson said.

The guy in the blue suit pulled his phone away from his ear and shook his head. The group seemed to relax. They hadn't seemed particularly eager to be here in the first place. The noise of the traffic was too loud to make out what anyone was saying, though he definitely didn't seem pleased.

I dipped into Wyatt Jackson's head.

Tell me what to do, Lord. I don't fear jail. Your righteousness is my guide. This den of sin awaits.

I bit my lip. Obviously there'd been a change of plans of some sort. I wondered what had happened.

"Did someone talk to them or something?" I asked.

"Pride committee sent an official cease-and-desist or something. Filed paperwork with the police," Tyson said. "Served them with trespass papers."

Ah. If they came into the bar, the police could easily haul them off—and have reason to keep them jailed. I tapped my fingers against my side for a few seconds, then went back into Jackson's head.

...fight another day. It was the oily and slick voice of Jackson's God. The anger in the thoughts seethed, but seemed to be controlled. *My judgment will come, and the world will see you as the righteous warrior you are. Your time—my time—will come.*

The bouncer let out a breath when the group started to break up and head down the street to where I now noticed their white vans were parked.

"Looks like they're giving up," Tyson said.

I shivered. That so-called voice of God wasn't giving up at all.

It was waiting for a better time to strike.

❖

Pilot was all too pleased to see me, and I washed all the slobber off my face while Sebastien took him downstairs and outside to do his business. When they came back and the hairy black beast tried to crawl all over me again, Sebastien finally put him in his crate for the night, and I tried not to laugh at the mournful little woofs that came from down the hallway after us.

"I need to take him on a good long walk," Sebastien said. "He's been cooped up inside too much this week. I've never seen him like this. He really likes you."

"It's not his fault. Dogs pick up on the telepathy thing. This is why cats are so much better. Though Easter's getting miffed at how much time I'm spending away."

"Cats are not better than dogs."

"Are we having our first argument?" I grinned.

"We already had our first argument," Sebastien said. "When

you wouldn't do what I said at the picnic." He sat down on his couch, and I joined him.

"You're pretty used to people doing what you tell them to do, aren't you?"

"Yes." He wrapped his arm around my neck and tugged me a bit closer.

I laughed. He was wearing a black tank top now, having shed the harness before we left the bar. My head fit perfectly on his warm shoulder, and I closed my eyes for a minute.

"How's your back?" Sebastien asked.

"Sore, but not too bad. Why?" I opened my eyes again and looked at him. He looked down at me, a sly smile tucked in the corner of his mouth. His arm slid down my side, pulling me even tighter against him, and he leaned down to kiss me. The silver stud flicked against the tip of my tongue.

I smiled, pulling back from him, and formed my teke. When a faintly purple glow shone from his belt, Sebastien's head tilted and he laughed as the belt slowly unwound itself from his jeans.

"Look, Ma," I said. "No hands."

"Very impressive," he said, and smiled as the belt slid completely free and fell to the floor. He frowned. "Can you undo knots?"

I leaned back. "I have no idea. Why?"

His smile was almost a leer. "Because we need to work up to handcuffs."

Oh my. "Uh, maybe we could save that for later?"

He kissed me again. *Bon.* Tonight I'll just hold you down the way I want you."

"Uh," I began, but he put a finger over my lips.

"I like to be obeyed, remember?"

I laughed. "Yes, sir."

His smile was wicked. "Now you're getting it."

❖

I woke up cold. I sat up on my elbow and looked over at Sebastien, sleeping beside me, in the pale light of the street lamps. He'd rolled up tight and taken all the blankets.

"Well," I said quietly. "I suppose you had to have at least one flaw."

He shifted slightly in his sleep, and the light fell across his face, the strong lines of his jaw in shadowy relief. His chin was stubbled and his mouth open slightly. I was overwhelmed by the sheer masculinity of him and closed my eyes. His thoughts, soft and gentle in sleep, were a muted susurrus, and I let myself be drawn into them. It was lovely, like riding a gentle surf while soft music rose and fell with every wave. I caught myself rocking back and forth.

Sebastien snored, very soft. My eyes opened, and I lost the connection to his mind. Chilled, I tried to tug the blanket from under Sebastien, but he weighed more than me and let out a little grunt and tugged it tighter to himself, even sliding the edge over his face. Not a single inch of his flesh was exposed to air, more was the pity.

I chuckled to myself and gave up. I got out of bed and padded barefoot around the room. I found Sebastien's housecoat and tugged it on. It smelled like him, and I held it against my nose, breathing deeply.

Jesus. I was officially off the deep end. I looked at the handcuffs on the bedside table and felt my face heating up. This was moving very quickly. Sebastien was definitely used to being in charge.

Did I mind? I hadn't minded that much a few orgasms ago.

Smiling, I sat back on the bed and closed my eyes again, listening for the music that Rachel said was the sound of thought. I found it, soft tones, after only a moment. It was so gentle, so kind. My chest tightened with it, and I tried to home in on the beauty of Sebastien's thoughts.

Sebastien's song was regular, like a heartbeat. Measured. In some ways it reminded me of my own song, the one Rachel had reflected back to me in my dream. What she'd called resonance. But Sebastien's song wasn't independent so much as it was confident. It invited you to follow along and held the promise of making it worthwhile. There was so much more than sound involved, now that I was really listening. The tones weren't just tones, they were feelings and emotions. I could almost grasp the whole of him—like everything Sebastien was had been distilled into this sound.

His song. Not at all like the music I heard when I was around Stigmatic Jack and his lunatics.

Suddenly, I caught that awful music—the discordant tones, the harsh counterpoints. It was so loud I looked at Sebastien, afraid he'd wake, before realizing how stupid that was.

Loud and clashing, Stigmatic Jack's song blasted in my head. I pressed my hands against my temples.

Kill the fucking faggots at their own fucking parade. Crush them. Cut them. Show them not to defy me! Show them they can't fucking mock me! The thoughts dripped with anger and contempt, and a vile enjoyment. I was in his head. I could hear Wyatt Jackson's thoughts, or at least, the thoughts of his other personality. It was so much colder, nastier, and darker than the thoughts I'd caught before. Bile rose in my throat.

I slid off the bed and made it to the bathroom where I dry-heaved into the sink. I built a mental wall around my head, and the music, and those wretched thoughts, died out.

I sat on the edge of the bathtub and breathed slowly and deeply.

Kill the fucking faggots at their own fucking parade, he'd thought. And he'd thought it loud enough that I'd heard it over the minds of every other sleeping person in the city, from wherever the hell Stigmatic Jack was.

The man was completely unhinged.

The parade was tomorrow. Stigmatic Jack was going to

assault the parade, and all the police in the world wouldn't be able to do much to stop him. Those thoughts. I shivered.

He'd kill people. With those vile thoughts. It would be like City Hall, and the hotel, and the picnic, only worse. Jesus...

I could handle this. I could. Every problem has a solution. What was it?

I rubbed my eyes. Stigmatic Jack was hearing what he thought was the voice of God, telling him to kill people. That he was a psychokinetic with a particularly specific gift was certainly no help, but the problem was the voice Jack was hearing.

What if...I bit my lip.

What if the voice stopped? Could I do that? Could I reach into Wyatt Jackson's damaged mind and shut off his multiple personality? Probably not. But maybe I could keep him level for the Pride Parade. If I went deep enough, maybe could I find this other voice before it started to rant and...And do what? I could tell it to go to sleep, like I'd tried at the picnic, but instead of trying to focus on Stigmatic Jack, I could try to single out the other voice.

Sitting on the edge of the bath in Sebastien's bathroom, I made up my mind.

I stood up and took another, cleansing breath. It wasn't hard to find that awful, discordant music a second time—it was easier. Once again it occurred to me that practice with telepathy should have been a priority all along.

Play?

I flinched. I'd woken Pilot.

Not right now, buddy, I projected. I got a sad little woof in return, muffled by the two doors and hallway between us.

I pulled down my mental wall again and tried to hold on to the tones without getting the thoughts—I'd heard all I wanted to hear from Stigmatic Jack's schizophrenic God voice. I stood in my lover's bathroom, in his housecoat, listening to the music of a madman's thoughts.

Boy, did I know how to have a good time.

I turned in a slow circle, carefully listening to the notes as they jangled and clashed.

When I finished a circle, I stopped and opened my eyes again.

There was direction to the sound. I knew which way Stigmatic Jack was.

In Sebastien's kitchen, the microwave told me it was just past four in the morning. I wrote a note on a piece of paper and put it on the fridge with a magnet.

See you at the Parade, I wrote. *Kieran.*

Then I went to find my clothes and my gym bag.

❖

For a kid, playing hot-warm-cold provides endless entertainment. For an adult? Not so much.

At the base of Sebastien's apartment complex, I did another slow turn in a circle. Oddly, when I faced his building door, I could hear the softest musical tones—Sebastien himself—upstairs in his apartment, even over the noise of the minds of the sleeping city. It was comforting, like having an anchor. A sexy anchor that liked handcuffs.

The other sound, Stigmatic Jack, was a cacophony that seemed to be coming from farther downtown. I had about nine hours between now and the Pride Parade. Judging by the loudness, it seemed like Stigmatic Jack was also awake. At least, I hoped he was. If he made that much noise telepathically while he was asleep, I was way outclassed.

I started walking.

Every third block or so, I stopped, did another round of hot-warm-cold, until I realized which direction I was heading and did a mental head slap.

I checked to be sure, but yes, I was heading straight for the hotel where Jackson was renting a board room for his "church" meetings.

Well, duh.

It took me twenty five minutes to walk there, and once I was there, another ten to figure out a plan. The last time I'd been here, I'd run out with the thicknecks chasing after me and bled all over the carpet. I'd also done a strobe at the front window and then taken off. I didn't think the hotel staff had had an actual good look at me, but even if they had, I was in different clothes, with messier hair, and how likely was it that the same single person I could see at the front desk was the one of the three from two days ago?

So I walked in, smiled at the desk clerk as if everything was grand, and he nodded back. I didn't manage to hook into his thoughts, I was walking past him too quickly, but he didn't seem worried. Bored and tired, but not worried.

I hit the elevator, but got off on the first floor and moved to the stairwell.

This would be harder.

I listened again to the telepathic noise of Wyatt Jackson and felt, vaguely, that he was higher up. My temples were starting to ache and I gave myself a little pep talk as I hoofed it to the third floor.

You can handle this.

There, at the doorway, I made a telekinetic lens just outside the small window, bending the light to get a reflected view of the hallway. No one. I stepped out into the floor and did another telepathic listen check.

Still higher, I thought.

On the fifth floor I repeated and got the sense that he was lower this time.

On the fourth I flickered my telekinetic lens through the glass window and was rewarded with a brief glimpse of one of the thicknecks—the blond one—standing outside a door at the far end of the hall. Poor guy hadn't even been given a chair. I let the light go, and pondered.

I needed to get thickneck number one away from the door. How?

Fire alarm? No good, given that it would also wake everyone up and empty the building.

What I needed was a distraction, but nothing that made the thickneck feel like it was a true threat. I snuck my thoughts into his mind. It was definitely getting easier, though I was still careful not to think anything myself in case he "heard" me.

He was bored. He wasn't sleepy. He needed to pee.

Bingo.

He jerked. I cringed and pulled out of his mind. Oops. I held my breath and counted out a full minute, then put another teked lens on the other side of the window. He hadn't moved, though he was definitely more alert than before. He had his arms crossed and bore a frown.

Damn. I snuck back into his mind.

Shouldn't have had that coffee, he was thinking.

Okay. I could handle this.

Have you ever noticed how when you need the bathroom, the sound of running water makes you *really* need the bathroom? Or how when you need the bathroom and nothing else is going on, all you can think about is how you need the bathroom? Thickneck wasn't quite in that zone, but I was pretty sure I could give him a few nudges.

Of course, if he went into the room he was guarding, which I assumed was Wyatt Jackson's, that wasn't so cool, but it was worth a shot. I was betting he wouldn't risk waking the prophet and would have a room of his own, probably with the darker-haired thickneck.

Into his mind, I pushed the sound of water, like the last drips of a shower just after you've turned off the tap. I moved on to the image of a waterfall. Then rain.

I kept this up for about ten minutes, until he shifted his stance. It was all I could do not to pump a fist into the sky and yell "hallelujah!" I knew the pee-pee dance when I saw it. Sure enough, he shifted again a moment later, grimacing. I let it play out. He checked his watch, sighed, then glanced carefully up and down the hallway before stepping into the room across from the door he was guarding.

As soon as the door closed behind him, I did a fast walk down the hallway, hoping to hell I wasn't being too loud, and grabbed the handle of the door the thickneck had been guarding. I let myself hunt for the cacophony of Stigmatic Jack's vile music, and found it. It was dead ahead.

I was breathing too quickly, holding the handle. It could be locked. I turned it, slowly, and pushed once the handle stopped turning.

The door opened quietly enough, and I slipped inside, into the darkness, and closed the door just as carefully behind me.

"What is it, Gavin?" came a voice. It wasn't Stigmatic Jack's. I didn't quite recognize this voice, though somehow it was familiar. Was it the other thickneck?

I froze.

"Gavin?" Someone shifted in the bed, and then, with a click, the room lit up.

Lying there on the bed, very much awake, in a pair of white shorts and a T-shirt, was a slim guy with brown hair, hazel eyes, and a confused look on his face. His hand was on the light switch beside the bad.

"You're not Wyatt Jackson," I said.

"Who are you, and why are you in my room?" He didn't seem ruffled at all by my standing there. He wasn't a big guy, he was slim, like me, though he had a bit of a potbelly. He seemed sort of familiar, like when I saw a client in a different setting and didn't recognize them right away.

"I was looking for Wyatt Jackson," I said, thinking fast. "I was hoping for a blessing."

The guy on the bed didn't sit up.

"At five in the morning?" he asked. "Without calling up from the front desk?"

"He's the prophet," I said, trying to put a bit of religious fervor into my voice. This really wasn't going to plan. I'd sensed Jackson *in here*. Where was he? In the next room, beside this guy?

It clicked.

"You're the guy in the blue suit," I said.

"Yes." He nodded. "You need to go now."

I was actually quite surprised he was taking this so well. I decided to count myself lucky and raised my arms apologetically.

"I'm really sorry to have bothered you." I'd have to find another way to get to Stigmatic Jack. At the door, backing up awkwardly, I opened my mind to see if I could feel to which side Stigmatic Jack was staying. The room filled with the discordant noise—and it was screaming from the mind of the man on the bed. I opened my mouth and threw up my mental walls to shield him out. His thoughts were horrible.

Shit. I'd had it all wrong.

The guy on the bed sat up quickly, whipping around to look at me. He was on to me. When I'd listened, he'd caught me hearing, or maybe he'd felt me put my walls in place.

"And I thought he was schizophrenic," I said, and started working the light. I went for the funhouse-mirror effect again, cursing my own stupidity, and threw open the door to make a hasty retreat while I heard the guy on the bed crash to his knees and swear, trying to follow me when his eyes said up was down.

I bounced off the thickneck, who had apparently peed at

something close to light speed. He staggered forward one step, and I nearly fell over backward.

"Stop him!" the man yelled from behind me.

I lit up, reflecting light all around me, and Thickneck threw up a hand. It was by no means the sun, but between the lamp in the room behind me and the brightly lit hotel hallway, it was enough to make Thickneck blink and look away.

I made it about three steps before whatever it was the guy in the bedroom threw at me connected with the back of my head. Then I was on my hands and knees, the light was gone, and I was trying very hard to put my thoughts back in order and avoid throwing up.

Then someone—the thickneck, I think—hit me again, with a fist this time, and I clocked out.

VIOLET

I came to feeling dizzy and too warm. There was the taste of bile in my throat. I couldn't open my eyes, and had the sensation of motion. It took me a second to realize I couldn't move my hands, either, or my feet. I was bound. And blindfolded. And moving. I tried to speak, and the realization of a gag in my mouth tipped me over the edge into real panic.

I had to get free. I thrashed, and tried to put together my teke, but I couldn't seem to concentrate, and my movements were sluggish. I felt nauseous. After a few attempts, I fell back, already exhausted. What was wrong with me?

"You're drugged," a voice said, heavy with contempt. "I find it's easier to get inside when someone is pliant." I knew that voice. It was the voice of Stigmatic Jack's "God." I shivered. I'd been such an idiot.

Stigmatic Jack didn't have multiple personalities. He really *was* hearing a voice. A telepathic one. From the guy in the blue suit, whose name I didn't even know. He was the telepath. And, I supposed, the psychokinetic. Emphasis on the psycho.

The motion slowed, stopped. Then, a short time later, we moved again.

We were in a car. Or a van, I guessed, remembering the Church of the Testifying Prophet vans with their bloody hands on the sides.

"How do you make light?" the voice asked me.

Gagged, I choked on the words I wanted to say to him.

Don't worry, his horrible voice filled my mind, *I can hear you.*

I had to concentrate not to throw up. His thoughts were oily. Vile, horrible dark words that were icy cold and angry. You cannot lie with your thoughts. This man was one fucked-up individual.

That's not very nice.

Get out of my head! I thought-yelled. His laughter filled the van.

"How do you make the light?" he asked again.

I don't, I thought truthfully. *I can't make light.* I was trying to build my mental wall, brick by brick, but it wouldn't hold together. Whatever he'd given me, it made me sway, and every time the van turned a corner, I lost my concentration and the wall tumbled down.

"Don't lie to me," the man snarled. "I was there. At City Hall. My eyes took two days to recover from that light show. So don't you fucking lie to me."

I felt a hot sharp pain flash across my left calf and yelped into my gag. He'd cut me.

I'll do more than cut you, faggot, if you don't tell me how you make the light!

You're insane, I thought clearly, past the pain, past the drugs. *You're a right fucking lunatic.*

"Fine, then," he said, with a false sadness. "I guess we'll do it the hard way."

An icy black wave slammed into my thoughts. He was inside my mind.

❖

I remembered.

"Relax," I said to the client, who was lying stiffly on the

massage table. He was uncomfortable, his shoulders were tight, and with the first few touches, I could tell this was not someone who knew how to handle stress. With my telepathy barely working, I could feel where his aches and pains were and started to send little mental nudges to the pain centers of his brain to turn it down.

It was slow work, to do so without alerting him to my telepathic presence, and not something I was incredibly confident in doing. But he had seemed nice, if nervous, and he was a new client. I wanted to make a good impression.

It took me nearly fifteen minutes to get his shoulders to slump, and I worked on his arms, shoulders, and neck for most of that time. Curious, I opened my mind a little wider, trying to skim, and immediately my head filled with his worries and doubts.

"I have to ask," I said conversationally, "is there something you're dreading right now?"

He laughed. "That obvious?"

"You carry a lot of stress up here." I rubbed at his neck and shoulders, which were continuing to loosen. I planted my elbow in the small of his back and rubbed at the pressure point. "And it's not helping the ache down here."

"I'm up for a promotion," he said.

"Congratulations," I said, and started working on his calves. They, too, were balls of tension. It was a wonder he could walk.

"Well, it's more money," he said.

Aha.

"You'll forgive me for giving advice," I said, "but if the money isn't worth the stress, I'd stick with something you enjoy."

He laughed. "That's sort of what I've been trying to figure out. I love what I do. But…"

"It's more money," I said with him. He laughed.

The massage continued in silence, and he truly relaxed. By

the end of it, I thought he might have fallen asleep. I smiled to myself. I loved my job, too.

When he got up to go, he tipped me a twenty.

"That's too much," I said.

"It is on my salary," he smiled, "but I think I'll keep the job I like."

This is how you use your power? Psycho's thoughts were sudden, and broke the memory into fragments. I swayed, my massage table and the client dissipating into a kind of mental blur. *You whore yourself out?*

Whore myself out? *I'm a masseuse,* I thought, angry. *Not a fucking prostitute. I help people feel good, you ignorant prick.*

He did something, and my world filled with pain. I realized in a vague sort of way that he was doing the opposite of what I did when I found sore places and traced them backward to the source. He'd found the pain centers of the mind and was turning them higher. My shoulders exploded with pain from being tied behind me, and my wrists burned with the tightness of the rope. But it was a clumsy effort—it had no deftness, no grace to it.

Which didn't mean it wasn't effective. My tears were soaking the blindfold.

Show me how to make the light! he yelled.

And I remembered.

❖

I was in my bedroom, one evening after high school. Dad was out with Callum at one of his hockey games, and I was alone. Across my bed were a dozen *Scientific American* magazines, all a few years old, a prism, and my bag of marbles.

I wrapped my mental fingers around a marble and lifted it into the air. It blurred a slightly red color when it moved away from me, and slightly blue when it brought it closer.

Red shift and blue shift, I'd just read. In space, at phenomenal speeds, stars moving away from Earth, relatively speaking, shone redder. Galaxies or stars that were moving toward the Earth shone bluer. It shouldn't be happening at such low speeds, nor so obviously, but somehow when I was moving the marbles...

I rocked the marble back and forth in the air and then tried to dim it down to no light. It took nearly five minutes before the glow was completely gone, and when I felt a satisfied thrill of success, it flashed with a yellow spark and lit back up again with a golden glow.

I sighed and sent it into an orbit around my head.

In none of the other documented cases of psychokinesis was there this light issue. Why did things glow when I moved them? And why didn't they always glow the same amount?

I mentally put the marble down, looked back at the article on light, and picked up the prism I'd bought at the toy store.

With a glance at the curtains, I teked them closed enough to block out the sunlight, and then I glanced at the light switch and flicked it off with a mental hand. The room was dark.

I lifted the marble again, and it barely flickered, even when I really moved it around.

I'm not making light, I realized with a rush, and stared at the prism. *I'm bending it!*

I teked the curtains, opening them up only about an inch, and sailed the marble past the line of sunlight that fell into the room. The marble flashed with rainbows as it passed the sunbeam.

I started gyrating around the room, doing what Callum called his "touchdown" dance.

Pathetic, Psycho's voice crashed into my mind.

I whirled, my younger self dissolving away into nothing.

There! See? I can't make light. I refract it! I howled back at him, and in my anger, I felt my focus return long enough to shove back telepathically. I struck out blindly, reaching into his mind at random, and tried to numb him, knock him cold. I felt him stumble, then recover.

What did you just do to me? He was furious.

Even as I cringed away from his raging torrent of oily thoughts, I felt a small kind of satisfaction. I'd surprised him, again. He couldn't touch minds like I did, either, to stop pain, or soothe, or push toward sleep. All he knew how to do was hurt people.

Show me, he demanded. Again, I remembered.

❖

She didn't look better anymore. She looked frail, and pale, and ready to die.

"What have you got today?" my mother asked me, once my father and brother had left. Callum had rolled his eyes at me when he was leaving, like he always did when I got to spend time alone with Mom, but I didn't feel bad about it anymore. This was our time. And even I knew it wasn't going to be much longer.

"I brought the marbles," I said, and held out my hand. Three cat-eye marbles lay in my palm. I was eleven. This was close to the end. I didn't want to live through this again.

Psycho's laughter was cold.

My mother smiled, then coughed. There was a deep pain in her chest, and she pressed her hand against it, trying to rub it out.

I could feel the pain in my head.

"Mom," I said, tears filling my eyes. "I can feel it."

She looked at me, and bit her lip. "I'm sorry, honey. Try the wall again?"

The young me tried to build a mental wall, but her pain was strong, and it battered through my adolescent attempts at keeping it out. The younger me rubbed at his chest and then frowned.

"It hurts here," I said, "but it comes from up here." I touched my head.

Then, suddenly, I was in my mom's head, and I could feel

the where the pain was, where her brain was telling her that something was wrong with her body, that she was dying, that she should do something about it—not that there was anything she could do.

And the eleven-year-old version of me told that part of her mind to *shut up.*

My mom gasped.

"It's gone…"

I looked at her, lip trembling. "I'm sorry. I didn't mean to go in your head. But it hurt, and I wanted it to stop."

She gazed at me, and tears fell from her eyes. I realized she wasn't mad. She was happy.

"Thank you, Kieran," she said.

I threw myself into her arms and hugged her, and when I pulled back, I had sent the three marbles—the third one wobbling terribly—into the air. They all glowed, one bluish, one reddish, and one just a soft yellow-white.

"Three at once," she said, impressed. "And not even looking at them."

I grinned. "Marbles are easier than Legos to float."

"Why do you think that is?" she asked.

I shrugged and snuggled down beside her in the bed. "I dunno. Round is easier. Pennies are easier than Legos, too."

She watched them float around for a while.

"Have you told your dad yet?" she asked me.

Hide. I fell silent.

"You can, you know."

"It's our secret," I said, and in my child's mind, the word repeated. *Hide. Hide. Hide.*

She stroked my hair. "Honey, when I'm gone…"

I frowned and started to speak, but she shushed me.

"When I'm gone, if you need to talk to someone, talk to your dad, okay?"

I sighed. "Okay." I wouldn't. It wasn't safe.

"You promise?"

I looked away. "I promise." I twisted, uncomfortable. I was lying to my mom.

"And you'll practice, all the games we made up?" She was looking at me sadly, but smiling. It was weird now, being able to know that she wasn't happy when she was pretending to be.

I rubbed my forehead, then leaned against her. "Yes."

"You're losing one of the marbles."

I looked over and saw that my mom was right. The yellow-white marble, the wobbly one, was falling lower and lower. I thought at it with my mental hand and pushed it back into the air. It held still, and my mom smiled at me.

I heard her love for me, and how much she didn't want to leave me, in my head.

Touching. Psycho's ugly voice filled my head.

Not this, I thought at him, angrier than I knew I could be. *You do not get to intrude on this.* Even through the drugs, and the mental beating he'd already thrown at me, I was livid. Off in the distance, I heard the soft chimes of thought music, and whoever it was, it wasn't the clanging dissonance of hatred and fury that was my tormentor. I filled myself with that music and pushed at him, willing him to get out of my head.

He laughed, pouring more and more of himself into my mind, until the room turned smudgy and gray, and darkness filled every corner. My mother's face grew ever more waxen, and I felt like I was drowning under his thoughts and his laughter.

His laughter flooded into me, filling every corner of my thoughts, and the room started to dissolve. I tried to fight back, tried to rally some sort of defense, but it was like fighting a river.

A river.

Mentally, I tucked, flipped over, and braced my feet against the edge of my own mind.

Then kicked off, as hard as I could, against the stream of thoughts.

I love to swim.

❖

The psycho's mind was a cold and horrible place.

I was somewhere in his young adulthood, and he stood in the middle of a field, surrounded by rusted farming equipment in various stages of disrepair. He was in pain—broad burning welts covered his back, and his anger was equaled by his humiliation.

His father had done that. Had whipped him until he bled. For being insolent, I thought, though I couldn't quite get deep enough into his thoughts to trigger the memory.

Dimly, I was aware that he was still digging around in my own head, but I felt removed. Hidden. I could hear him growing angry in the distance—he couldn't find me.

This version of himself—perhaps fifteen, maybe sixteen—was lifting a lone brick with his mind. Once, twice, three times, he lifted it into the air. He smiled with a dark happiness. This was the only time he felt in control.

He dropped the brick and walked away.

At the same time, a blurred image of him walking back into the field appeared, and this time the cuts on his back weren't as horrible, but he had a black eye. Days had passed, I realized.

And this time, he lifted a tire. Once, twice, three times.

The scenario repeated, time after time. Sometimes he was freshly hurt, a new beating from his father inspiring him to the field, sometimes he was just alone for a while. Always, he was angry.

He moved from the tire to a small boulder.

From the small boulder to a rusted old propane tank.

From the tank to a larger boulder.

From that boulder to a broken-down trailer.

Get out of my mind! His thoughts suddenly shrieked at me. Mentally, I jumped, but at the same time, I couldn't help but feel a mix of pity and disgust for him.

Don't you dare pity me, you faggot! His thoughts slammed into me.

I feel bad for you, I thought back, *because of what happened to you, but you're a right raving lunatic.*

I dove deeper into his thoughts and felt his anger as he lost me for a second time.

A church appeared around me. He was sitting there, in a suit, beside the man I assumed was his father. A collection plate was being passed around, and when it came to their place, his father put a twenty-dollar bill onto the plate.

The younger memory of my tormentor scowled. He hated this. Hated that his father gave these people money. Hated that they had so little, and what they did have was wasted on this stupid church with their stupid stories and singing.

People were stupid, he thought. Gullible and pathetic, and they deserved to be broke and think like sheep.

He glared at the preacher, who didn't even notice the hatred that was aimed his way. The preacher was an older man, and charismatic. People flocked to his sermons, gave him money, and got empty words in return. The whole church was nothing but a sham.

But it wouldn't suck to be the guy getting all the cash.

Get. Out.

The church shivered, shifted, and faded. I was back to being blindfolded, aching and tired.

You are nothing compared to me. He sneered. *Marbles and light.*

And what are you? I thought back at him. *I saw your childhood. Lift a thing. Lift a heavier thing. Lift an even heavier thing. Grow an imagination! Do you have any idea how annoying it is for me to finally get a nemesis and have him turn out to be a glorified size queen?*

That pushed him over the edge. He kicked me, hard, and our mental connection collapsed.

"I can cut people, too," he reminded me, like a gloating child.

I laughed around my gag. *Bloodying someone is nothing to be proud of,* I sent to him. *Just ask your dad.*

He kicked me a second time, harder. "You won't laugh when I kill them," he said aloud. "I'm going to blow them right off the street in their 'parade of sin.' Do you have any idea how generous people will be to the so-called prophet after that?"

You make me sick. I thought of the young woman at the picnic, who'd been about my age. And I thought about the memory of this man at the church. He didn't believe a word of what he was projecting into the mind of his "prophet." *You're doing all this for money.*

He smirked, and I could feel him looking down at me like I was the crazy psycho, not him. "Of course. Why else? I'm gonna blow your little faggot parade apart. Then I'll come back, and I will wring all your tricks from your head and show the 'glory of the Lord' to all my followers." His voice was dripping with amusement. "Then I'm going to buy myself a whole fucking island and be done with this shit forever."

My answer was lost in the gag and the force of his third kick. By the time I got my breath back and stopped seeing stars, the van had stopped and he had stepped out of it. The door slammed hard, and I realized I was alone.

Finally.

❖

I lay on my back in the van. My hands were bound beneath me, my feet tied together. My whole body was shivering. The blindfold across my eyes was wet with my tears. I was breathing hard, through my gag. My jaw ached.

People were going to die.

I tried to put my teke together, but it wouldn't quite work. I couldn't even feel what was around me. I took a deep breath. I'd been drugged. Right. I could handle this. I just had to focus more. There is no problem that doesn't have a solution.

Even though I was blindfolded, I closed my eyes.

People were going to die.

I can do this. It was no different than Sebastien's belt. Though now I really wished I'd let him use rope instead of handcuffs, if only for the practice.

I tried again. I felt the mental fingers forming, but they wouldn't move right. It took me nearly ten minutes just to slide the blindfold up to my forehead and away from my face, and by the time I did, tears were streaming from my eyes. Light fell on me through the small glass window that led to the front of the van. It was definitely midday. I was so fucking weak. I shivered, shaking and limp against the floor of the van. My gym bag lay against the far wall of the van. I tried to tug it toward me, but it didn't budge.

I could hear, muted, the sound of a crowd of people. It wasn't close, and with a gag, I couldn't make enough noise to be heard. Where had that psycho parked the van?

I reformed the teke, behind and beneath me, but no matter how hard I tried to tug or twist the ropes on my hands, it wasn't working. I couldn't get a clear enough sense of how the knots were knotted to untie them, and my mental hands were too clumsy.

I yelled into my gag in frustration.

People were going to die.

He was going to kill people.

I could fucking handle this, damnit.

The gag, Kieran. Get the gag off, and then yell for help.

My shoulders were burning with a hot pain by this point, and

I had to concentrate to push past it. Making my teke was even harder than before, and I wrapped it around the thick roll of cloth that the psychopath had tied in my mouth. I could handle this. I tugged it, but it barely moved. I tried feeling around for the knot or buckle, but I couldn't grab it. I closed my eyes tight and pushed. It shifted, but didn't come out. I even pushed at it with my tongue, but it wasn't enough.

I slumped back again and opened my eyes. My shoulders burned and throbbed. In the distance, I could hear loud music with a heavy beat. The Pride Parade must be starting. I was running out of time.

I threw my teke together and shoved, hard. The teke crumbled apart, and it didn't even nudge the gag slightly. I tried again. Again. Again.

I couldn't get past the ache in my shoulders, the dizziness from the drugs. I was starting to hear the echoes of thoughts of the people on the street, waiting for the parade. It was a muted white noise, but it was making it harder to concentrate.

I heard a single, horrid note.

It was starting. Wherever the hell that psychopath had gone, he was starting to put together his own brand of psychokinetic power. I'd seen what he wanted to do when I was upstream in his mind. He was going to kill anyone and everyone in his way, and then claim it was divine. And there would be enough weak-willed people who believed him and his puppet prophet. He'd rake in profit from misery, then ditch it all just to live somewhere in comfort, and no one would ever know. He was insane. I had to stop him.

I pushed again, but the excitement of the parade watchers was loud, and I couldn't keep them out. My shoulders were screaming.

I started to sob. Big, racking sobs of misery. I couldn't do it. People were going to die because I just couldn't do anything about it.

The noise of the people was driving me crazy. Too many thoughts. The pain in my shoulders, the fog in my head from the drug. The drug hadn't just taken down my mental walls, it had left my head open wider than it had ever been. I couldn't shut it off.

I was going to have to listen to it all, I realized with horror.

I was going to have to listen to people dying, sliced by that lunatic's power.

God. Sebastien was out there. Waiting for me.

I heard him. The lovely soft music that was his thoughts. Even among the noise of the rest, I heard him. It was easier to hear him than anything else. I was going to have to hear him die.

I can't handle this, I thought, and sobbed into my gag.

Kieran? Est ce toi?

Sebastien! I thought.

Kieran... Où es-tu? Je ne peux pas voir...

Sebastien, I thought wildly, *I was wrong, it wasn't Wyatt Jackson. It's the guy that goes around with him, the one in the suit and sunglasses. He caught me. I'm tied up in one of the vans, and they drugged me and I can't get myself out... He's going to kill people...* I was sobbing again. *I can't get out. I can't...* I shivered.

Sit! Sit! Sebastien's thoughts were worried, shaken. *Sorry, Pilot is going crazy.*

Pilot. My eyes filled with tears. This time, though, it was with relief.

Sebastien, I sent, as clearly as I could manage. *Follow Pilot.*

Then I took a deep breath, tried to center myself, and blasted one thought as loud as I could.

Hey, Pilot, let's play!

❖

I'm coming. I heard Sebastien's voice in my mind. *He can hear you, and we're coming. Shit!* I had the sense he'd nearly tripped, and started to laugh at the insanity of it all. *He's running.* Thinking in English was clumsy for him. The worry in his thoughts was not.

You can't lie with your thoughts.

Je t'aime, I thought carefully, just as clumsy with French as he was with English.

Plus comme ça, I heard him, louder now. *More thoughts. Pilot can hear you, and we're coming.* The music in his thoughts, the rising and falling tones and counter tones, were calming. My head swam, and I closed my eyes. I was so sore.

More thoughts, Sebastien was thinking, *Pilot is slowing down. More thoughts!*

He got inside my head, I admitted. *That psycho. He went into my head, Sebastien. He tore into my mind, and he took things from me.* I shivered against the cold metal floor.

I see the vans. Sebastien's thoughts, and the music of his mind, were so loud now. I'd never heard thoughts this clearly before. I could hear barking and sagged with relief. Pilot. He was frantic to get to me. I heard the music that was Sebastien's thoughts and tried to echo it back to him the way Rachel had done with me. Strength filled my mind. The music doubled in volume, and the interior of the van suddenly lit with a bright light that made me flinch. It startled me, and the light went out.

I'd teked a lens and lit the van. It had barely taken any effort at all.

What the hell?

I tried again, but the light I made was weak at best, redirected from the small window to the front of the van. It was hard to maintain a lens. It fell apart again.

Play! Play! Play!

There was a bang on the side of the van. I groaned in relief.

"Kieran!" Sebastien's voice yelled.

I let out a roar through the gag, muffled but loud enough, I hoped.

I'm in here, I thought clearly. *You just hit the right van.* Pilot was barking like crazy. I heard Sebastien yank on the driver's side handle and curse in frustration. Of course it was locked. He came around to the back and yanked at the handle for the rear doors. Also locked. I looked at the inside of the door, inching myself up against the side of the van with an agony of burning from my shoulders, and fierce aching in my wrists.

I heard his voice again as he bellowed out his frustration and kicked the van's doors.

Wait, I thought to him. I tuned in again to his music of his thoughts. The tones, up and down the scales, made me smile even around the agony of my shoulders. Again, I tried to reflect it back to Sebastien. It doubled, rising in notes of beauty.

Again, my mind seemed to fill with strength.

Qu'est-ce que c'est? I heard him think, and then, holding the music, I sent my teke out, fully formed, and tried to push the latch on the van's rear doors.

Instead, I tore both doors off their hinges and sent them sailing into the back of the Jeep parked behind the van with a loud crash. I blinked, and the music was gone.

"Tabernac!" Sebastien said, climbing into the back of the van. Pilot scrambled in after him and nearly knocked Sebastien over trying to get to me. Pilot's tongue lashed at my face with log, wet swipes. I twisted to pull my face away, but couldn't. Sebastien started to laugh despite himself, pushing Pilot to the side. The dog whined, but stayed down while Sebastien tore the gag from my mouth and then started working on my feet. I couldn't help but grin—he was wearing his leather harness and black leather chaps over jeans. He looked amazing.

"Please," I begged. "My hands?" Pilot barked.

"You are such a good dog," I said. "I'm not even kidding.

The best. Best. Dog. Ever." Pilot's tail thumped against the metal floor of the van. His whole body was tensed, ready to jump. His doggy thoughts were overwhelming. He was exuberant to see me. He liked this game.

Sebastien pushed me gently forward and started tugging at the bonds on my hands.

"I could hear you in my head," he said, breathlessly. "And music."

I shook my head, and it made the whole world tip sideways. "I know. Asshole drugged me. I'm leaking all over the place." I glanced at him, hearing and feeling something as he undid the knots. "Tell me you didn't just think you liked seeing me tied up like this."

"Sorry." He had the grace to look ashamed.

My hands came free and I pulled my arms in front of me with a hiss of pain. My shoulder pain was nothing compared to the feel of blood running back into my fingertips.

"Jesus, that hurts," I said, clenching and unclenching my hands. Pilot helped by licking them. I winced and then gave his head a quick pat.

"Ow," Sebastien said, and looked at his hands. "That hurts."

"Sorry," I said. "Like I said, I'm leaking." The drugs were making it impossible to control my telepathy. I was pretty sure I was projecting my pain into Sebastien's mind. I tried to clamp down on it.

He rubbed his forehead, then started untying my ankles. I was still dizzy.

"We have to stop him," I said.

Sebastien looked at me. "How? Can you even walk?"

"That is not a helpful attitude," I said, frowning. I grabbed my gym bag and awkwardly got it onto my shoulder, then I tried to slide to the edge of the van. My ankles were all pins and needles, like my hands, and my shoulders wouldn't cooperate. I stayed upright once I slid off the edge, but not by much. Sebastien wrapped one arm around my waist. Pilot jumped down and barked. He was ready for the next game.

"We need to call the police," Sebastien said. "They kidnapped you."

I looked around. We were a few blocks over from Bank Street, where the parade had obviously begun, judging by the noise and applause and voices on microphones.

I caught the broken sound of the psychopath's music. Atonal. Rising.

"What *is* that sound?" Sebastien asked again. His forehead was shining with sweat.

"Sorry." I looked at him. I was definitely leaking my thoughts into him. Then I remembered what those tones meant. Damn, it was hard to think properly…

"We're out of time," I said. I looked at Pilot. "Where can we leave him?"

Sebastien left my side long enough to tie Pilot's leash to a tree. I wasn't entirely sure Pilot couldn't just chew the tree in half, but the dog sat willingly enough, though he let out a kind of breathy sigh, his dark eyes looking at me with mournful reproach.

"We'll be back," I said to myself as much as to the dog.

I couldn't run, but I managed a quick walk back toward Bank Street. The noise of the crowd was loud in my head, and with Sebastien's worry and fear pounding on me from right beside, adrenaline kicked in, and the aches of my shoulders, legs, and wrists moved off into the back of my head. The broken notes were growing in volume, but I couldn't see where the hell Stigmatic Jack's group was standing.

"Where are they?" I asked. "Did you see them?"

Sebastien gripped my shoulder tightly. "No."

I frowned and closed my eyes. Played hot-warm-cold with my mind. At least that was one benefit of not being able to screen people out properly. It was much easier to feel which direction the nutjob was in. I pointed.

"That way."

We pushed into the back of the gathered crowd and tried to move against them. A float from Chances was going by, with half-naked dancing go-go boys moving to the thump of a heavy beat and an arching rainbow made of balloons. And beyond it, on the other side of the road, I caught sight of a group all dressed in white, holding signs aloft and chanting in counterpoint to the celebration going on around them. They were a very large group. At the front, between the thicknecks, stood Stigmatic Jack, his palms raised high. He was crying out about sins, but drowned out by the music of the bar float passing by.

One of the go-go boys tossed them some condoms. I couldn't help but smirk. I was definitely still feeling the effects of the drug.

The psycho in glasses wasn't with him. Crap. That was new.

I tuned in to Stigmatic Jack.

Warn them! Warn them that I am not pleased! Tell them to repent now! Tell them that they are to be punished for their sodomy and lust! I could hear the psycho's voice in Wyatt Jackson's mind. I frowned and tried to push further. Where was it coming from?

Three sharp notes sounded—and Wyatt Jackson's palms began to bleed.

I bit my lip, then saw Detective Stone approach Wyatt Jackson and his group, two uniformed police with him. Now was definitely not the time to hide.

No, I sent to him, loud and clearly. *Detective Stone, it's not Wyatt Jackson. It's the guy that's always with him. Blue suit and sunglasses. He's the one. Do you see him?*

Stone froze, obviously startled. He looked left, then right. He said something to one of the men with him. The cop shook his head. I concentrated.

He wasn't sure who was talking to him.

Crap. Well, in for a penny…

Detective, it's Kieran Quinn. The psychokinetic we're looking for is the handler that's always with Wyatt Jackson. Blue suit and sunglasses. Can you see him? I wondered if my voice sounded as panicked as I felt.

Stone started looking around with an angry scowl on his face, hunting. The cops to either side of him spoke, and he snapped something to them. They all started looking.

Stone's thoughts were hard to catch from across the street, but I felt a surge of satisfaction from him. He pointed left.

I followed his finger. Tucked back beside a recessed storefront stood the psycho in the blue suit, mirror shades and all. He was staring into the crowd, watching, lips curled in amusement. I knew, behind the glasses, he was looking at the parade and getting ready to attack.

He raised his hand an inch, and I felt the music clash loudly.

Don't you fucking dare! I yelled into his mind, and lit up.

❖

Sebastian let go of my shoulder as the people around us began to move and jostle. There were gasps and yells.

You really think you're going to convince anyone this isn't an act of God? the psycho's voice thundered back in my head.

There were screams from the crowd. Three of the go-go boys on the float yelped and staggered as bloody cuts opened on their chests.

"You are *not* God!" I yelled, and pushed out into the road. The rainbow-bedecked float had just moved past me, and I was facing the psycho. He held up one hand, and between that and his shades, didn't seem too bothered by my light. He flicked his other wrist at me, but nothing happened to me. He still couldn't affect me without seeing exactly where I was.

He snarled and raised his hand. One of the speakers on the bar float shot from the float and sailed at me. I threw myself to the ground and heard it crash beyond me.

People were screaming. Running. The floats stopped moving, and I heard doors opening. The psycho raised his hand again, and a trash can flipped end over end toward where I was lying on the street. I threw up my hands and pushed with my teke, but he was still stronger than me. The trash can deflected to the left with a burst of indigo light, but it clipped my wrist and made me yell out in pain, knocking me onto my stomach. When I tried to get up, my hand wouldn't work right, and a stabbing pain shot all the way up my arm. Something in my wrist was broken. My gym bag, hastily thrown over one shoulder, had fallen off into the road. For a second, the pain made my light falter. Almost immediately, a cut flashed across the small of my back.

I'll kill you, faggot!

I scowled and made a lens in front of me, between us, and reflected the light back at him. As far as he was concerned, there was a mirror between us.

Another trash can flew at me, but I rolled out of the way. I tried to catch it, but only managed to slow it with a blue flash before it hurled itself into the crowd, where two people went down under it, crying out in pain.

My head was spinning.

Get out of here! I blasted the thought in all directions, something I'd never tried to do before. But it seemed to work. The assault of terrified minds all around me reacted, and most of the crowd began to move away as fast as they could.

I'm going to cut you, and beat you, and break your bones. I'm going to kill you. His thoughts dripped like oil into my mind, coating everything with a blackness. I mentally snatched up a crumpled can from one of the tossed garbage cans and flung it at his head. He batted it away with a mere gesture and sent it sailing off down the street.

He was a stronger teke than me. He was a louder telepath than me.

Someone took my hand. I looked up and saw Sebastien, a cut across his eyebrow, looking down at me with concern. He pulled me up.

"Your back is cut," he said.

"It's okay."

The psycho raised his hands, and the windows of the storefront exploded in a rain of glass. I threw up both my hands, as did Sebastien, and suddenly, the wonderful song that was Sebastien's thoughts was back and echoing between the both of us, and my mind cleared completely, overflowing with a rich, cool confidence.

And *power*.

The glass veered around us in an arc, shattering against the pavement. Retreating people screamed all around, cut and sliced by the fragments, including Wyatt Jackson and his group, who'd been huddled together behind the thicknecked guards. I lost the teked pane, and the mirror effect vanished, though I managed to keep myself shrouded in light. We rose, untouched, a circle of clear ground around us.

"How...?" Sebastien said, looking at his hands.

"I'm not leaking," I said, stunned. "It's not me. It's *you*."

Sebastien looked at me, squinting into the light around me, obviously confused.

The psycho stepped out of the storefront, and with a jerk, the Chances float lifted off the ground, the three wounded go-go boys sliding off the edge and hitting the ground with grunts and cries. It rose, as Psycho raised his arms, and I saw blood trickle from his nose. It glided out above us.

I'll crush you, he gloated into my mind. Then flicked his arms down.

I snagged out with my thoughts and felt myself link again with Sebastien's glorious music, and heard my own as well, magnified by the resonance between us. I wrapped the light around both of us and smiled. I was going to handle the living shit out of this.

I threw up my arms as the float hurtled down, and wrapped my teke and Sebastien's teke in one resonating glow that burst into violet light above us, bathing the whole street in a kind of false twilight. The float jerked to a halt a few inches above my head.

Sebastien dropped to his knees. *"Tabernac!"* His nose was bleeding, too.

My head felt like it was going to bust.

Even with both of us, we weren't stronger than the psycho. Sebastien hadn't practiced, and I was drugged. Light tricks weren't going to cut it. I felt the float give an inch, and dropped to my knees as well.

Crush! You! The man's thoughts were dripping icily into my head.

I saw my gym bag.

Can you hold it? I asked Sebastien in my mind.

Comment? Je fais ça?

I'm aiming, you're firing, I thought, hoping that made sense. I was using his ability, but he was providing a good chunk of the oomph.

Sebastien rose slowly, fists clenched at his side. The float shuddered down, once, but didn't fall and crush us completely.

I gestured with my good hand, and my gym bag jumped up. I felt blood burst in my nose and pour down my face. It was so hard to keep the resonance going between my own thoughts and Sebastien's, keep the light up around us so we didn't end up sliced to bits, to show Sebastien how to hold the float in a teke, and to still teke something myself. A few things at once I could do, sure, but one of them was a fucking huge parade float...

I dug my hand into the bag and found what I was looking for.

Don't let go, I thought.

"Crush you!" The blue-suited freak was yelling it out loud now. He'd raised both fists and was clenching them so tightly his fingers were white. I groaned as I felt the pressure of the float increase above us. Sebastien let out a long, angry growl. I looked ahead, my left hand gripping tightly. My right hand had gone completely numb.

Psycho staggered forward a step and swung his arms wide. He was pushing himself very hard, I realized, when I saw the streams of blood pumping from his nose. With a groan, the pub float dipped another few inches above us, clipping Sebastien's head. He ducked.

"Colis!" Sebastien swore.

I opened my hand. A single small ball of light lit up in my hand. I flicked my wrist, and it shot out at the psycho.

Psycho saw it coming and let go of the float. Sebastien screamed, and I helped him flip the float up and to the left, where it landed behind us with a crash. I hoped no one was hurt. I glanced around, seeing almost no one. The sidewalks were pretty much clear. My head throbbed and I felt Sebastien sag beside me even as my full, if weak, teke returned to me, no longer resonating. Psycho spread his fingers in midair, sneering at me. The marble I'd shot at him floated in front of his hand.

"A marble?" He laughed. "You think I can't stop a marble?"

"No," I said. "I think you can't stop seven."

I lit the seven marbles with a prismatic burst and launched them at him. To his credit, he managed to stop two of them, but the other five slammed into his forehead as fast as I could shoot them, with a sickening series of wet crunches.

He toppled over backward with a grunt.

The awful tones stopped.

I saw Detective Stone, covered in dirt and bloody-knuckled, run up the steps to where he lay.

Don't let him wake up, I sent to Stone. He turned and looked over his shoulder, and then saw me, on my knees beside the broken float.

I looked at Sebastien and smiled. Everything seemed really far away. "You okay, big guy?" Sebastien nodded at me, though he was rubbing his temples. He was okay.

That was good.

I fainted.

WHITE

The light from the moon reflected a brilliant white, and I watched it for a moment, hovering in space before it.

"Beautiful desolation," I said.

"What?" Rachel asked me.

"The moon. Neil Armstrong, or…" I shrugged. "I'm not sure which astronaut said it."

"Turning your back on Earth?" she said.

I rotated around until the blue marble appeared. Rachel, beside me, was in a long, yellow nightgown, her braids flowing gently behind her head. I was wearing the same clothes I'd been wearing when I'd battled it out in the street. I had no idea if that was true in the real world or not.

"So I'm pretty sure I broke his skull with a half dozen marbles," I said. "Which would maybe make me a murderer. Also, I telepathically outed myself to a police officer. Oh, and Sebastien's psychokinetic, too. And I passed out in the middle of the street right after, so for all I know, I'm in prison right now." I felt so incredibly numb about it all. Tired.

Rachel's eyes were wide. I couldn't tell if she was in shock at my own stupidity, or if she was feeling genuine concern.

You can handle it, she sent to me.

"Having that attitude kind of buggered it all up," I admitted.

"I can't believe I didn't notice that Sebastien was psychic. Or that it wasn't Stigmatic Jack, but his freaking blue-suited handler who was the psychokinetic cutting people and throwing bicycles and parade floats at people."

"Parade floats?" she repeated. "Shit."

"Yeah, you wouldn't like him when he's angry." I cracked a weak grin.

She smiled at my pathetic joke. She really was one of the coolest people I knew. Or knew astrally, anyway.

Not for the first time, she reminded me of Karen.

"You'll be okay," she said. "I've gotten used to you. If you have to bust out of prison, you will." She shrugged a little.

I wasn't sure she was joking.

"The part that really bothers me," I said softly, "is that I can't decide which would be worse—that I killed him with that marble, or that I didn't."

Rachel's eyes softened. "Oh, honey."

"What do we do with him, if he's still alive and kicking? Seriously? Tranquilize him for the rest of his life? Give him a lobotomy? How do I even convince people he's dangerous enough to do that? Who'll believe me that he's a psychic, let alone a really strong psychokinetic with a hard-on for cutting people?" I sighed in the airlessness of the wonderful dream. "Oh, and it turns out he's just a money-grubbing asshole using scared people to fill his collection plates. He doesn't even believe the shit he's spouting."

"Hard choices," Rachel said.

"Have you ever yet met anyone—and I mean, here, or in the awake world—like this? Someone who has the same abilities, but isn't...well...isn't nice?"

She shook her head. "So far, most people I've met here have been pretty tame. And not very strong, the way I am—uh, we are." I smiled at her quick, and generous, correction. "And it's rare that they even show up—they've gotta be pretty deep asleep to make it here. You're the first person I've met on a regular basis, and that's why I think you're such a powerful telepath."

"You should see me when I work as a team," I muttered.

"What?" she asked.

"Remember the resonance?" I said. "When we both sort of linked into each other, and shared thoughts a bit, and hearing thoughts got easier?"

"Yes."

"Well, you can do that with telekinesis, too. Sebastien and I sort of…hooked arms, I guess…and we were almost the equal of that creep when we did. On my own, I can barely lift thirty pounds at my best."

She thought about that.

"Resonance," she said quietly. We floated there in silence.

"I'll watch the news," she said, after a while. "If I so much as hear a peep that you're in jail, I'm not kidding, you bust your ass out of there." She crossed her arms. "Pretty boys like you do not want to end up in jail."

"Thanks," I said, and laughed. I meant it. "I'm more worried about the other guy."

Rachel sighed.

"I have an idea," I finally said, miserable. "But…Well. It's pretty horrible."

She looked at me, and I felt her move into my mind and listen to the only solution I'd managed to come up with so far.

❖

I woke up in a hospital with a cast on my wrist and the worst pain in my stomach I'd ever had. I was in one of those horrendous green hospital gowns, and I came to with a moan. My head was aching dully, and given the onslaught of words drifting through my head, I'd been given more drugs at some point. Groggily, I opened my eyes, then shut them. The light was a bad, bad thing. Someone took my hand, a bit too tightly. I winced. "Ow."

"You're awake."

I rolled my head to the side, gently, and opened my eyes. Sebastien came into view. He had a bandage wrapped around his head, but no ugly hospital gown. He wore a white tank top and jeans. He had absolutely no business looking sexy when I felt this bad, shadows under his eyes or not.

"Ugh," I said. "I feel like garbage and you still look like a porn star."

He raised his eyebrow. "A porn star?"

Someone on the other side of the room moved, and I tilted my head—slowly—back in that direction. It was a uniformed police officer, a younger man with buzzed brown hair and a neatly trimmed goatee. He was dialing his cell phone.

"Am I under arrest?" I asked. My voice was raw.

"He's awake," the police officer said into the phone.

"No," Sebastien said.

Are you okay? I sent into Sebastien's mind. My head ached like mad to do it, but I wasn't going to speak in front of the policeman, who was nodding and saying "yes" into the phone.

Oui. Sebastien's thoughts—so formed and strong, which should have been a dead giveaway to his psychic nature—filled my mind. They were also edgy with kind of confused excitement. *Mais je pense que je—*

En anglais? I begged. *English, please.* My brain hurt.

Sorry. He looked down at me. *I think I'm like you. Psychic.*

Yeah. I smiled up at him. *You are.* I thought back, to the number of times I'd been amazed at how organized and strong his mind seemed, how his thoughts made that wonderful music—like, say, Miracle Woman—and felt intensely stupid. *I should have caught that a bit earlier.* I frowned. *Just try not to do anything psychokinetic in front of anyone, okay? At least until I'm out of here and we can practice. Oh, and for God's sake, don't let them call my family!*

He cringed. *Too late, they're in the cafeteria right now.*

"I'm sorry, sir," the policeman said to Sebastien. "You'll have to wait outside now."

I sighed, and it made my head spin. "Why? He's my boyfriend. Partner. Whatever. He handcuffs me up for fun, he can handle anything I have to say to you." I blinked. Yep. I'd been given drugs.

Sebastien grinned.

The policeman cleared his throat. "Detective Stone wants to speak with you alone," he said. I caught a flush of pleasure from him at speaking Stone's name. I resisted the urge to taunt him for his crush. It seemed inappropriate.

Stone wanted to talk to me.

For crying out loud, how much did one guy have to do around here to get a break?

❖

By the time Stone arrived, I had worked out the contraption that raised and lowered my bed so that I was slightly bent at the waist—a waist that I'd peeked at under the sheets and seen was a wide swath of black and blue. Apparently, dodging heavy things aimed at your head left you bruised.

Someone should explain that to raging lunatics.

When he walked in, Brian Stone closed the door behind him and then sat in the chair beside my bed and crossed his arms.

"Hi," I offered.

"Hi," he replied. "Your family is outside. They're anxious to see you."

I winced. "I'll bet."

Stone waited, just watching me.

I felt nauseous, and it wasn't the drugs.

"So, uh, you got my message, then?" I said.

Stone nodded warily, then shook his head, letting out a puff of breath.

"So it *was* you. The voice sounded like you," he said.

I leaned my head back and looked at the ceiling. "So my cover's blown, then."

He laughed, and I looked back at him, surprised.

"I wasn't going to put down hearing voices in my report, Mr. Quinn." He smiled. He had a nice smile, actually. He had one dimple. Left cheek.

I blinked. "You...didn't tell anyone? About me?" I was stunned. "But I killed him. Blue-suit guy."

"His name is Dennis Contret." Stone shook his head. "You fractured his skull, twice. He's not dead. He's currently three floors down, though, and drugged." He rubbed his chin. "I took what you...said...seriously. I told them that Contret was mentally unbalanced and that he needed to be sedated. By the time you were done, everyone had either run away or wasn't in a good position to see who was left behind when the light went out. What with the glass and the float and the big purple flash and all."

Tears came to my eyes. "Oh."

"But what do I do with him when he wakes up?" Stone asked me.

I groaned, leaning back. "Can we cross that bridge when breathing doesn't hurt so much?"

He looked at me oddly, but pursed his lips.

"Okay. What about the Rainbow Man?" he asked.

I groaned. "I *really* hate that name."

He laughed. "I won't argue there. Why did you pick it?"

"I *didn't*." I glared at him, but he was smiling, so I didn't explain about the website. "Between you and me, I think Rainbow Man is going to take a vacation," I muttered. "A real one. Where he gets to have unhealthy breakfasts, and even some sex. No. Scratch that. A lot of sex. I have earned handcuff sex."

Stone raised his eyebrows.

"Not with you. You're cute, but I met a leather guy."

Stone raised his hand. "I don't need to know. So no plans for Rainbow Man?"

I closed my eyes. "None."

"Well, I guess it's lucky that no one really knows who he is, then."

I opened my eyes again. He shrugged.

"Yeah," I said, choking up. "Though if you ever did need his help or anything, if something like this happened again, I'm sure he'd be willing. In fact, I'm sure if it happened again, he'd probably come to the police right away, instead of maybe not telling the whole truth when he had the chance."

Stone regarded me frankly. "That would be a very good idea."

I dropped all pretense. "Thank you. I mean it. You could have totally messed up my life."

He shook his head. "And you could have bolted at any time. You didn't."

I smiled. He made me sound awfully heroic.

"You threw a float around with your mind," he said, with a kind of worried shake of his head. "I can barely believe it, and I saw it."

He thought I'd done it on my own, without Sebastien's help. That was good. I wasn't going to correct him. I felt a little guilty. What was that I'd just said about being honest with the police from now on?

"I'd rather just massage people," I said. "It's way less stressful. And the pay is better."

"I'll take you up on that massage," he said, leaning forward with an obvious twinge of pain. "But for the record, I'm not one for handcuff sex."

I laughed, which made my belly hurt. "I know. And so does the police officer outside, who really wishes you'd hurry up and ask him out already."

He gaped.

"Just a suggestion," I said. "But seriously, guy. He's been sending you signals."

He blushed. "I, uh. Well." He smiled again, full dimple.

He rose, and paused at the door, his face sobering.

"About Contret. He'll probably shake off most of the medication by tomorrow morning…"

I groaned. "It's not like you can throw him in jail and expect him to stay there." I bit my lip.

"And he'd have to be assessed before being moved to an asylum, and they don't keep you drugged unconscious during a psychological evaluation." Stone crossed his arms again. "I didn't lie about him in my report. I put down that he was a suspected psychokinetic/telekinetic, and how it really was the only explanation for the events. But I'm not sure if even half the people involved will believe in that."

"I could demonstrate the reality," I offered, though I wasn't really sure I meant it. "In private, maybe?" It seemed like a good idea, though. If people had psychokinesis shown to their faces, how could they discount it? He seemed to consider that.

"Let me think about it. I'll call you later if I think that's the way to go," he said.

I nodded.

"I'll let your family in now."

"Could you get me more drugs first?"

He laughed and opened the door.

❖

My father burst into the hospital telling me that I was reckless and should have run away the moment something went wrong.

Callum had asked me why I hadn't taken off the moment things had gotten out of control, and whether or not I had to be crushed by a parade float to gain some common sense. I was just glad Karen was at work, or she'd have shined a spotlight into my face while Dad and Callum played bad cop/worse cop. I'm sure I was due for a major chewing out from her later.

I'd introduced them to Sebastien and watched my brother give him the evil eye and listened to my father's thoughts scramble to reconcile "the big strong fella" with the whole gay thing. Sebastien had been smooth, though he'd excused himself for the majority of their interrogation. It took me nearly an hour to calm them down and then send them on their way.

"You do realize I'm the one in the hospital bed, right?" I said, which had made them both sheepish. "Maybe one of you could do the invalid a favor and go feed his cat?"

When they left, I buzzed a nurse, who arrived with Sebastien.

"Can I go for a walk?" I asked the nurse.

"If you're not too sore. You shouldn't do much, but it would be a good idea to stay mobile so you don't get too stiff. You're pretty bruised, but you didn't break any ribs. Just be careful with your wrist."

I offered up puppy eyes. "I promise I'll be gentle. It hurts to be rough."

"I won't let him overdo it," Sebastien said.

The nurse was smiling as she left.

"Please tell me there are pants available?" I begged Sebastien.

"I like you in that gown." He wagged his eyebrows.

"Ugh," I muttered. "I'm feeling the least sexy I have ever felt, big guy."

"I brought you a dressing gown," he said, and unfolded the long, fluffy white bathrobe from where he'd left it folded on the countertop.

"I think I'll keep you," I said.

He smiled. Then, glancing to see that the door was shut, he held the robe out in his open hands.

The bathrobe lurched about a foot in the air toward me, then fell in a heap on the floor. There was no light. I guessed that was still my own quirk.

I smiled. "You'll want to start with marbles," I said.

He nodded, looking dejected. "It was so much easier with you."

"I think it'll be easier to learn that way, too."

He picked up the robe and I got out of the bed and struggled into it.

"Where do you want to go?" he asked me once we were in the elevator.

"Three floors down," I said, opening my mind and pointing. "And that direction."

❖

Dennis Contret was pretty bandaged, from what we could see through the window, especially his head. A police officer, a brawny man who made Sebastien look slender, sat outside his room, so Sebastien and I didn't approach very closely, just enough to see him from where we stood near the hallway. Three floors down had turned out to be the step-down unit, one step removed from I.C.U.

"Why did you want to see him?" Sebastien asked me.

I looked at him. "When he wakes up and shakes off the drugs, what do you think he'll do?"

Sebastien clenched his jaw. "I don't know."

"Exactly. But I'm betting on bad things."

Sebastien nodded.

"I need to ask your help," I said. "What I want to do is what I did to you when you couldn't sleep, but I want to do it...more."

Sebastien paled. "You want to kill him?" He was whispering.

I shook my head. "No. But I don't want him to wake up tomorrow."

Sebastien watched me, his forehead furrowed.

"Or ever," I said. "At least, until maybe we can come up with something better."

"A coma?"

"I guess," I said. "Yeah. A coma."

"You can do that?" he asked me.

I took his hand. "We can. Remember how much stronger our teke was together?"

He nodded.

"Well, I'm pretty sure it'll work that way for telepathy, too."

"Pretty sure." Sebastien squeezed my hand.

I shrugged. "I am making all of this up as I go along."

D'accord, he thought into my mind. *I can't think of anything else*. He sighed. *Is it wrong that I wish he had died instead?*

"You and me both," I muttered, and then we slipped into the resonance of our minds, then into the drugged and sleeping mind of Dennis Contret. It terrified me how much stronger I was like this, with Sebastien helping me, but everything about Contret's mind was cold, hard, and oily. I found the places where I knew sleep came from, and with much more power than I had on my own, they obeyed without question. With Sebastien's help, it was easy. I told those parts to go to work, and not to stop.

Ever.

Contret did not wake in the morning.

LIGHT

The closing party of Pride Week was in full swing by the time I arrived. My wrist was in a cast, and I had a small orange bottle of painkillers in my cargo pants. I'd skipped my latest pill given the crowd of minds I knew to expect, but apart from my wrist, it wasn't so bad. I was wearing a simple white button-down shirt to hide the bruises on my arms, and I was already growing warm. The arena was packed, the music pulsed, and the floor was full of gyrating happy dancers.

I smiled, paid my entrance fee, and walked in slowly, avoiding the crush and hugging the edge of the hall. I didn't want anyone to jostle my wrist, stomach, back, or shoulder blades.

"Hey, Irish."

I turned just in time to be enfolded—albeit gingerly—in Sebastien's arms. He rested his forehead down on mine and let out a long, deep, sigh.

"Hey there," I said.

"I'm glad you came," Sebastien said. "I know you're not feeling well."

"And you are?" I asked, raising an eyebrow.

He shook his head. "No, but I wanted to be here." He, too, had chosen a long-sleeved shirt, his black, and I could see a telltale bulge where his wrist bandages were. His forehead looked better—it had been a pretty small cut, all things considered.

"My stomach looks like a sunrise," I said. "It only hurts to breathe."

"I took a float to the head," he pointed out.

"Hrm. True." I leaned into him and pressed my face into his chest. He smelled wonderful.

"Did you see the news?" he asked me.

I had. Contret hadn't woken and had been moved to a long-term care facility. And Stigmatic Jack? Not stigmatic even once since the parade. He'd been on the television, saying he had lost the voice of God. Most of his church has left him, especially after they'd been sprayed with shattered glass. Wyatt Jackson was quoted saying he was "sure he was being tested."

I hoped he fucking flunked.

"I got you something," Sebastien said.

I smiled. "When did you have time to get a present?"

"When your family arrived."

"Oh, when you ran away and abandoned me to them."

"They were worried," he said, but he smiled.

"Yeah," I said.

"Your dad is really nice," Sebastien said. "But I think your brother doesn't trust me."

I laughed, which hurt. "Callum doesn't think anyone is good enough for me. It's a big-brother thing."

"My family isn't close," he said. "It was nice. They really like you."

It made me sad to think his own family wasn't the same. "Well, Dad is all ready with the adoption papers," I warned him. "I told him you restored furniture. You're the tool-wielding manly-man son he always wanted."

Sebastien laughed. "Maybe I should wear the harness next time I see him. Here." He tugged a small white thing out of his back pocket.

I unfolded it. It was white leather. Where did you even buy

white leather? Long and narrow. I frowned, turning it over, until I saw the two holes.

"A mask?"

He nodded. "If you're still going to go through with this, I thought it was a good idea."

I smiled. It was a very good idea. I looked around, but predictably, no one was watching the dark walls since there were half-naked gyrating folks in spotlights all over the dance floor. I put my glasses in my pocket, then tied the mask over my eyes.

"Look, ma," I said. "I'm a superhero." My throat felt tight.

He hugged me.

"I like you in leather," he growled into my ear.

"You carry it off way better," I growled back, and grabbed his ass with my left hand.

He laughed and let go, then took me by the shoulders. "You're sure?"

I tried to make him understand. "If people know it's real, then maybe the next psycho won't get so far before the police can do anything about it. I'm sure Detective Stone will appreciate the support." He'd called me and told me that he was—his words—"meeting with some extreme skepticism."

Sebastien looked up. "I should go to the organizer table."

"Go ahead. I'll be fine. I'll…uh…let you know when I'm ready."

Sebastien gave my ass one more grope, then walked off to the front of the arena, smiling. His butt was amazing in those jeans.

"Why on Earth are you wearing a mask?"

I turned, and grinned. Karen and Callum were behind me, arm in arm. "You came!"

She smiled at me. "Yeah, well, like I said. I assume that's the hunk?"

I gushed. "Isn't he the hunkiest?"

"That ever hunked," she said. "He's built."

"I'm standing right here," Callum said.

"Let the adults talk, honey," Karen said, and gave my brother a peck on the cheek. He blushed.

"I take it back. You two are perfect together." I grinned.

Callum rolled his eyes at me, but the smile he gave Karen was sloppy and romantic. Aw.

"So, the mask?" Karen raised an eyebrow. "Because if that's the only way he can get off with you, I think you should give Justin another shot."

"Justin said the Pride Parade was trashy."

"The Pride Parade landed on you," Karen pointed out. "Also—again—why the mask?"

I smiled. God, she was unstoppable. I loved her. "Just wait for it. And don't be mad. I'm telling you guys now, and you'll be pretty much the first people to know, okay?"

They stared at me, but I turned to the stage to wait for my cue.

"You're weird," Karen said. "Even for a Pisces."

"It runs in the family," Callum said.

❖

"Folks," came the voice of Mizz Anne Thrope, "I hate to interrupt the music to make you listen to me…no, wait, actually I adore it. Shut the fuck up and listen to me."

Cheers and laughter from the floor. She was wearing a bright yellow ensemble, complete with a yellow hat covered in yellow faux feathers and a tiny beaded yellow purse. She held the microphone to her lips and stood on the small stage where the Pride organizers had earlier announced the money raised for charities throughout the week and thanked all the sponsors. Or so I assumed, given how late I was to the party. It's what they usually did, anyway.

"The reason I'm interrupting your soiree," Mizz Anne said, "is to tell you that we have a special guest star almost as fabulous as myself, and to announce the winning name of the contest on our website to name this special guest." She swung the microphone around in a circle on its cord, then caught it. "Which I suppose should be enough of a hint for even you dullards to suss out?"

"Rainbow Man!" someone yelled and Mizz Anne nodded.

"My faith in humanity is restored." She paused. "Wait, no. There it went again."

People started to applaud, and I smiled. A few chanted out "Rainbow Man!" and a few others shouted "Disco!"

"Now, I would say we should dim the lights, but I hear tell he can handle the lighting himself," Mizz Anne was saying. "Which, incidentally, would make him perfect to be my stage director, assuming he's also cute, mute, and a masochist."

I reached out mentally and felt Sebastien, standing with the Pride organizers by the stage.

May I? I asked him, listening for the music of his thoughts.

Bien sûr, he thought back.

We joined, and with the resonance powering up between us, I sent telekinetic lenses through the room, turning and twisting in front of the various spotlights. The room lit in every shade of the rainbow, with light bending and reflecting above us in a prismatic spray of colors. It took almost no effort at all.

The applause was wild.

"You see what I mean?" Mizz Anne said, her voice almost lost in the noise.

"Kieran," Karen said. Beside her, Callum stared, mouth open.

I'd started glowing.

"Keep my name to yourself, would you?" I asked them, and winked.

Karen just shook her head, somewhere between annoyed and proud.

My brother smiled. "You get to tell Da," he said.

"I'll call him."

"Liar."

I winked behind my mask.

Then, with the resonance between myself and Sebastien, I lifted myself into the air, lit myself with a reflective teke with just enough light to drown out my features, mask or no, and floated above the crowd, sending flashes of light in all directions.

People started to notice. Some pointed, some yelled, and some applauded.

"I am sad to say that nobody won the naming contest," Mizz Anne said into the microphone above the sound of the cheers and applause. "It turns out this fellow had his own idea for a name all along. So it is at this time I'd like to introduce you all to the man who whomped the crap out of those bigoted freaks, saved the go-go boys from Chances, and put the fabulous back in our week."

She smiled and raised her arms dramatically. "Ladies and gentlemen, I give you our own gay super-fucking-hero: Pride."

The applause was overwhelming, and in the tide of thoughts that flared in the room, I heard Sebastien's voice in my mind the loudest.

If you're Pride, should I be Wrath? Maybe Envy?

You, I sent back, *are Lust.*

Je t'aime, his thoughts said, rich with laughter. And I felt myself crying in midair, overwhelmed with the words.

You can't lie with your thoughts.

Me too, I sent back to him. I rotated in the air and sent beams of light flashing through the crowd. The music had started up again—someone doing a techno version of "I Need a Hero," which made me laugh—and people were dancing and looking up at the same time.

Kieran? Sebastien's thoughts were amused.

Yeah?

How are you going to get down without someone seeing who you are?

For crying out loud.

Good thing I have a mask.

I thought so, he thought smugly. *Just asking.*

I'll be down right after this song, I thought to him. Then I lost myself in the music, the love, and the light.

About the Author

'Nathan Burgoine grew up a reader and studied literature in university while making a living as a bookseller—a job he still does, and still loves. His first published short story was "Heart" in the collection *Fool for Love: New Gay Fiction*. Since then, he has had over a dozen short stories published, including Bold Strokes titles *Men of the Mean Streets, Boys of Summer, Night Shadows,* and *Saints and Sinners 2013: New Fiction from the Festival*, as well as *I Do Two, The Touch of the Sea, Mortis Operandi, This Is How You Die* (the second Machine of Death anthology), and *Lavender Menace*. 'Nathan also has a series of paranormal erotic short stories that begin in the Bold Strokes anthology *Blood Sacraments* and continues with further installments in *Wings, Erotica Exotica,* and *Raising Hell*. His standalone short erotic fiction pieces can be found in the Lambda Literary Award finalist *Tented, Sweat, Tales from the Den,* and *Afternoon Pleasures*. 'Nathan's nonfiction pieces have appeared in *I Like It Like That* and *5x5* Literary Magazine.

A cat lover, 'Nathan managed to fall in love with and marry Daniel, who is a confirmed dog person. Their ongoing "cat or dog?" détente continues (and will likely soon end with the acquisition of a dog). They live in Ottawa, Canada, where socialized health care and gay marriage have yet to cause the sky to cave in.

Books Available From Bold Strokes Books

Light by 'Nathan Burgoine. Openly gay (and secretly psychokinetic) Kieran Quinn is forced into action when self-styled prophet Wyatt Jackson arrives during Pride Week and things take a violent turn. (978-1-60282-953-4)

Baton Rouge Bingo by Greg Herren. The murder of an animal rights activist involves Scotty and the boys in a decades-old mystery revolving around Huey Long's murder and a missing fortune. (978-1-60282-954-1)

Anything for a Dollar, edited by Todd Gregory. Bodies for hire, bodies for sale—enter the steaming hot world of men who make a living from their bodies—whether they star in porn, model, strip, or hustle—or all of the above. (978-1-60282-955-8)

Mind Fields by Dylan Madrid. When college student Adam Parsh accepts a tutoring position, he finds himself the object of the dangerous desires of one of the most powerful men in the world—his married employer. (978-1-60282-945-9)

Greg Honey by Russ Gregory. Detective Greg Honey is steering his way through new love, business failure, and bruises when all his cases indicate trouble brewing for his wealthy family. (978-1-60282-946-6)

Jacob's Diary by Sam Sommer. Nothing exciting ever happens to David Jacobs until the day he and his son are thrown into the most fascinating and disturbing adventure of a lifetime. (978-1-60282-947-3)

Lake Thirteen by Greg Herren. A visit to an old cemetery seems like fun to a group of five teenagers, who soon learn that sometimes it's best to leave old ghosts alone. (978-1-60282-894-0)

Deadly Cult by Joel Gomez-Dossi. One nation under MY God, or you die. (978-1-60282-895-7)

The Case of the Rising Star: A Derrick Steele Mystery by Zavo. Derrick Steele's next case involves blackmail, revenge, and a new romance as Derrick races to save a young movie star from a dangerous killer. Meanwhile, will a new threat from within destroy him, along with the entire Steele family? (978-1-60282-888-9)

Big Bad Wolf by Logan Zachary. After a wolf attack, Paavo Wolfe begins to suspect one of the victims is turning into a werewolf. Things become hairy as his ex-partner helps him find the killer. Can Paavo solve the mystery before he runs into the Big Bad Wolf? (978-1-60282-890-2)

The Plain of Bitter Honey by Alan Chin. Trapped within the bleak prospect of a society in chaos, twin brothers Aaron and Hayden Swann discover inner strength in the face of tragedy and search for atonement after betraying the one you most love. (978-1-60282-883-4)

In His Secret Life by Mel Bossa. The only man Allan wants is the one he can't have. (978-1-60282-875-9)

The Moon's Deep Circle by David Holly. Tip Trencher wants to find out what happened to his long-lost brothers, but what he finds is a sizzling circle of gay sex and pagan ritual. (978-1-60282-870-4)

Straight Boy Roommate by Kevin Troughton. Tom isn't expecting much from his first term at University, but a chance encounter with straight boy Dan catapults him into an extraordinary, wild weekend of sex and self-discovery, which turns his life upside down, and leads him into his first love affair. (978-1-60282-782-0)

Raising Hell: Demonic Gay Erotica, edited by Todd Gregory. Hot stories of gay erotica featuring demons. (978-1-60282-768-4)

Pursued by Joel Gomez-Dossi. Openly gay college student Jamie Bradford becomes romantically involved with two men at the same time, and his hell begins when one of his boyfriends becomes intent on killing him. (978-1-60282-769-1)

Timothy by Greg Herren. Timothy is a romantic suspense thriller from award-winning mystery writer Greg Herren set in the fabulous Hamptons. (978-1-60282-760-8)

In Stone by Jeremy Jordan King. A young New Yorker is rescued from a hate crime by a mysterious someone who turns out to be more of a something. (978-1-60282-761-5)

The Jesus Injection by Eric Andrews-Katz. Murderous statues, demented drag queens, political bombings, ex-gay ministries, espionage, and romance are all in a day's work for a top secret agent. But the gloves are off when Agent Buck 98 comes up against the Jesus Injection. (978-1-60282-762-2)

Combustion by Daniel W. Kelly. Bearish detective Deck Waxer comes to the city of Kremfort Cove to investigate why the hottest men in town are bursting into flames in broad daylight. (978-1-60282-763-9)

Night Shadows: Queer Horror edited by Greg Herren and J.M. Redmann. *Night Shadows* features delightfully wicked stories by some of the biggest names in queer publishing. (978-1-60282-751-6)

Wyatt: Doc Holliday's Account of an Intimate Friendship by Dale Chase. Erotica writer Dale Chase takes the remarkable friendship between Wyatt Earp, upright lawman, and Doc Holliday, Southern gentlemen turned gambler and killer, to an entirely new level: hot! (978-1-60282-755-4)